Chapter One
David Henderson Kibblesworth, Gateshead, Tyne &
Wear. June 2018

What man in his right mind could resist her? I can tell
by the look in her eyes when she sweeps aside her long
copper curls and sips her wine that she wants me.
When she's feeling passionate her green eyes darken
and there's just a slight raise of her eyebrows. My
wife, Erin has small eyes with slightly hooded eyelids.
When she is roused and staring at me, I'm completely
transfixed. It's as though I'm hooked inside her. I've
felt like this from the very first time I met her.

'It does make sense, David,' she coos softly. She
leans very slightly towards me resting her elbows on
the small dining table. She has finished her wine and
placed the glass carefully to her left. 'Even if you just
go along for the interview and meet them it'll give you
a feel for the place.'

I manage to drag my eyes from hers and lower my
head while I lay my knife and fork together across my
plate. We're about to have the same discussion we'd
had this morning before we both left for work. Now
we're back in the cottage I know she will continue
until I give her some type of answer.

I've been approached by another bakery to head up
their development team. This is a great compliment
and my chance for promotion to a manager's role
which I'm more than ready for. But, and isn't there
always a but in life, the job is sixteen miles outside of

London and we live in a small village in the north east of England.

I look back to Erin who is wearing one of my favourite camisoles under her black fitted jacket.

She doesn't like fashionable clothes but prefers vintage pieces, and at times creates a hippy-gypsy look with flowing skirts and brightly coloured blouses. However, for work she begrudgingly conforms and wears trouser suits. This camisole is the special red one with a fine line of lace along the edge. Now she has moved forwards over the table it has formed an amazing cleavage. I swallow hard.

'Hmm,' I nod in answer to her question. 'Well, I haven't really had time to think about it today because I've been so busy. Can we talk about it tomorrow?'

Memories of special nights when she was wearing the red camisole fleet through my mind and I fill with desire. Sitting on the hard dining chair I wriggle slightly and try to move into a more comfortable position. I smile hoping my answer won't disappoint her. I love Erin so much that I never want to upset her. Pleasing my wife fills me with satisfaction and makes me feel happy too, so it's a win-win situation. A no-brainer, as they say.

She shrugs her shoulders a little and pouts her lips together. I'm waiting for her tongue. If I see her little tongue dart out and lick her top lip, then I know we'll soon be making love. It's a tiny idiosyncrasy she does when she is ready and cannot wait.

While I stare at her mouth in anticipation, I think how ridiculous this must seem to other couples. Most men would try to get in a romantic mood first, but I've never been that organised. We've always been spontaneous and take each other when and wherever we want. This is one of the many things I love about being with Erin. I wouldn't have our marriage, or her, any other way.

I can't suppress a smile that is pulling at the corners of my mouth because she knows I'm waiting for her. I know she will pounce soon. It's as though we're animals circling each other each waiting to see who makes the first move. Inevitably, it is Erin who does so first.

I look into her bright sparkly eyes and we are at one with each other. I feel a tingle run up my back. Suddenly I see her little tongue dart out. Is this it? Just when I'm hoping I don't have to wait too long she grabs at the knot in my tie and pulls my face towards her devouring the whole of my mouth with her huge lips.

And I'm gone. I'm lost in a sea of desire so strong that I cannot escape even if I wanted to, which of course I don't. I respond greedily and groan when she takes her lips from mine gasping for breath. I jump up from my seat and hurry around the table. She flings herself at me wrapping her arms around my neck and her legs around my back.

Erin is skinny and only five-foot-four but has amazing long legs for a small woman which can grip like a vice when she feels the need. She moans into my neck while I carry her into the lounge. We topple onto the large leather settee tearing off each other's jackets. I sink my face into the camisole and want to cry for joy that I have this amazing passionate woman with me.

I know she will do things in her own time. I concede and let her control this side of our marriage because she always gives me as much pleasure as she takes herself. I'm concentrating now on not finishing before she does and have learnt to think about other things until she reaches her release. I often recite scores from football matches while kissing her in places which drive her wild. I want her to feel the same irresistible desire that is cursing through my body.

The smile of absolute joy spreads lazily on her full lips and I can feel her toes curl on the outsides of my thighs. My chest swells with pride knowing I have helped her reach her own private place and have made her happy.

Now she is satisfied, I know her goal in life is to please me. She positions me so I'll receive the very best her love making can bring. When Erin takes me like this, I cannot deny her anything. If it is within my power to give her what she wants, then I will because I love her: totally, utterly, completely. She is my everything.

I tell her this as she manoeuvres me, and I grin like an idiot. Erin makes me feel like the king of England and puts me right up there on a throne. And she is my own special queen.

She teases me relentlessly, and every time she begs, 'Please go for the interview, David. Please do it just for me.'

When she allows me to reach my glorious release, I shout, 'Yesss, I'll go, Erin.'

And that's it. I'm done and spent. She's lying on top of me with her abundance of wild red hair in my face. I gasp for breath and still feel my toes tingling minutes afterwards. I hug her so close to me that I can feel her ribs sticking into my chest. She is panting with emotional exertion and we start to breathe together in unison. Sometimes when we are like this, I feel that she is the breath inside my own body. Although I know that's not possible, I feel safe and whole when we're together as we are now.

'Christ, you've no idea how much I love you, Erin,' I whisper, and she nods her agreement.

I know other women might call this emotional blackmail and berate Erin for being the type of woman who resorts to sex to get what she wants.

Logically though, she has long since established that this works for me every time. And I do want her to be as happy with me as I am with her. Also, there might be men reading this who would scoff at my weakness. But all I'm going to say, is that if you were lucky enough to have this gorgeous woman screaming for more, you'd probably do the same and not be able to resist her either.

Chapter Two

My mind is full of Erin when I drive to work the next morning. Although its Saturday I'm popping into the bakery to oversee the production of our new white chocolate cake.

Usually, I moan when I go into work on a weekend. However, at just after seven on the first day of June, I look up at the sun shining with a promise to be a lovely day. I feel so happy I can't complain. There is very little traffic which makes it a quick fifteen-minute drive to work.

I've always been an early morning type of guy. I love to be up and about especially in the spring and summer to hear the birds tweeting and see what the sky has in store for us. Of course, like everyone else I do enjoy the occasional lie in bed on a weekend although nine o'clock is about my limit. I'm usually itching to be up and getting on with the day.

The muscles in my legs are aching after last night's furious lovemaking and as if that hadn't been enough, we'd made love again in bed a couple of hours later.

'It's just a little top up,' she'd said. 'Because I'll miss you in the morning when you've gone to work.'

I can't help smiling when I think of her. I'm rather proud of the fact that after two years of being together, we are still so into one another that she makes me tingle with happiness. I worship the very bones of her.

Sitting at traffic lights strumming my fingers on the steering wheel I give a little sigh remembering that I've agreed to give Erin what she wants and contact the London company.

I recall how I'd felt when I'd agreed and smile.

Although my darling wife uses lovemaking as a bargaining tool, I also know she would never do the opposite and withhold it as a punishment. Her sex drive is the same as mine and I know she would miss our lovemaking as much as I would.

When I've been with my mates in the pub after the football match, I've listened to them complaining about their wives. 'We hardly ever do it now and sex is nothing like it was when we first met!'

When this happens, I stare into my beer and don't comment. I never want to tell them that I don't have that problem because I'd sound too smug for words.

When the lights change to green and the traffic moves in front of me, I whistle between my teeth knowing how lucky I am to have her.

Driving down the road to the factory I swing my silver hatch-back into the car park. There aren't many cars parked up today as we run on a skeleton staff at weekends as opposed to weekdays when the car park is full to bursting.

When I climb out of the car and look up at the familiar outline of the factory building, I decide that applying for the position can't do me any harm. I've worked for the same company for eighteen years and would like to see how far I could get through the recruitment process. If I reach second stage interview, I'll be proud of myself. And I want Erin to be proud of me, too.

I smile imagining the delight on her face if I am successful then hurry through the swing doors into the building. Calling hello to a colleague I speed downstairs into our development office.

My desk as senior technologist is in the corner of the small dismal office which has no windows.

The walls are a pale grey colour and the strip lighting flickers needing a new tube. I sit down in my chair in front of the computer and quickly sign in.

Looking across to my boss, Alfie's, messy desk I sigh at the thought of him. He's a great guy and we've always got along well, but I've often thought how I would run the department differently if I was in his place.

Alfie is stuck in the past and if any change or re-development is necessary which involves hard work or sustained effort, he is adamantly against it. Development is all about moving forward and it's the reason why I love my job and the challenge. New ideas always excite me, and I like working towards an end goal, especially when I get it right. And if it isn't right, then I'll work my socks off until I get it perfect.

This would be the biggest advantage of the new job. I'd be able to run the department in London in my own way and put my ideas into practise.

Conscious of the time and knowing the guys on the production line will be waiting for me I retrieve my factory safety boots from under the desk. Undoing the laces in my brown leather shoes I push my feet into the boots. I've always loved Italian shoes and expensive clothes. Although where this comes from in my background I don't know. As my mam would have said, I certainly wasn't born with a silver spoon in my mouth.

Mam and Uncle Geoff brought me up because my father wasn't around. Uncle had often said, 'He'd been kicked into touch years before for being a bad sort who was too handy with his fists.'

Apparently, or so the story goes, I'd been born on a small farm just outside our village. As a seven-year-old boy, my memories of this time are scant and vague, but I can remember the old kitchen which had a big blackened range in the corner. I can also remember how mam often sported a black eye and on a couple of occasions her wrist was so swollen that she winced in pain lifting the saucepan.

When I try to remember more about these episodes the images are hazy. I can only recall words and sentences she'd used. 'Oh, I'm so clumsy I'm always banging myself on things,' she'd say. Or, 'I opened the door too quickly and it bashed my face.'

According to Uncle Geoff this had happened on a regular basis until one day when my father had been working in the bottom field, mam had packed our belongings and taken us to his home. We'd arrived at his big stone cottage in Lamesley, which is a small hamlet down the bank from Kibblesworth village. He'd been waiting for us with open arms. 'Come in, come in,' he'd shouted, and hugged mam tightly then ruffled the top of my hair.

Geoff is mam's only brother who was then a six-foot-three burly bricklayer. Growing up I mostly remember him as a jovial man who loved to joke and spoil me with treats.

Although I can't remember anything about my father, when I was about nine, I do remember mam saying that he'd sold the farm and gone to Scotland to live with another woman. And then years later, she'd heard he had died in a car accident. 'Good riddance to bad rubbish,' Uncle Geoff had pronounced.

Shaking the sad memories of mam from my mind, who died five years ago I pull on my white coat and head out onto the factory floor.

I watch the new chocolate cake being assembled on the production line and check-off the criteria to ensure we produce a top-quality cake.

When I return to the office with the necessary cake samples to send out on Monday morning I glance at my mobile. I read a text from Erin. 'How about lunch at The Ravensworth Arms?'

I grin. Spontaneous, unplanned and after last night I'm longing to be with her again.

I text back. 'I'll be there in twenty minutes.'

Looking around the office before turning off the light, I grimace. Maybe Erin is right. I know deep down that I am ready for a change, but, I sigh, if only it wasn't so far away from home.

Chapter Three

The sun is shining through a few billowing clouds
when I pull into the car park at The Ravensworth Arms
and head off to find Erin. She will have walked down
the bank from the village because Erin doesn't drive. I
find her sitting outside in the beer garden enjoying the
sunshine. She loves the sun as much as I do. Children
are playing in the corner sandpit while their parents sit
in groups around the tables enjoying drinks. The food
here is consistently good and it's one of our favourite
places to eat.

I smile and nod at the manager who is talking to a
group of people at the side gate. We've known each
other for years because her mother worked with my
mam in the library. I've always thought the great
advantage to living in a village is that everyone knows
everyone else. It's the sense of community and
friendship that I love. Of course, sometimes this
doesn't suit everyone, and after what happened to us, I
know Erin still struggles with this issue.

Erin is sitting with a glass of white-wine spritzer on
the table in front of her. She looks gorgeous and is
easily the most attractive woman in the garden. I grin
then hurry towards her. Dressed in a black flowing
skirt and a white gypsy top, she smiles, and I kiss her
bright red painted lips.

'I can smell white chocolate on your lips,' she says.
'Have you been eating cake?'

I slide in beside her on the wooden seat just as a
young waiter approaches us. I look at the lad with his
black spikey hair and vivid blue eyes and a spark of

recognition comes to my mind. When he addresses me as, Mr. Henderson, I remember him being one of my daughter's friends. We chat briefly about his course at college and how he is working for extra cash.

Erin grins with pleasure with his news that today's special on the lunch menu is Seabass. We both order then he leaves us to talk.

I remember how Erin had asked me about the chocolate cake. 'Well, I only had two mouthfuls of cake just to make sure the recipe is correct and that we got the chocolate ganache spread evenly in the centre,' I say then raise an eyebrow. 'But you know I don't eat the cakes I bake. And I didn't bring any home because I always end up binning it.'

It was on the tip of my tongue to say that I always took cakes home for my daughter, Sally, and my first wife, Beth. However, I know that sometimes it's all right to mention them and sometimes it's not. I also know, if ever there is going to be cross words between us it will usually centre around them. Thankfully, arguments are rare between us now-a-days.

I smile but remain silent because it's too much of a gorgeous day to risk spoiling our lunch with awkward conversation or upset. The waiter arrives with my cold glass of coke and I gulp it down relishing the cool liquid in the back of my dry throat.

Erin nods in agreement. 'I've never been one for cakes and pastries. Probably because it was too hot in Australia to have afternoon tea and cakes. It was usually cold lemonade and the occasional cookie at snack time.'

Easing myself back against the wood slats on the seat I relax my shoulders and drape my arm around her playing with the lace on the sleeve of her blouse. 'I love hearing about your life in Australia and often wish things had been different and we'd met up again earlier.'

She turns slightly towards me and places a hand on my thigh.

There's a melancholy look in her eyes while she rubs the seam on my black jeans with her fingers. 'They're just memories, David. And, from a long time ago. Some happy, but quite a lot of them are sad,' she says. 'I don't often think of my childhood in Australia.'

Our plates of Seabass and salad are brought to the table with cutlery and napkins in a tall wooden container. This seems to break her reverie and I remove my arm to sit up straight again.

Erin moans softly when she savours her first mouthful of the delicately grilled fish claiming it is delicious. I nod in agreement and she mentions the Seabass we had in France last year. We chat easily about the mackerel and salmon at the hotel restaurant and I watch her smile with our holiday memories.

Although we are not vegetarians, we eat very little meat now-a-days, but we both love fish. Which is quite different to how I ate with Beth and Sally. I pierce a cherry tomato then pop it into my mouth while we continue eating in companionable silence. I let my mind drift back to my life before I met Erin.

Looking back now I can't honestly say with hand on my heart it wasn't what is laughingly called the male menopause. But, at 38 years old when I was heading towards the dreaded, big 40, I fell in love with Erin and subsequently left Beth.

At the time, Beth had a steady job working as a secretary for a firm of solicitors in Newcastle that she loved. Aged sixteen, Sally, had just secured a work placement in a dental practice in Gateshead and our mortgage was paid off. Which meant most of the time I'd felt content, as they say, with my lot in life. I know now that if I hadn't met Erin I would have stayed with my family because there was basically nothing amiss with our marriage. I hadn't stopped loving Beth; it had just been a different kind of love.

I'd met Beth when I was in my last year of my degree at Newcastle University. We'd clicked together so comfortably that aged twenty-one I'd felt my life was somehow mapped out. One hot summers day, I'd taken Beth to Lamesley Woods and we'd lain in a field supposedly swatting for exams. She'd rolled over to me and I'd tickled her chin with a daisy. Her gentle eyes had washed with tears. 'Oh, Dave,' she'd whispered. 'I've got something to tell you.'

My heart had sunk. I'd thought she was going to finish with me. I knew I'd never find another Beth. We loved being together. We had the same taste in music, books, and equally enjoyed the same films at the cinema. Even our personalities were similar. Quiet, studious, and kind, but neither of us had much confidence in ourselves. I'd only been with one other girl before I'd met Beth and had made a botched job of making love. Being a virgin, Beth had no experience either. So, once we'd clumsily figured things out between us I'd been deliriously happy.

My throat had been dry waiting for her words. If she had met someone else, I didn't want to know about it. 'What is it?' I'd asked and taken a deep breath dreading the outcome.

Her eyes had filled with tears. 'I…I'm pregnant,' she'd whispered.

It had been a huge shock for both of us. When I think back now, I realise how immature and vulnerable we'd both been. However, once we'd come to terms with the shock, it had seemed like the most natural step was to get married. Mam and Uncle Geoff both loved Beth from meeting her. 'She's already one of us, David,' mam had said proudly. And this had been important to me because they were my family.

Beth's own large family had taken me into their open arms immediately. Especially her mother who had the biggest chest I've ever seen. I'd scarily felt on the point of suffocation in one of her big hugs. She'd told me, 'You're the best son-in-law anyone could ask for.'

After we married, and with a small loan from Uncle Geoff, we bought a three-bed semi-detached house which had been ideal. It was near mam who was an instant babysitter when required. Sally had grown up loved and cherished by us all.

However, two years ago our old cat went under the wheels of a car one day. I rushed him into Gateshead to the vet's surgery. And that's when I'd met Erin. She had been the receptionist behind the desk and I'd vaguely remembered her from Kibblesworth primary school with her bright red hair. While Erin had inputted our cat's details into the computer, I'd desperately tried to remember her name. Erin had thrown her head back and laughed at my puzzled expression.

'Yes, I did go to Kibblesworth primary,' she'd explained. 'My father was the history teacher, but we immigrated to Australia when I was seven.'

I'd nodded with understanding and that's when I'd felt latched into those eyes of hers. From that very first day I couldn't stay away from her. After three months with Erin, and I don't want to use the word, affair, because we were so much more than that, I buckled under the guilt and confessed my feelings to Beth. My wife had been devastated. The only word I could use to describe the look on her little face when I'd left them had been crestfallen. I'd moved straight into Erin's cottage further up in the village.

I shake myself back to Erin now when she asks if there is anything wrong with my Seabass because I've obviously drifted so far away in my thoughts.

'No, darling, it's fine,' I reassure her.

I'm rewarded with one of her big smiles. Did I mention that Erin has a smile that can warm you from a few feet away? Sometimes when she is laughing the corners of her big lips seem to almost reach her ears. If I get an okay sort of smile when her lips aren't wide, I'm left feeling cheated. Realising she has finished her meal I suggest a dessert, but we agree to have fruit and cheese with coffee at home.

Chapter Four

Erin's cottage is a single floor building with an extension. I don't like saying her cottage now because it has quickly become my home. I suppose in estate agents speak it is classed as a bungalow. It is built of old stone; therefore, it does have more of a cottagey feel. It's detached with grassy waste ground behind, so we're not overlooked, and the front area is paved. The paving suits us great because I've never liked gardening, and Erin feels the same.

The inside of the cottage had been renovated before she bought the property which created one big open-plan space. In one corner there are two large windows which Erin states is the main reason why she bought the cottage on return from Australia.

Erin is an artist and a damn good one at that. I tell everyone about her remarkable gift and boast about her paintings. On moving into the cottage she'd made full use of the exceptional light from the windows to paint and swiftly turned the corner into her studio.

When I first saw her paintings, I'd gasped in awe at her talent. I'd decided that not only was this bewitching woman beautiful, but she was also very clever. I'd pulled her close to me in a tight embrace. 'Oh, Erin, they're amazing,' I'd gushed. 'I'd love to learn more about your art world and get involved in some way.'

She'd giggled. 'Well, Mr Henderson,' she'd teased. 'I'm so pleased you're interested. Maybe when I'm famous you can be my manager.'

We pull up outside the cottage now which is on the corner of the last row of houses at the top of the village.

It's a good position because we don't get much traffic down the road which leads out into the countryside. Most of the villager's cars are in the centre next to the pub, shop, library, and community centre.

Even though we've had a light-hearted good lunch, I can sense an atmosphere building between us. An unresolved atmosphere. It's as if we both know something is pending and needs to be sorted out. Although she hasn't said the actual words, we need to talk about this, it is there. I know she wants to discuss the new job and for me, the dreaded thought of moving south.

Erin switches on the kettle in the kitchen area while I remove my shoes and pad along the wood floor to join her. We put fruit and cheese onto a plate and make coffee.

She places the cafetière onto the coffee table in front of us and sits next to me on the settee, then sighs. 'Okay, do you want to go first?'

I could pretend that I don't know what she means, but that would just waste time and be an insult to our mutual understanding of one another.

So, I take a deep breath. 'It's not really about the job, Erin,' I hedge warily. 'You know, if the job was even an hour's drive from here, I wouldn't give it a second thought. I'd be looking forward to having a shot at the manager's position. It's just the thought of leaving home to live in a city. That's what I can't get my head around. I mean, this…' I wave my arm towards the big lounge window and the fields beyond. 'Well, this is all I've ever known.'

Erin expertly peels the skin from a satsuma. She pops two segments into her mouth and offers me the rest.

I shake my head and pour hot coffee into my mug. I try again. 'You know how I love the countryside.

Whenever I finish work and drive home through Newcastle I cannot wait to get away from the hustle and bustle. As soon as I see fields and meadows, I can feel the peace and quiet again and unwind.'

'I know,' she begins slowly while I watch her mouth chewing the juicy segments. 'I suppose it's easier for me because I've travelled to pastures anew in my lifetime. The thought of moving is bound to be more difficult for you and I am trying to understand your reluctance to leave the village which you think of as home,' she says. 'But what exactly is holding you back?'

I can tell she is trying to understand my ties to the village. When I think back to the fall out after I left Beth and Sally, I decide that Erin really is being reasonable. She endured a lot of accusation and aggression from the villagers. I take a sip of my coffee and feel a comfortable warmth in my face not just from the hot drink, but from a sense of gratitude.

It had been a terrible upheaval. And as our Queen had said the year Prince Charles and Diana split up, it had been annus horribilis. Sally refused to speak to me at all. Beth had been devastated and refused to go to work while taking antidepressant medication prescribed by the doctor. I'd felt like a villain of the worst kind.

Before my confession, Beth had quietly accepted all my excuses about working late and meeting my mates for drinks. 'Are you going out again, Dave?' she'd ask looking at me with huge doleful eyes wondering why I was behaving so differently. I knew she hadn't figured out what was happening and that I'd met someone else. Our usual pattern of life had changed. I'd changed. I'd stopped touching her. Bedtimes had turned into simply a place to sleep.

The night I'd cracked and told Beth about falling in love with Erin had been because I couldn't carry on telling lies. It had been torturous. However, after I'd left and saw what our marriage break-up had done to my wife, I'd felt even more guilty.

The villagers had been downright nasty to us. They gossiped in corners of the general store when we entered and moved away from us in the local pub. Erin had come home in tears on many occasions when people were rude to her.

One morning, a middle-aged woman, who I'd class as a relative newcomer to the village had stopped in front of us on the pavement outside the shop. She'd hissed, *devious bitch*, at Erin when we'd walked past. I'd glared at her, livid with outrage that this woman felt she had the right to speak to us in this manner. Let alone use the word, bitch.

I'd shouted back, 'Don't speak to Erin like that! It's not her doing, it's mine!'

But Erin had dragged me away pulling on my arm. 'Shush,' she'd whispered. 'I don't want any more upset and retaliating will only make them worse!'

I'd seethed inside wanting to protect her from the narrow-minded idiots who thought they had a right to make her life miserable. Their gossip was upsetting her, and she didn't deserve the accusations.

I'd tried to explain hoping to make her feel better. 'It's just that they've known Beth for many years, and they think their loyalty should lie with her. Whereas, even though you were born in Kibblesworth you only returned two years ago. In their eyes, you've upset the equilibrium with what they see as scandalous behaviour,' I'd said. 'It's bloody ridiculous, just feudal rubbish!'

She'd nodded in agreement as though she understood but I'd wanted to wrap her up and shield her from their harassment. It had been the first time that I questioned village life and all it entails.

I look at Erin now and slot a finger into one of her ringlets. My insides melt with pleasure as I stare at her small body but strong resilient personality. I'm so proud of her and everything she is.

'David?' she prompts. 'Please just talk to me.'

I take a deep breath and try to explain. 'Well, I'll be leaving all my friends and family for a start, and…' I stop mid-sentence when Erin slowly shakes her head. I can see the reasonable understanding leave her eyes now and they narrow.

'Family?' Erin repeats the word and her face tightens. 'And what family are we talking about here?'

I can tell she's bristling, and I rack my brains to think of a way of getting through this without hurting her. I can't bear to wound her in any way. 'Well, I mean, Sally, Beth, Uncle Geoff, and my mates,' I say.

She folds her arms across her chest. 'Oh, I see. You mean your daughter who ignored you for nearly a year, and only now talks polite conversation unless of course she wants money from you,' she smirks. 'Well, if that's the case you can always do an internet bank transfer for her. You have heard of them; I suppose?'

I lick my lips and feel my stomach start to churn. This is the bitchy side of Erin's personality that I often struggle with. Speaking from the only experience I have, and not that I'm comparing the two women for one minute, it's just that Erin's character is so different to Beth's easy-going, empathetic personality.

'W…well, I think that's a little unfair,' I answer. 'Sally has been through a lot and she was only sixteen when I left them.'

'Ah, right,' Erin purses her lips. 'And, Beth? Is she included as family? Because stupidly I thought she was your *ex-wife* and I was your current wife.' She crosses her legs tightly and stiffens her shoulders. 'I'd hoped that after two years I was your family now, David. After all, I am the one who has stood by you through all of this!'

Oh, God, I've gone and done it now. I know I've hurt her feelings and I try to gather her into my arms, but she stiffens her whole body against me. 'I'm sorry, love, I didn't mean it like that. Of course, you're my family, I love you to bits, you know that!'

Erin relaxes a little and raises an eyebrow. 'And, David, considering there's only two of your pals still live here in the village now because the rest have all moved into Newcastle, I cannot see how they'd be such a miss,' she says and puts her head onto one side. 'Other than the football season you hardly see them in the summer.'

'I know,' I try to soothe and explain. 'It's more of a tradition really that we still all meet up here in The Plough after the match. But I suppose we can always meet in Newcastle.'

Erin grunts slightly in satisfaction. 'David, for God's sake, London is not the end of the world, you know. It's only three hours on the train from King's Cross into Newcastle,' she pouts. 'You can come back for the big matches and travel back down the same day. It is possible to jig your life around.'

I swallow hard because my throat is dry and take another sip of the coffee. 'I know, darling. Of course, I could.'

An uneasy silence settles between us and I desperately try to think of what to say to make up for my family faux pas.

I resort to information. 'Mam used to say, it was the closure of the pit in 1974 that was the downfall of the village because historically Kibblesworth had always been a mining village and when the pit closed, droves of men had to find work in Gateshead and Newcastle,' I say then raise an eyebrow at her. 'And, did you also know that the name Kibblesworth means, Cybbel's Enclosure. I remember that in our history lessons at school from your dad. I think he would be pleased to see that not all his efforts were in vain and at least one of his pupils remembered something from his lessons.'

At the mention of her father her eyes water a little and soften. Her shoulders sag and I feel her relax into my arm.

Keep going, I think, she's coming around. I try one of my best lop-sided grins. This often does the trick and I'm hoping that it will work this time. The grin is meant to let her know that it is still me. The man that loves and worships her to distraction.

I can tell she's relenting because she shakes her head and gives me a watery smile. She teases, 'Yeah, right, Mr. Henderson. The know it all.'

I lie my head on the back of the settee and pull her further into my arms. She is now resting her head against my chest. 'I'm sorry, love. I've been trying to explain how I feel about living here and as usual I've made a pig's ear of it all.'

I squeeze her tightly against me and rub my chin on top of her hair. 'I loved it here when I was little. There used to be cricket and bowls on the green and mam would take us for tea and iced buns into the Methodist church. Mam loved working in the small library and although she never married again and lived with Uncle Geoff, she was very happy here.'

I sigh and wish for the hundredth time that mam hadn't ignored the lump in her breast and had told me about it.

But she'd been too scared to go to the hospital. If she had gone, they might have been able to save her. By the time the symptoms began to show the cancer had spread and it was too late.

Erin must know that I'm thinking of mam because she puts her arm right around my chest now and hugs me close. Absurdly, I can feel tears sting at the back of my eyes. I swallow hard.

Erin sighs, 'I know your mam loved it here, but that was years ago, when you were a little boy, David. They're just old memories. Which are lovely to have but she's gone now. We can't live our lives here just because you don't want to leave her memory behind…' she pauses then stares up into my eyes, 'and, for the rest. When have either of us been to a cricket match or played bowls. I mean that's not what we do together, is it?'

I nod my head in agreement. I try one more shot. 'And, there's Uncle Geoff. What would I do about him?'

She sits up a little from my chest and smiles. She places a cool hand on my cheek. 'David, he's in a nursing home and has Alzheimer's. I know he's the only family you have left, and you used to visit him regularly, but at your last visit he didn't even know you. And you haven't been back for six weeks now.'

I groan at her words and sigh heavily. 'Is it that long?'

Erin reminds me of the short train journey and suggests that I could visit him before I go to the match on weekends at home.

I feel the back of my neck flush knowing I've lapsed with the visiting. Mam would be upset that I'd not been to see him. I can almost hear her saying, 'Just because he doesn't know who you are doesn't mean you don't know who he is. He shouldn't be left alone without family around him.'

I determine to go and see him as soon as possible.

'It'll be great to be in a new place,' she says. 'A fresh start for both of us where no one knows about our previous troubles.'

I decide to throw one last ditch attempt to her. 'Plus, we are semi-rural here which I've always loved, and I know you like it too. Are you sure about being so close to London? You might not be able to walk around safely like you do here.'

She chuckles slightly. 'The address is not in the capital as well you know. It's thirty minutes out of London,' she states reaching across the coffee table for her iPad. 'Let's google Bexley Heath and see if it is in a built-up area?'

And I know I've lost the battle.

Chapter Five

Erin Henderson, *Kibblesworth, Gateshead, Tyne & Wear. June 2018*

After establishing the fact that Bexley Heath is a built-up area sixteen miles south east of London near the bakery, we found a nearby smaller town called Bexley. This is only another mile down the road and being much older it looks the ideal place.

David seemed to perk up looking at the relatively large area of open spaces amongst the quaint streets and avenues. 'Yes,' he'd agreed. 'It looks a good place to settle.'

He's sloped off now to have a shower. I know this is just an excuse to be on his own and digest what we've looked at online and think about things. It's what he does. When he's quiet and non-talkative I know he's brooding but will soon snap out of it.

I'd already looked at Bexley on my own yesterday so when we went online, I knew exactly which links to use to show the area at its best. Am I devious or clever? Neither, it is simply that I know David very well and how his brain ticks. I also love every inch of him and cannot imagine my life without him.

Bexley is where I want to live now and I'm praying that David gets the job, so we can make a fresh start in the south. I comfort myself with the fact that I really can't see a reason why he shouldn't get the job. I know from talking to his colleagues at Christmas parties that he is good at his job.

Alfie had said, 'David is brilliant at developing new cakes and is super to work with because he loves what he does. In our line of business that's what makes the difference.'

I smile knowing my husband will make an amazing manager.

He'll be great with his team of workers. Kind and generous but when it's something important he will be firm and stand his ground.

I peel another satsuma and look at the two properties that are up for sale in Bexley. I calculate the price. With my sale for this cottage, David's monthly contributions, and some of my father's money we will be in a comfortable situation to buy either one of the houses. Even though the prices are much more expensive than here in the north, I simply cannot wait to leave this village.

My mind goes back over the two years and I shake my head in disbelief at what we've been through. There are a couple of situations that arose which David doesn't know about. At the time I'd felt he had enough to cope with and didn't tell him. But now I grimace knowing how awful it feels to be the outcast.

When David had turned up with suitcases that night at my cottage door it had shattered my equilibrium. I'd got used to our affair over the three months and the fact that if we wanted to be together, we had to sneak around and keep it secret. I hadn't minded this although David had seemed more troubled about it than I was. I was just deliriously happy to have him in my life whatever price there was to pay. I'd spent those first months not quite believing that such a gorgeous looking guy could be interested in me. I'd been determined to love the very life out of him for as long as it lasted. Nothing in my past had lasted with any type of longevity so I wasn't used to declarations for the future. I've always lived in the here and now.

In Australia, I did have relationships in my twenties but none of them lasted very long. Although they were nice guys, they hadn't turned me into a tizzy like David had done. And still does.

I'd met a Scotsman who I nick-named, Scottie, and went out with him for six months. He lived near our house, but father never really liked him.

'Scottie asked me to marry him,' I'd told my father one morning. He'd looked flustered and scratched his beard with a sad expression on his face. This immediately had lifted into a huge grin when I'd continued. 'But I've refused him. He's not what I thought he was.'

Scottie had been exciting and fun to be with. Later I discovered he had two children from his first marriage that he'd somehow omitted to tell me about because they lived in Glasgow.

'I thought you'd think they were excess baggage,' he'd said which sounded heartless and uncaring. When this happened, I'd known father had been right all along not to trust in his easy-going manner. Scottie turned out to be shallow and a liar.

So, when I'd met David, I approached our sexual relationship with a devil-may-care attitude determined to enjoy him for as long as he lasted. With the news that he'd left Beth and Sally that night, I'd felt my whole insides flip into a state of wariness and apprehension.

I'm not good at surprises and shocks. I'd had enough of them in my childhood when my mother left us. I like time to digest news and make my own controlled decisions. We'd never talked about him leaving Beth. He'd never made promises and I'd never asked for them. I remember standing behind him in the hallway and staring mutely at his suitcases while he told me how devastated Beth had been and Sally's hysterical reaction.

My first thoughts had been, yes, I want you with me but not until I'm ready. I couldn't voice those thoughts to him as he suffered dreadfully during the first few weeks.

I had suffered too, but with a different range of problems. Not only did I have to cope with being stared at in the village, with the older women jeering and calling me a whore and homewrecker, but I had to get used to someone living with me.

I'd been alone since my father had died suddenly with a heart attack in Australia when I was thirty-five. Our beloved housekeeper, Josie, who had stepped into the breach when my mother left had announced her intention to move across to Bondi Beach to be near her brother.

'You'll be fine,' Josie had stated giving me a hug. She'd pulled away from me and smiled but the smile hadn't quite reached her eyes. 'And you can come over to me for holidays.'

I'd felt the offer had been a throw-a-way comment as if she'd hoped I wouldn't take her up on the suggestion. Within weeks of her departure and longing for a new start somewhere myself I decided to return to my birth town of Kibblesworth.

So, although I love David unreservedly, having him in the cottage 24/7 hadn't been easy and it took a while to get used to him being with me. Once I had, of course, I knew I'd never want to live without him again.

I'd liked Kibblesworth at first. Everyone in the village had been pleasant and welcoming towards me. Not being much for socialising I hadn't exactly thrown myself into community events, but I had used the shop and the library. They'd kindly ordered some large art books for me and I'd spent many hours reading through them and photocopying the paintings to work on at home. I knew the names of the women working in the local shop and had been into the pub on a few occasions for lunch. However, the pleasantness all ended abruptly when David moved in with me.

Within the first year we'd weathered the storm. Beth and Sally eventually got on with their own lives again and David was convinced that life in the village would soon settle down. But there were two singular incidents that will always be uppermost in my mind and proved to me that I'd never be accepted by the villagers.

We'd converted my single bedroom into an office for David to use with his computer. After decorating and changing the soft furnishings I'd popped into the village jumble sale with old cushions and bed linen. The sale was held at The Millennium Community

Centre which has been re-developed from the old village hall by lottery money and was now a modern bright room with new facilities.

When I'd asked at the door where to leave my contributions, I'd been met with a hostile stare from a woman around my own age who worked part time in the shop. If she'd been an older lady, I could have accepted the fact that she believed it was scandalous to live with a man who wasn't your husband. But at our age and in the 21st century, I'd thought her mind-set could be more liberal.

She'd grunted, 'Put them over there.' I'd scurried past her with my head down.

I'd decided, even after a year that the anger and hatred I saw in the eyes of the village women astounded me. The atmosphere had hung around me while I strolled from stall to stall. I'd felt their eyes bore into my back. The older lady on the bric-a-brac stall had openly glared at me, as if to say, how dare you come in here after what you've done.

This occurrence had a detrimental effect upon me, and I began to withdraw further into myself dreading more encounters with the villagers.

The second incident took place about a month later when I'd called into the pub one night to buy a bottle of David's favourite red wine. I'd spotted one of his friends who caught up with me just inside the door when I'd been leaving.

At dusk, and with only a single light in the doorway, I'd been able to see he was drunk. He'd pushed his ugly face up to mine and the smell of beer had made me recoil. I'd been appalled when he made a pass at me. He'd grabbed a handful of my skirt in his rough hands and tried to hike it up. I'd shoved him aside then hurried to get outside into the fresh night air. As I'd rushed down the street clutching my bottle of wine he'd jeered after me, 'What's wrong! I thought you were a good-time girl who would be up for anything?'

I'd decided that night I would never feel at peace living in the village and wouldn't fit in with the local people supposing it took another fifty years.

After this, when I'd been alone, and David was at work or out with his friends I'd been happiest to stay inside the cottage. Even going out for a walk some days had made me feel anxious. The thought of going to the village shop had made me cringe inside and I'd felt my self-confidence slowly ebb away.

Following one disastrous morning walk where my heart had begun to race, sweat had stood on my forehead, and I'd felt as though the trees were all leaning in towards me like a canopy, I'd hurried home and wondered if it had been a panic attack. The feelings had been all the scarier because I've always had a gregarious personality and am well-used to doing many activities on my own.

However, once David and I were married I began to feel more secure in our relationship. He thought this would help to cement us as a couple in the area but in my opinion, it hasn't.

When David had proposed, I'd quickly accepted. I mean, what woman in her right mind wouldn't? But at the time, and even now, I know our marriage hasn't made any real difference to the villager's opinions.

It did make a difference to me, however. Now I go out and about again with the attitude that I won't let a bunch of narrow-minded people get the better of me. At the same time, I know I will always be thought of as the homewrecker. The bit on the side. The other woman. The woman who had nearly destroyed Beth and Sally lives.

Sighing now I close the laptop and begin to wander around the lounge. There's a photograph standing proudly on top of the polished bureau. I pick it up and peer at David's face smiling easily into the camera. He is with his pals in the pub and one of them has inscribed, Dave and chums, in the corner of the photograph with a red pen.

I grimace. I've never liked the photograph because more than anything I hate him being called, Dave.

Dave is what Beth used to call him. Apart from the fact that it was her special name for him, he is so unlike a man I would associate with the name Dave that it just sounds ludicrous. To me, Dave sounds like he should be in a rock group or an old has-been hippie.

My David is too manly with an authoritative air and couldn't be called anything else but, David. Although he comes across to people as modest in an understated manner, he is self-assured and very comfortable in his own skin.

I put the photograph back into place and think about our lunch. I could tell David had stopped himself from

repeating the fact that he used to take cake home to
Beth and Sally.

I know I shouldn't mind him talking about them, but
sometimes I can't bear it. I feel a burning sensation in
my stomach, and I clench my jaw thinking about the
two of them with him. This jealous streak in me is a
failing. I should be content and confident in his love
for me that I'll happily let him regale me with their
cosy family stories, but I can't.

Very often I know my emotions are volatile especially
when I'm hormonal. In the past I've blamed this for
reacting badly to situations that are beyond my control.
But David's previous life which he shared with his
daughter and ex-wife is something I can't do anything
about. This frustrates me beyond belief.

I sigh. It's not as if Beth has been any type of threat to
me because as far as I can see she's never looked after
herself. Chubby to the point of being fat, probably with
all the cake she's eaten over the years, she is a plain
mousey woman with broad flat features who seems
devoid of any real personality.

'Beth is just quiet and shy meeting new people,'
David has said in the past. 'But when she comes out of
her shell, she's really very nice.'

Upon that I can't comment because I've never
actually spoken to her. However, apart from going to
work all she ever seemed to do was clean her house,
visit her mum in a care home, and watch TV. What
type of existence is that? David reckons if they went on
holiday abroad after three days she was longing to be

home again. She didn't like the sun and never joined in any sight-seeing activities. No wonder he was bored.

And Sally, so far as I can see is destined to become a carbon copy of her mother. As a teenager she was plump and looked horrendous in the leggings she wore. Even now, she doesn't appear to have many friends and seems to spend most of her days in front of the TV or a computer screen.

So, I reason brightly, I've made sure our life together is the total opposite. We don't watch much TV. Although I do like to watch Lost Masterpieces and anything arty, and David of course, loves his sports channel. Together, we enjoy the travel programmes where we daydream about all the places we'd like to visit by train and see as much of the scenery as possible.

Michael Portillo is one of our favourites. When we'd watched an episode filmed in Florence, David had joked, 'Yes, I'd love to go there. But I'm not wearing those pink trousers!'

I sigh and recap over Sally. The one thing I am glad about now is that she does speak to David. Her abandonment was cutting him up. Even though she still refuses to talk to me, he reckons she will come to terms with our marriage in time.

I won't lose any sleep over this not unless it hurts David, of course. I have and always will do anything in my power to prevent David being upset. Since meeting me, he's been through so much already. I love him too much to watch him suffer. When I see his sad eyes or when he bites the inside of his lip, I feel wretched myself. It's almost a physical pain in my stomach and I find it unbearable. I shudder.

Sitting back down onto the settee I gulp at the warm coffee. I hear the shower running and think of my gorgeous man. I hug myself with pleasure. I always feel like this when he's on my mind. David is blonde with a little grey peppered in his sideburns and has a lovely face. He has a longish nose and is always clean-shaven and smells good.

I like to buy him classy after-shaves because I love to smell him. I often sink my face into his neck and breath him into me. He's not overly tall, around five-foot-seven I think, but because I'm a shorty we fit together perfectly.

He has a good body too and likes to keep himself fit. If he has a heavy weekend where we eat and drink too much, he does extra running sessions because he doesn't want to have a middle-aged-spread. Or as he calls it, a potbelly.

The very thought of David makes me want him and deciding a woman can never be too clean I head along the corridor to join him in the shower.

Chapter Six

Monday morning dawns and I have a day off work. The vet has closed the surgery for a training session. I know David is going to ring HR at the London bakery this morning to arrange the interview. I feel a bundle of nerves for him. And for me too. I decide the best way to keep my myself distracted is to spend the whole day painting in my studio.

It's not a studio as such but the folding wood doors create a section apart from the rest of the lounge. When I have the blinds fully open the light floods the room and is amazing, It's the main reason why I bought the cottage. I tie my hair back from my face with a scarf and pull on paint splattered dungarees. I hate anything which irritates me when I'm in the throes of my work.

Some people wouldn't class this as my work because I do have what is commonly known as a proper job. But I like to think of this as my future career and not just a hobby.

From the day I'd met David he'd raved about my paintings.

'Oh, Erin,' he'd said. 'They're amazing!'

At first, I'd thought his compliments were said through kindness. However, on my good days I do agree with him. I've sold a few paintings to people at work who have been delighted. My main ambition is to become proficient and make an income from the sale of my paintings. I've long since decided it's what I do best in life.

Carrying my mug of coffee, I stride purposively towards my easel. The smell of oil paint hits my senses while I stare at the canvas I'm painting. I smile. It's a scene of Venice from a postcard David bought me when we were there on our honeymoon.

This is proving to be quite a challenge because I usually work with bright colours. However, the Venetian narrow alleyways and canals hold a typically subdued light.

Years ago, when I first started to paint, I began with watercolours but soon found the delicate pastel colour palette uninspiring and I longed for more boldness. I changed to oils and love the vibrancy of rich scarlet reds, bold bright blues, with sunny yellow colour palettes.

I'd once said to David, 'If I'm going to paint a grassy field, I want the grass to look luscious green, a grass that sheep would want to nibble, not brown dried-up vegetation.'

He'd nodded in agreement, and over the years I've become more skilled at my work.

The old saying, practise makes perfect, has certainly worked for me. It's the only activity I've found that completely empties my mind of all other thoughts. When I'm painting, I'm so engrossed that I lose track of all time. David often reprimands me because I forget to eat and drink for hours on end.

I stand back sipping my coffee wondering how I can capture the water in the canal that gently laps up the side of the house in the postcard. It looks murky and almost grey. I remember the night times in the dark when we strolled along the sides of the canals. I start to mix colours on my palette until I find a blend which suits the eerie, evening light.

I'm transported back to Venice and remember everything about our honeymoon. I'd longed to visit the small Italian city for years. When David asked where I'd like to go on honeymoon, I hadn't thought twice.

'Venice!' I'd cried, and he'd picked me up and spun me around in the air until I'd felt quite dizzy.

I'd started grinning from the moment we walked up the steps onto the aeroplane and hadn't stopped for the whole week we were there. Thankfully, David was as enchanted by the city as I was. When we came home, he made a beautiful album with all the photographs he'd taken. I look across to it now propped open on the window ledge and grin. One of my favourite photographs is of David wearing a white tuxedo when we went to a Venetian ball.

Now, you need to know that David looks good in a simple pair of jeans and T-shirt. But that night in our hotel room when he emerged from the bathroom wearing the tuxedo, I'd gasped in awe. He was so damn handsome.

I'd bought myself a long, red velvet dress from a vintage shop in Newcastle, and when he saw me, he'd whistled through his teeth. Playfully, he'd held out his arm for me to link while we'd glided through the hotel lobby. We'd stepped gingerly on board the boat that took us down the canal to the Palazzo.

I'd giggled, 'I feel like Julia Roberts in the film, Pretty Woman.'

He'd looked deep into my eyes and squeezed my hand. 'No, Erin, you are way more beautiful than she is,' he'd said.

I grin now and hug myself with the special memories then begin to mix a brown colour on my palette. I look at the cat sitting outside the house on the postcard. Maybe I'll make the cat a tabby colour and I think about the first day I'd met David.

David's cat had died in my arms. The vet had told him, 'Tiddles, is just too old to survive any type of surgery and it's not fair to watch him suffer.'

I'd seen a cloud pass through David's blue eyes when he bit the inside of his lip. And that is when I remembered him from schooldays.

Before we'd moved to Australia, our small terraced house had backed onto the boundary of the farm where David had lived. I could vaguely remember him crossing the fields to school with his mum. But then they'd left the farm and moved down to Lamesley with his uncle. After that, I'd only seen him in classes at school.

I'd smiled at David stroking the cat. He'd looked up and teased me, 'I remember your wild red hair.'

We'd looked into each other's eyes and I felt something hit me. A connection, a bolt of lightning, it sounds corny, but there it was, something deep down inside flipped and joined me to him. I'd fallen for him in an instant and knew without a doubt that David was the one. The special one I felt was in harmony in everything I did. He'd slotted one of his long fingers into a ringlet in my hair and I'd melted inside.

I'd gone through school hating my red hair because the other kids had taunted me. 'Ginger nut and freckle face,' they'd chant. At the time, I'd blamed my father for this because he had the same bright red hair. Whereas mum, and baby Neil had blonde hair.

These days, I'm not bothered by the red colour and have been accepting of it since my twenties. I've never coloured my hair although hairdressers have suggested toning the brightness down, but I've refused. David reckons, it sets me aside from millions of other women.

However, there are still some comments that irritate me. One day, the vet had said, 'You look just like Demelza in the Poldark series.' I'd snorted to myself in derision. This was more because the man himself irks me, than the actual hair comment.

I'd met David for lunch the day after his cat died and we'd come back to the cottage afterwards.

I'd known within minutes of sitting opposite to him in the restaurant that he wanted me as much as I'd wanted him. Because I hadn't been able to think of a reason we should delay or ignore our feelings, I'd invited him back for coffee. When I'd shown him around the cottage, he'd murmured appreciative comments about the décor and how it was an incredible transformation of an old property. I'd opened the doors to my studio, and he'd gasped in awe at the sight of my canvases strewn around the room.

'But Erin,' he'd gushed. 'These are brilliant!'

He'd made me grin and blush like a teenager. Standing close behind me while we looked at the canvas on my easel, I'd felt his hot breath on the back of my neck and ear. My hair was fastened into a top knot and I'd sighed in pleasure when he'd pulled it lose and gently scrunched both his hands into my hair.

'Oh, Erin,' he'd whispered. 'I've been longing to do this.'

My knees had weakened at the touch of his hands. Within seconds we were writhing around on the pine wood floor scattering my paints, pots, and bottles of water all over the floor. Afterwards, we'd laughed conspiratorially while I'd tried to wipe red paint from the top of his thigh with a cloth before he'd left.

'It doesn't matter,' he'd protested. 'I want the smell of oil paint and you on me forever.'

At the door when we'd kissed each other longingly. He'd smudged a streak of green paint from my cheek with his thumb. And that was it. We were hooked.

The sound of my mobile ringing brings me back to the here and now. I glance at the clock and realise David will be on his lunch break and might have news of the interview. I can feel myself holding my breath for a few seconds.

He tells me the appointment is arranged for the following Monday. I can hear the excitement in his voice as if he is grinning at the news.

'This is it!' I punch the air feeling quite giddy with excitement. Maybe it will be our chance to get away from this bloody backwater village. I hurry through to the lounge and sign-in on my iPad. David has suggested we weekend in London first and I busy myself booking train tickets, hotel, and a West End show.

Chapter Seven

'But I have to get the job first, Erin,' I say in the most soothing manner I can muster. It's Saturday morning and we are sitting on the train travelling down to London.

Erin flaps a hand nonchalantly at me. 'Of course, you'll get it,' she states confidently. 'There's no reason why you shouldn't get the job, David.'

I raise an eyebrow. 'Well, I don't want to see you build yourself up and then be crushed if I'm not successful for one reason or another,' I say gazing out of the window. 'I don't want to disappoint you.'

Erin lays a hand over mine on the small drop-down table on the back of the seat in front of me. I turn to look at her.

She squeezes my hand. 'You could never do anything to disappoint me, darling.'

I look into her eyes and we are at one.

A lady pushing the refreshment trolley clatters towards us. She calls out, 'Tea or coffee?'

Erin busies herself paying for tea and milk jiggers and I can almost feel the excitement oozing out of her body. Erin chats to the woman explaining why we are going to London and what she plans to see.

The further towards King's Cross we get, the exhilaration seems to intensify. I don't mind admitting myself that I'm also a little excited. I've been to London before, of course, but mainly to visit the cake retailers head offices. Like Erin, I'm looking forward to behaving like a typical tourist and seeing as many of the sights as possible.

Erin is now chatting about the exhibition at Tate Modern that she plans to visit on Monday while I'm at the interview.

She has her hand on my thigh and is tracing the material of my trousers by rubbing her thumb around in circles.

I turn my face away to stare out of the window trying to ignore the instant reaction to her touch. This response is not surprising because Erin oozes sex appeal from every inch of her. It takes very little contact and closeness to make me want to show her how much I love her. Erin has always been, in my eyes everything a woman should be. Sexy and passionate which comes naturally to her. The attraction between us had been mind-blowing from the first time I'd slept with her.

When I think of my sex-life before Erin it had been very different. Beth had been meek and unadventurous in bed probably because I was too in our early days. We knew no different. I'd felt for many years that as lovely as Beth was, she often saw sex as a chore. An inconvenience she could well live without. I remember distinctly one night in our late twenties when we'd began to make love. I'd been feeling particularly frisky but halfway through I'd looked down at Beth and noticed her eyes were closed. 'Beth,' I'd whispered in her ear. 'Beth are you awake?' She'd shaken herself and hurriedly tried to join in. But I'd known she'd dozed off to sleep midway. This had done nothing for my self-esteem and confidence. I'd felt a sense of total inadequacy.

I continue to stare out of the window now at the trees and fields of the countryside rushing past as the train races down the track. I sigh then shake myself. I feel bad about thinking of Beth in this way because as the saying goes, it takes two to tango. If we were boring and conservative, then I need to take my equal share of the blame. If I hadn't been exciting enough to keep her awake when we were making love, then that's down to me and not her.

I wonder where I'd be now and how my life would have panned out if I hadn't met Erin. Probably the same as it was before I met her. I shrug, I hadn't been unhappy with Beth. I hadn't been purposely looking for someone else when I fell in love with Erin. I'd probably have drifted along thinking this was it. This was how marriage worked. And yes, it was perfectly natural for your wife to fall asleep during making love. As a couple that was all we could expect to have.

I peek at Erin out of the corner of my eye and smile contentedly because she has taught me that it's not all we can expect. There is so much more we can have as a couple. Every day with Erin seems to be filled with desire which makes me want her even more. And because she feels the same my self-confidence has soared to an all-time high. I may still have insecurities about other issues in my life but not about making love.

I turn my head towards her now because she has stopped talking and has removed her hand to look for something in her handbag. I feel a coolness on my thigh where her hand had lain. She brings out a packet of chewing gum and we both take a piece and begin to chew. The spearmint flavour freshens my dry mouth and I smile at her gratefully.

We both stare out of the window when we pull into Peterborough station looking at passengers waiting on the platform. We'll be in the capital within the next fifty minutes. She snuggles into my shoulder while I drape my arm around her and hug her close.

Of course, like other couples our relationship is not one hundred percent perfection. We have slight ups and downs. Erin's challenging and sometimes sulky personality is the total opposite of Beth's easy-going nature.

But I've long since decided this is easily overlooked because her artistic and physical attributes make up for a few tantrums. Thinking back over the last two years I can honestly claim that most nights when I lie next to her, I'm filled with genuine happiness. Or to use a friends' expression, I feel like I've died and gone to heaven.

**

Arriving in King's Cross we alight from the train and walk through into the entrance hall. A train to Edinburgh has just been announced and hundreds of people pulling suitcases and carrying bags start to hurry through the opposite ticket gates.

We step outside into the sunshine. Standing still for a moment I feel a buzz of anticipation while people mill around a food fair which is under way. Small stalls are set up selling everything from honey to cheese.

Ordinarily I would love to browse, but Erin is waving our tickets that she has bought for the tube.

Pulling the suitcase, I follow Erin towards the tube entrance. She flounces in front of me in her short flowery dress with flat strappy sandals. I can see a couple of men standing in the taxi rank turn to stare at the wild red hair flowing around her smiling face. I grin. I'm not a jealous type of man but I'd love to shout, hands off guys, she's all mine.

We walk along the underground corridor towards the tube platform and Erin slows down to link my arm. We're amidst hordes of people hurrying towards their destinations.

I've done this walk many times with Alfie when crossing over to Paddington. I chuckle. 'Alfie always says that Londoners down here in the tunnels are like rats scuttling along the depths of the earth.'

Erin giggles and nods her head. 'He's right,' she states happily as we step straight onto a tube to London Bridge. 'It's giving me some amazing ideas for paintings.'

***

The weekend has flown over. I've left Erin in the hotel and I'm on a train out to Bexley Heath for the interview. My black leather briefcase is on the vacant seat next to me because the train is not busy. I go through a mental checklist to make sure I have everything. I've already done this twice and know I'm over-reacting with a slight case of the jitters. Two copies of my CV, the portfolio of cakes I've developed, my skill set, and a personnel questionnaire I've been asked to complete.

My mouth feels a little dry and I gulp at the bottle of water Erin has put in my briefcase. I take a deep breath. The train guard has made an announcement that the air conditioning is not working. Already my shirt collar is stuck on the back of my neck in the hot atmosphere. I gulp at more water and reassure myself that the butterflies in my stomach are simply the fear of an unknown situation. Once I get into the interview, I'll be fine.

The young train guard approaches and I show him my ticket. I smile hoping for a few words of conversation, but he grumpily stamps the ticket then moves on down the carriage. I shrug my shoulders and look at my watch for what seems like the umpteenth time since we left the station.

I read through my list of answers that I've prepared. It's hard to imagine what questions I'm going to be asked. But I did ring an old work colleague who has recently been in a similar interview situation. He told me the questions he'd been asked. The hardest being, *what were his three best qualities, and in turn, what were his three worst qualities?*

I chew the side of my lip deciding these questions are not easy to answer. The first answers will sound like I'm bragging. And the second will be difficult because no one wants to admit their worst traits. I shrug, this question can never be answered with total honesty. The next question, *what skills can I bring to the team?*

makes me feel much easier. I've bullet-pointed my attributes and development experience.

There's a taxi waiting outside the station and I climb into the back giving the taxi driver the address. We speed off into the traffic. Opposed to the train guard, the taxi driver chats continually all the way to the bakery. Glancing in his mirror he establishes by my accent that I'm from the north. We joke about the differences in the weather. I can feel my shoulders relax with his conversation and his further well-wishes as I stand on the pavement outside the reception doors.

Turning behind to look at the huge bakery plant which looks at least three times bigger than where I currently work. I gasp in awe. I take a slow deep breath then walk into the reception to announce my arrival.

***

Two hours later I'm back on the train heading for London Bridge. I'm grinning to myself and feel all my senses are heightened. The interview had gone well. The upshot is that HR have already asked me to return for a second interview with the development team. I feel like punching the air and giving a loud whoop.

The train is busier going back into London and a young girl is sitting next to me. Although she has his ear plugs into her mobile, I can hear the beat of the music and tap my foot on the side of my briefcase which is wedged on the floor.

I think about the questions they'd asked and how they liked my answers. I remember a couple of things I was going to say but had forgotten. I loosen the knot in my tie and look out of the train window. These answers couldn't have been important because it hasn't affected the outcome.

My main feeling, and no one is more surprised at this than I am, is how much I want the job. Ever since agreeing with Erin to come for the interview I've honestly had mixed emotions. There was a small part of me thought I'd not get past the first stage interview and would be crushingly disappointed in myself. Worse still, I'd let Erin down.

My phone tingles with an email and I skim-read the message from HR with possible dates for the second interview. My stomach tumbles. I'm looking forward to returning already.

The train is heading onto the station platform and I pick up my briefcase from the floor. I know I've done well and feel a surge of energy and adrenalin race through my body. I pull my shoulders back and hop off the train then hurry towards the exit and outside into the warm sunshine.

I hold my face up to the sun then continue up the road to the hotel. I think about the team of technologists I will have working for me and know I can run the department to a high standard.

***

I hurry through the hotel reception hoping Erin is back from the art gallery. I'm on such a high I can't wait to hug her. I think she has had more confidence in me than I had in myself and want to show my gratitude.

I ride up in the lift deep in thought. For some reason I remember how I'd struggled during the first few months after I'd left Beth.

Although I'd been deliriously happy living with Erin, the guilt of tearing my family apart had hung around my shoulders like the proverbial black cloud.

Erin had been the one who'd held us together with her never-failing faith in our love for each other. 'We'll be fine, once we get through this rough patch,' she'd insist. 'Just give them time. Beth and Sally will eventually get on with their lives again, you'll see.'

On those days, all it took was one glimpse of Erin to make me feel the sunshine break through that black cloud. I knew back then, as I do right at this moment that if I have her at my side, I'll survive whatever life throws at me.

While I push the key-card into room 401 and hurry inside calling out her name I drop the briefcase to the floor. She side-steps out of the bathroom.

She stares at my face searching for an answer. 'Well…'

'I think I've got it!' I cry and scoop her up into my arms then spin her around in the air. I shout, 'Whoopee!!'

Erin shrieks. 'Oh, well done, David. I knew you could do it!'

I set her to the floor again but keep my arms securely around her waist hugging her tightly. 'They want me to go back for a second interview next week to meet the team I'd be working with. That's if I get it, of course.'

She looks up into my eyes and squeezes me. 'You'll get it. That's for sure,' she gabbles. 'They wouldn't want you to go back if they didn't like you.'

I can see the excitement shinning in her eyes. I feel a little breathless and can't stop grinning. 'Well, I was a bit nervous before I got there. I must admit my interview skills were a little rusty, to say the least, but I surprised myself at how easy it all felt.'

Erin peels the jacket back off my shoulders while I tell her about the questions they'd asked. I explain how many technologists there are in the team and about the different retailers. I keep taking quick gasps of breath because I'm talking so fast. Without realising what we are doing I have pulled off my tie and flung it over the chair.

'So, who was with the personnel lady,' she asks starting to unbuckle my belt.

'Oh, there was a manager called June,' I say. 'She is leaving and moving up to Scotland.' I look down at Erin's nimble hands undoing the button on my trousers.

I laugh out loud. I'm not sure if she realises that she is undressing me, and I wonder. Is it such a habitual response between us now that when we're excited, we strip off each other's clothes? We stare at each other. I feel like I'm on the starting blocks of a 100-metre dash with my heart beginning to race.

'What did she say?' Erin asks and shakes her hair loose until it flows wildly around her face.

In my own humble thoughts, I know she is getting ready for me just as a peacock proudly spreads its feathers. I shake my head trying to remember what I had been saying then swallow hard at the sight of her hurriedly undressing.

'W…well,' I stutter licking my dry lips, 'June said that my natural passion and enthusiasm for the job shines out of my eyes when I talk. She was amazed at my portfolio of the cakes that I've developed.'

'Oh, did she now?' Erin purrs sexily with a catch in her throat. 'Well I'm glad she is moving on if she is looking into my husband's eyes!'

I look at her mouth and see her tongue dart out. I throw my head back whooping loudly. I know this is my green light and she is as excited as I am. My heart begins to pound. I need her now. Right now. There's not a minute to lose.

The adrenalin surging through me is indescribable. I feel drunk. Heady. I'm so charged up I can hardly think straight. The tension and anxiety that had built up over the last two hours screams to be released from my body. I can't think of a better way to achieve this. Erin yells with encouragement and squeals loudly as passion overtakes us both and I achieve my blessed relief in her body.

We spend the afternoon in bed. Well, not just in the bed, but on the floor, and in the bathroom. We make love with such ferocity that it is quite simply three hours of my life that I will never forget. After our first session, I ring room service and order a bottle of champagne which we drink from long stem glasses. 'Here's a toast to your success,' she calls out.

I pour out a second glass. 'And, here's a toast to moving down to Bexley Heath and the start of our new life together!'

By the third glass I'm too drunk to remember what we're toasting. Erin's energy is boundless, and her voice rises to new crescendo's in her abandoned lust. The hotel receptionist rings and asks us to keep the noise down because we are disturbing guests in the next room.

This is like waving a red flag to my she-devil tigress who screams and yells even louder. And for once in my life I don't worry about disturbing other people. I love Erin totally and utterly for who she is. Her happiness is paramount to me.

Chapter Eight

I once heard Josie, say, 'You've grown up with a distorted view of family life because of what happened.'

And maybe she is right. Apart from David, who I class as my soul mate and other half in life, I don't have what most people call close friends. Even at school I've never had a best friend. The people I've worked with over the years, or neighbours, or old family friends, are what I call acquaintances. And because I'm not digitally aware and never take part in any social online activities, I am on my own.

I did try Twitter once. Other staff in the vet's surgery spend most of their lunch hour glued to the screens of their mobiles. One of the girls had said. 'Start with joining Twitter and then you can learn Facebook.'

But it wasn't for me. After reading tweets where people wished each other, Happy Friday, and one woman's account of trip to a supermarket, I decided it was nothing but meaningless rubbish and closed the account.

I do have one close acquaintance, who is the vet's wife, Vicky. She is not an artist but does love art works and paintings. On a few occasions, we've been to exhibitions in Newcastle and York. Early in our friendship I'd asked her to the cottage, and she had gushed over my work. 'I love the colours, Erin,' she'd said. 'And the paintings of Venice look magical!'

She'd bought a painting from me that day and it had cemented our friendship. There again, if I took our love of art away from the friendship, I'm not entirely sure what would be left. Being the same age, we get along well together, but I'd still struggle to talk about my feelings with her.

The only person I can open my heart to is David, of course. I suppose this makes me quite singular in a way.

I can be friendly and chatty even amusing at times but the moment anyone starts to feel close enough to want to share their dreams or fears with me, I clam up. Quite literally.

Previously when we've met new people David has said, 'She seems a nice woman, why not join her for dinner or go to the cinema?'

I've stubbornly shaken my head. 'If I wanted to do either of those things, I'd much rather do them with you.'

My excuse, and I cannot seem to waver from this belief, is that I don't like people getting too close to me. I've learned in life that relationships are fragile and can be whipped away in seconds. The intelligent and rational side of my brain tells me this is simply a result of the family trauma I suffered. I know I should recognise this, deal with it, and move forwards to believe in people. But I simply can't put my trust in anyone.

Hence, on days like today when I am on my own and David is having his second interview, it would be great to have a close friend to talk over this monumental leap we are about to make. Or, a mother to give me advice and support. Neither of which I have.

David has only travelled down for the day and will be home later tonight. I will hear all his news then. Right now, I'm sitting on the floor in my studio with my legs crossed and staring at the knots in the wood. My mind seems heavy with raging tumultuous thoughts. I know I've bolstered David up into making this move south because I really do want to leave this village. However, this wish is not without its own problems.

Now, I don't have any involvement in David's workplace other than the annual Christmas party. His colleagues know that I prefer things this way.

But his new team in the south won't know this and I'm worried they might insist I join groups or clubs. Also, will his team expect a certain amount of commitment from the new managers wife? In short, will I have to alter my lifestyle to fit in with his promotion.

I sigh heavily and wish I'd had a normal family background and hadn't been blighted by what my mother did to me when I was seven. I mean, a girl needs her mum when she's growing up, doesn't she? In fact, she needs her mum whatever age, but I've never had that. My mother robbed me of this support because she was never there.

Just before Christmas when I was six years old, I remember reading in a storybook about bad things happening to naughty girls. On the day my mother checked-out, I'd asked, 'Is it my fault she's gone?'

I figured it had to be something I'd done wrong and that I must have been truly bad for her to want to leave me. I missed her voice singing in the kitchen, her bedtime kiss and tuck-in, but most of all I just missed her being there.

From then onwards there'd been no motherly hugs. When I'd been frightened of the dark and had nightmares, it had been my father who'd sat on the end of my bed reading to me until I fell asleep again. 'You're okay,' he'd soothe. 'Close your eyes and go back to sleep. I'm here.'

I'd clung to him for years and he was the only one who knew exactly how much I hated my mother.

I wish I could be the happy well-adjusted woman that people think I am from the outside. Not the person they soon discover when they get to know me better. My misgivings and hang-ups soon chase them away. I wish this for David more than anything else.

However, I do know David thinks I'm fine and my problem is that I simply over-react to situations. He'd once said, 'You're just a bit of a loner, but a gorgeous one all the same.'

This memory makes me smile. He'd said this not long after he moved in with me. At first, I'd worried that being a bit of a loner might deter him. I needn't have worried though because I know how infatuated he is with me. And me him.

David left early for the six o'clock train down to Kings Cross. I've been sitting here on the floor since eight this morning when I phoned the surgery to take a sick day.

I'm still in my pyjamas and haven't showered nor brushed my teeth yet. My hair is knotted and needs de-tangling. I am craving another cup of strong coffee but cannot shake off this morbid mood and do anything constructive. I look around at the canvasses propped against the walls. David has offered to hang them, but I've refused. I like my room the way it is. Cluttered and haphazard. It's the way I work.

The mug of undrunk coffee that I'd made earlier sits beside me on the floor. It is cold with a thin layer of foam around the mug. I sigh knowing where this miserable mood will take me if I allow it. Be positive, I think and scramble to my knees with my heart beginning to race. The depressing dark pit is calling me. I know the awful memories will engulf me soon unless I do something concrete to stop them.

Even after thirty years the memory of how painful my early days were in Australia still haunts me. Sometimes it feels too much to bear. And it was all because of my mother. My bloody mother. Since that day I've hated her for what she did. And still do. Sitting on my hunkers I bend forward. I wrap my arms around my waist squeezing my eyes tight shut to blot out the start of that tragic day.

I try to concentrate on last weekend when me and David were at Tate Modern and the amazing paintings we saw. I remember wandering around London realising there are far   more artistic outlets living near the capital than being buried away in Kibblesworth village.

Sweat starts to form on my top lip.

I desperately struggle to focus on how happy and excited I'd felt with my new thoughts and dreams. And starting a new chapter in my life.

I lick my dry lips and rock gently backwards and forwards.

Sometimes I can hold the awful memories at bay by thinking about David. I remember our lovemaking in the hotel room. We'd been wild with each other and although I'm always carefree, even David who is usually reserved, had possessed a reckless attitude which I loved. Later that night I thought he would be shame-faced when we'd walked through reception to go into the restaurant.

But he'd taken my hand in his and whispered, 'I don't care what people think of us.' He'd pulled his shoulders back and walked tall swinging our hands together backwards and forwards as if he was showing us and our love to the whole world.

My breath is quickening, and my heart is beginning to pound.

No matter how hard I try now, the overwhelming smell of dirty river water fills my nose. I know that I won't be able to suppress the memories away today. I give in and slump to the floor curling my body into a foetal position. I wait for the image of baby Neil's waxen face to come into my mind. When it does, I choke back huge wracking sobs which escape from my throat.

I'm starting to relive the day in my mind. I have never been able to say the words aloud and talk about it.

Years ago, a therapist told me if I couldn't get the words out of my mouth then it might help the healing process to write it down. I did this and can practically remember what I wrote word for word. Here is the written account of what my mother did to our family.

We immigrated to Sidney in Australia when I was seven years old. Mum was pregnant with my brother, Neil, when we left Kibblesworth and my quiet history-teacher father fussed over her during the long flight. Mum had looked very pale faced, in contrast to her usual red-rosy cheeks. Father explained it was because she was tired and once the baby was born, she would look more like her old self again.

Settling into the Sidney suburb of Bankstown had been relatively easy for me and I loved the new school. I'd felt like a celebrity because my father taught there, and I'd realised the other children were impressed. They loved his history lessons. He entertained us all and made history come to life. Most of the kids were rapt and I'd once heard them say that he was cool. I'd simpered with pride.

One of his favourite sayings had been, 'Even if I can get one pupil interested in Oliver Cromwell then I'll feel like a champion.' The other teachers really liked him too.

Mum gave birth to my baby brother, Neil, and from the first day he was born I loved him unreservedly. Mum would let me hold the talcum powder and shake it on his tiny little body at bath time and we'd both sing lullabies to him while she rocked him in his cot. Our rented house was half a mile from the Georges river and we'd often amble down there with picnics at the weekend. I'd play at the water's edge and mum would cradle Neil feeding and changing him. Father would lie next to us with an opened book reading. We'd all bask in the warm weather which was such a contrast to the cold damp winters of Kibblesworth. It was idyllic.

It happened one day when Neil was around six months old. Apparently, the police had rung the school looking for my father. All I saw was him running out of the school gates and down towards the river. He'd looked so very different to his usual composed self. There'd been an air of panic about his flaying bright red hair and long dangly legs. I'd never seen him run before and I jumped up from my maths lesson and fled out of the room. Calling after him I ran as fast as I could down the lane towards the river wondering why he wasn't stopping to wait for me. Surely, he could hear me calling out!

I got to our usual picnic area and stopped dead in my tracks clinging to the trunk of a tree. I caught my breath at the sight before me. My father had slumped to his knees on the edge of the river as two burly policemen dragged my mother out of the water. Father leant his head back and howled. I will never forget the noise it was like a tiger or a lion from one of my storybooks. He simply roared and howled until one of the policemen placed a hand firmly upon his shoulder.

At the same time the other policeman shouted, 'Oh, God, there he is!' I crept around the other side of the tree trunk to see my baby brother floating on the top of the water.

'But he can't swim!' I'd cried aloud and staggered towards the water's edge to tug at the policeman's shirt sleeve.

The other policeman was soon behind me and hauled me up into the air and away from the riverbank. But not before I'd seen Neil's waxen-white face with dirty brown reeds clinging to his curly hair. His big pale-blue eyes had been wide open and staring straight at me as though he wanted me to help him. But of course, I couldn't. I'd sobbed his name repeatedly into the arms of the maths teacher who had followed us down to the river.

My mother had walked from our house down to the Georges river and waded into the water until both her and Neil were deep enough to drown. This is what I'd heard the ambulance man say that was leaning over Neil on the grass. The rest of that day is much of a blur. This shattered both me and my father for years afterwards. It was our babysitter and housekeeper, Josie Williams, who kept us together. She became the mother to me, that my own mother obviously didn't want to be until I was a young woman.

I wipe the tears away from my cheeks knowing the traumatic recollection is over. I feel exhausted as I often do after these events. I pull myself up from the floor staggering towards the kitchen for a long drink of juice. My body feels cold and shivery and I plod back to our bedroom then crawl under the duvet. It smells a little of David which echo's the fact that I am back in the here and now. The memories, as usual, were only what they are. Horrible memories that will never leave my mind. I drift off into an exhausting sleep.

Chapter Nine

Now I'm showered and dressed in clean jeans and a black T-shirt. I'm pacing around the lounge willing my mobile to tinkle with a text or a call. David should be in Newcastle by now if he has caught the three o'clock train from Kings Cross. He'd promised to ring as soon as he left the bakery. But he hasn't.

Has he missed the train and is stuck in London? Has something gone wrong? Have they changed their minds and they don't want him? Has there been an accident in the traffic and he's lying under a taxi?

I practise deep breathing exercises and feel restless. I begin to prowl around the kitchen opening and closing cupboards which I recognise as part of my agitated state. I'm not quite sure exactly what I hope to see in the cupboards. Answers to my problems or a note to say that David is safe.

I frown and look at the poor cactus plant on the windowsill which is dry. I pour a glass of water to soak the plant. Alfie gave us the cactus last year along with other plants which have all died. I know cacti are well used to dry climates in the desert, but this is Kibblesworth with plenty of running water. I reckon there's no need for it to die of thirst.

I watch the heavy rain run down the kitchen window remembering how we'd left each other this morning. Had our last words to each other been meaningful. I hate saying goodbye to someone because I always fret that they won't come back.

When my father had suffered the massive heart attack and had lain dead and alone over his desk for three hours, the first thing I remember thinking was that my last words to him had been, 'We're having Josie's special steak supper tonight.'

Afterwards during the overwhelming grief I'd tormented myself.

If I'd only known it would be his last day, I could have said something more profound. I wished I'd told him how much I loved and adored him.

I switch on the kettle and pop a teabag into a mug. David must have seen the look of trepidation in my face this morning because he'd cupped my cheeks with his hands then stated firmly, 'Erin, I will be back safe and sound later tonight.'

I'd wound my arms around his neck and whispered in his ear, 'Please do. I couldn't bear it if anything happened to you.'

I pour hot water onto the solitary teabag and stir it with a spoon. I've often thought that if I died tomorrow David would be devastated, but after time I know he would carry on without me. Whereas, I cannot say this. I know I wouldn't be able to carry on without him and, as dramatic as this sounds, I'd take my own life rather than face living without him.

Stirring sugar into my tea, I curse him under my breath for making me worry like this. Doesn't he think my day has been bad enough already? I shake myself knowing full well that he doesn't know how I suffer with the dreadful Australian flashbacks and traumatic episodes.

The sound of a taxi pulling up outside makes me jump and I fly to the door pulling it wide open. David is paying the taxi driver and turns to grin at me. While he hurries up the path towards me the grin on his face stretches from one ear to another. I can see the light shining in his eyes and know he has got the job.

'I'm so sorry, sweetheart,' he gasps in the doorway throwing his briefcase to the floor. 'My battery died the minute I got in the taxi. We got stuck in traffic and I had to run up the platform to catch the train with only minutes to spare!'

All the worry and apprehension floats away. I wrap my arms around him and reach up to kiss him full on his mouth. He tastes of stale coffee, but I cling to him with my arms around his neck while he pulls me in close for an extra hug.

I smile. 'I can tell by your grinning face that they want you.'

Taking a hand from me he punches his fist into the air. 'Whoopie! They want me to start as soon as I can. And if I go now,' he gabbles, 'then I can work alongside June before she leaves.'

I feel the excitement coming off him in droves. I grin back at him caressing his neck under his open shirt collar. I know he will have taken off his tie the moment he sat on the train.

'Oh, David, you've done so well,' I say. I stand back and hold him at arm's length. 'I couldn't be prouder of you, and I can tell you really want the job.'

I draw my eyebrows together and feel the tiny niggle at the back of my mind about the move. I know I must ask the question even if I won't like the answer. I owe it to him. I take a deep breath. 'David, do you honestly still have doubts about moving down the country?'

He grins. 'None whatsoever,' he says and drapes an arm casually along my shoulders while we saunter towards the kitchen.

David opens a bottle of red wine while I serve a vegetable casserole from the slow cooker. He tells me all about the day at the bakery and meeting the MD. We move around each other in the kitchen collecting cutlery and glasses. I cut crusty baguettes and we sit together at the small glass table. He tells me his plans for the team and how he wants to change their way of working with different accounts.

'Of course,' he mutters chewing a piece of carrot. 'I'll wait until I've been there a few weeks before I suggest any of this. I want to get them on my side and into my way of thinking before I make any big changes.'

I nod in understanding at his considerate nature. He's not the type of man to rush at things quickly and make a mess. I smile. 'And to think when we first talked about this promotion you were the one with misgivings and didn't really want to move away,' I say looking over his shoulder at the photograph of him with his pals. 'But I can tell now that you're totally up for it.'

He stops eating for a second and takes hold of my hand. 'Yes, Erin, and I've you to thank for pushing me forwards instead of letting me hang back in the shadows like I've always done in the past.'

I lean forwards over the table and grin. 'Oh, I knew it was there in you somewhere. We just had to dig deep to find it.'

David nods his head and stares back at me. We are hooked into each other. 'Erin, as long as you are by my side, I would live anywhere,' he states confidently. 'Our weekend in London made me realise that a house is just bricks and mortar. A place is just streets and fields. Because it's you that can make any place into our home.'

I gasp and feel an emotional tug in my throat at his words. David doesn't always wax lyrical, as the saying goes, but when he does talk it is always with such meaning and depth of his feelings that it often takes my breath away. 'Aaah, David, that's a lovely thing to say.'

He nods and finish's eating while I sip at my red wine slowly.

David's forehead creases slightly. 'Yet, you look tired?'

I tell him about calling in sick because of a troublesome headache which is a small white lie.

We move into the lounge area and snuggle down onto the settee wrapped around each other.

Usually, I wouldn't lie to David. In fact, there's only one biggish lie I've ever told him since we've been together. That came about in the early days when we first met. I hadn't lied to him on purpose or to be secretive, I'd just said it through panic when he'd asked about my mother.

I'd known I couldn't have talked about her without sounding like a vindictive nutcase. So, I'd said, 'My mother and baby brother were killed in a car crash when we'd first settled in Australia.'

After that he'd sort of presumed this was the reason that I don't drive. And I haven't corrected this assumption. I've simply let it carry on. Now, of course, it's too late to tell him the truth because he'll be so hurt that I've kept it from him.

Chapter Ten

I look at Uncle Geoff sitting in his armchair in the lounge of the nursing home and smile. He is wearing a bottle-green cardigan that I remember from years ago, and black corduroy trousers. It's warm and sunny outside for the first week in July and the large windows in the old building are open wide. The room is full of old people sitting in their chairs gazing around as though there are wondering why they're not in their own homes.

It is very warm and stuffy with what I can only describe as an old people smell, not urine or the other, just a musty smell. The collar on his grey shirt looks baggy around his neck and he seems shrunken from the big strong man he'd been when I was a young lad.

I remember him taking me to my first football match when I was nine and how he'd stood beside me in St. James Park to watch Newcastle United. That was in the days before the new stadium and way before the days of seating areas. Every Saturday we merged in with all the other dads and sons huddled together in the stand to keep warm. 'Here,' he'd said. 'Cup your hands around this mug of Bovril to keep you warm.' Which I'd done while munching into a hot meat pie at half time.

Although, of course, I knew he wasn't my dad, but he was the closest thing I had to a father figure. Now-a-days, I think we'd call him a role model, but back then I'd thought of him as a stand-in and knew I couldn't have asked for better. Since that day I've been a season ticket holder at St. James Park and have never missed a match.

Uncle Geoff's eyes are closed and although the nurse has given me a chair to sit on, she has now disappeared. I'm not sure whether to wake him up or just stay quiet until he wakes of his own accord.

I feel full of love and affection towards this old man sitting in front of me and know I probably wouldn't be the man I am today if it wasn't for him. He taught me the good attributes a man should possess. He taught me old northern traditions, how to behave towards other men with good manners and, protect the women in our lives.

I sigh, maybe it's a good thing that he had lost most of his memories because I know he'd have been disappointed in me for leaving Beth and Sally. Even though I've tried to protect them and made sure they still have the house and money in the bank. The suffering I caused wouldn't have gone down well with him. I cringe slightly knowing he would have thought me less of a man for leaving them. I believe everything I did was damage limitation, but he wouldn't have agreed.

Sadness fills me just as a nurse appears pushing a trolley with coffee and tea. She offers me a cup, but I shake my head and thank her. She leans forwards and pours coffee into uncle's blue plastic beaker.

'Geoff,' she says in a warm hushed tone. 'Wake up and drink your coffee you've got a visitor.'

At this, my uncle's eyes open. 'Hello, Davy,' he says sitting forward and smiling. 'I didn't know you were here.'

I feel happiness surge through me because he knows me, and my visit isn't going to be in vain. 'Yes, Uncle Geoff, it's me,' I say. 'Hey, it's great to see you looking so well.'

Geoff leans forward and strokes my arm. I'm wearing a white T-shirt with short sleeves and I feel the old crinkly skin on his hand brushing my skin. 'It's a sad business about your mother,' he says.

I realise he thinks mam has just died and the last five years don't figure in his mind. But I nod in agreement rather than correct him.

'Your mam was a lovely lass,' he says. 'I know I was biased because she was my sister but nevertheless, she was a little corker.'

I nod and feel a tightness in the back of my throat. 'Aye, Uncle Geoff, she was that.'

He shakes his head. 'I never knew what she saw in that rotten weasel she married. I told her at the time she was crazy, but she wouldn't listen and moved onto that crappy farm with him.'

It's obvious he wants to talk about mam and I'm just so glad that he at least knows me today. Even though I still feel emotional talking about her, I continue because I want to keep him with me in the here and now. 'You're right there, Uncle Geoff, from what we know about him now she was silly to go with him,' I say. 'But I suppose she did love him.'

Geoff sips his coffee and I sigh to see this great big man drinking out of a plastic beaker and not a man-size mug. It's sensible though because I see his hands shake and suppose it's safer than spilling the coffee and scalding himself. The coffee smells good and I wish I'd taken a cup now.

I shake my head. 'I've only scant memories of my father,' I say. 'But sometimes I do have flashbacks in my mind about the farm and that old barn.'

'Aye, well, it's probably for the best that you can't remember that awful place. She was besotted with him because he was good looking, and…' he pauses looking directly into my face, 'you look a lot like him with those big blue eyes, but thankfully you have your mams kindness and good nature.'

I smile and nod for him to continue.

'Well, you'd just been a few months old when your dad was playing around with other women. Your mum heard rumours in the village that he was shagging the barmaid from the local pub and she hadn't wanted to believe it. You know what the folks around here are like. There's none of them can mind their own business.'

I nod my head in understanding because it's only in the last few years that I've found that out. I wonder if mam had suffered at the hands of the gossipmongers when she brought me here to live with Uncle Geoff. Did they gossip about her leaving what they saw as, a good hard-working farmer?

I shake myself back to Uncle Geoff as he continues.

'Aye,' he says. 'And when she saw the barmaid in the post office one day with a black eye, your mam knew it must be true.'

I haven't heard this story before and lean towards uncle with my elbows on my knees and my hands clasped together. His voice is quieter now and I don't want to miss anything he tells me.

He tuts and shakes his head. 'He was nothing but a bully and beat your mam up on a regular basis especially when he was drunk in the bedroom and wanted sex,' he says staring down at his beaker. 'Now, Davy, call me old fashioned, but a man is not a man if he has to raise his hand to get what he wants in that department, if you catch my drift?'

I have a sudden flashback to one night in the farmhouse when I was little and how I'd woken to her screaming but thought I'd been dreaming and had gone back to sleep.

Sweat forms on my top lip and my heart fuels with anger at what my gentle mam had gone through at the hands of this scumbag. I can't help but grimace and pummel one fist into another at what I'd like to do to him.

Uncle Geoff lays a hand over my fists. 'Don't let it eat you up, Davy, it's in the past and he died under the wheels of a lorry. As soon as she left him and you got home to me, I knew you'd both be safe,' he says. 'Because if he had come looking for her, I'd have knocked seven shades of shit out of him. Bullies are cowards and only pick on smaller people who can't look out for themselves. They never tackle big men like me because they're scaredy-cats. And that weasel was rotten to the very core!'

An old lady in the corner of the room starts to cry and moan loudly and Geoff puts his head back against the rest on the chair. He closes his eyes as though he's used to the rumpus occurring as two nurses head over to her. I begin to explain how I'm moving down south for work but will call up as often as I can to visit him.

Uncle opens his eyes again. I can see they're glazed over now and not as bright and alert as they had been. He asks, 'Who are you, then? Are you the new doctor?'

I know I've lost him once more and his lucid train of thought has gone. I get up to leave and give him a small hug. I'm filled with a sense of gratification and am so pleased I've come. At least I've shared a few coherent thoughts with him before I leave home.

Chapter Eleven

Before we know where we are, we've both worked our notice periods, and the furniture removal van is arriving tomorrow for the journey down to our new house in Bexley. We've been lucky enough to find a detached three bedroomed house which is vacant. At this stage is only available to rent.

David thinks this is ideal. 'It'll give us the six-month rental period to decide if we like the area well enough before we buy our own home,' he'd said.

And I've had to agree. Yes, it does make sense, but it has a smack of transient living to me and given the choice I'd rather have found a permanent home.

David has gone to visit Uncle Geoff and is taking Sally out for lunch afterwards. He has left me to finish packing and the only thing I need to do is sort through the old trunk I brought with me from our home in Australia. It's not a job I'm looking forward to and have consoled myself with the fact that I could leave the trunk locked and take it with me to sort out later.

However, I grit my teeth with determination and drop to my knees on the well-worn carpet. I'm desperate to make a fresh start in Bexley and the last thing I need is unwanted baggage with me. Opening the clasp, I take a deep breath of wavering bravado. I haven't looked inside the trunk since the day I arrived in the cottage and pushed it to the back of the spare bedroom.

From what I can remember it should only contain a few keepsakes from the house which my father loved, documents, old clothes, and photographs. And, I decide

cheerfully, when we get settled in our new house, I
might display some of my father's beloved ornaments.

A musty smell invades my nose while I unwrap an
ornament and lift out a few of father's books. I'm
instantly transported back to Brankstone and remember
each area of the house where he'd kept everything for
over twenty years.

I'd once tried to paint Neil's face from memory. It
was just a few years before father had died. I'd been
especially troubled with dreams around February 18th
the day Neil was born and thought it might help.

From the year Neil died his birthday had remained,
unlike my mother's birthday, a hard day for me and
father. I'd thought if I could capture his likeness then it
would be a special thing to do for us both. I'd not had
much confidence in painting people because I knew
my facial expressions and body shapes were never
good enough. I'd always been more at ease painting
landscapes or animals. However, when I'd finished the
painting of Neil's blonde curly locks, his big blue eyes
and cute button nose I'd felt good about my work on
the small canvas.

When I'd shown it to father, he'd gasped then cried
out clasping his hand over his mouth. I'd thought at
first it was a reaction of surprise at the painting, but it
hadn't been. My father had fled from the room looking
distraught which had left me feeling hurt and confused.

However, later that evening father had come to me
and pulled me into his warm embrace. 'It was just
because the painting was so life-like,' he'd said. 'It

took my breath away and brought back such painful memories.'

We'd cried a little together but the next day I'd wallowed in my father's pride. Satisfied that my skill in painting a face had been so much better than I'd thought it could be and how I'd impressed father with such a great likeness. I'd obviously captured Neil's spirit and baby cuteness in the painting.

A week later when I'd arrived home from work Josie and father were standing in the hall looking at my painting which Josie had had framed and hung on the wall.

I smile now with the memories and unwrap a small framed photograph that father kept by his bedside of their wedding day. The only reason I've kept it is because the photograph was his most treasured possession. I would never want to see a photograph of my mother but at the same time I cannot help staring at her face. I'm loath to admit it is strikingly like my own now. In fact, it's like looking into a mirror.

Mum was in her early twenties when they were married. And, although I now have more fine lines and a wrinkle on my forehead, I do have her eyes, nose, and the same shaped face. She has masses of blonde hair under her veil and her dress is beautifully made with flowing white satin. I'm also the same build as her and in this photograph, she looks slim and dainty like I did in my wedding dress.

Her face is tilted upwards to my father and she is staring at him with such love and adoration that I bite my lip. For what seems the millionth time in my life I wonder how she could obviously love him so much but then kill herself.

I lay the photograph back into its cloth wrap and sigh heavily. I wonder. If she hadn't killed herself and had lived to be a lively sixty-year-old lady would we have been close. I've heard other women say their mothers are like their best friends. So, would she have been mine. Would I have been as close to her as I had been to my father. Maybe I would always have been daddy's little girl and Neil would have been a true mummy's boy. That, I sigh, is something we'll never know.

Stroking the soft material of the wrap I grimace.

I've hated my mother for so long now it just seems like the norm and it's a struggle to remember the years of my life that I didn't. I also tend to forget that there are people who have good relationships with their mothers, but unfortunately, my good memories were only until I was seven. It's plain to see that David had been lucky because his mother adored and worshipped him up until the day she died.

I bite my lip. As awful as this may seem, sometimes the green-eyed monster rears its ugly head when he is drooling over her memories and their old life together. And I feel jealous. Not that it's hard to understand why his mother loved him so much because David is such a good man and he is easy to love. But more that they shared such a loving family relationship. One that I would have loved to have had when growing up.

His mum had told David on her deathbed, 'Leaving you is the last thing I want to do.'

In contrast, my own bloody mother couldn't wait to get away from me, I seethe. I feel tears prick my eyes and shake my head. Stop it, I curse, determined not to spoil my mood and my father's memories by thinking about her.

I find another photograph in a frame taken by Josie which is of me and father together in his study. I'm about twenty sitting on his desk swinging my legs and grinning at him while he smiles shyly into the camera. I stroke his face on the photograph and smile. He had a thin face with a pointed chin and wiry red and peppered grey hair.

The children at school had said, 'Your dad looks like a mad professor with his gold-rimmed glasses perched on the end of his nose and his face stuck in a book.'

But they'd said it with affection because they all liked him. I moan with sadness at his loss.

The heart attack had come as such a shock and I'd railed against the unfairness. He'd never smoked and had a tall lean body. If he did have a glass of whisky, he often left it unfinished.

The doctor had explained, 'Although he'd had none of the pre-disposing factors associated with heart disease it was probably due to a genetic family history of coronary disease.'

We'd had to have a post-mortem because father hadn't been to the doctors for many years before a death certificate could be issued.

I swallow a lump in my throat. I might have had a terrible mother, but no one could have asked for a better father. He'd tried his utmost to make our lives bearable after the tragedy. I know everything he did was for my benefit.

'How could she do this to us,' I'd ranted. 'It was bad enough killing herself, but why take baby Neil? What did I do so wrong that she wanted to leave me?'

My father would try to soften my attitude towards her memory by making excuses for her suicide, but I'd remained steadfastly averse to any type of justification for her behaviour.

'It wasn't your fault,' he'd stress. 'It was nothing you did. If anything, the blame lies with me because I didn't see how unhappy she must have been. She had poor mental health and wasn't thinking straight, but I do know how much she loved you. You were her precious little girl!'

He'd tease using his nickname for me, little bonzer, and try his hardest to make me believe that mother had loved me. But I couldn't and wouldn't believe him. All I knew was that if you love someone, the last thing in the world you'd want to do is leave them. It had been her choice to walk into the river. Not mine. Nor my fathers.

My hatred had grown steadily over the years and by the time I'd reached eighteen whenever my father would mention her name or try to talk about her, I'd put my hand up in front of him. 'Stop, no more,' I'd say. 'I don't want to hear it.'

Eventually he gave up and her name became taboo. He'd even forbidden Josie to talk about her in front of me. Whether this was right or wrong, I'm not sure, but it was the way we plodded on through the years as a family.

Father had built a small annex onto the end of the house for Josie which she loved because it meant she had her own little bit of independence but was always there when needed. Although she was very good to me, I could never think of her as a replacement for my mother. I'd told my father, 'I'm terrified if I do, she will leave us too!'

Josie was there every morning to make breakfast and there every afternoon when I returned from school and then onwards to college. It was Josie who helped me find a dress for the prom. It was Josie who helped me when my monthlies arrived and explained the birds and the bees to me. It was Josie who I turned to one morning when my period was late and confessed to my first sexual experience with a boy.

Josie loved animals and helped at the local animal sanctuary. She often took me with her, and it was where I discovered my own fascination with animals. We brought stray dogs and cat's home to love and nurture. However, we always returned them when they'd recuperated because father didn't want the responsibility of looking after them. And to me, his word was law. I never did anything to upset or disobey him because I was terrified, he too, might leave me.

At school, I was never particularly bright although I did study and try hard.

Therefore, when it was obvious, I wasn't academically astute enough to become a vet, Josie pulled a few strings and got me a job in the reception of a large vet's surgery nearby.

In my late twenties, while I was cuddling a puppy one day, Josie had said, 'I think you transfer your maternal instincts and love onto the animals you care for.'

Now, I think, maybe she was right? When we have dogs and cats in the surgery, I love to cuddle them close, so they feel human warmth in the absence of their owners. But I never feel the weight of responsibility towards the animals because at the end of the day the vet is accountable for their health. However, I'm happy to know that in some respects I've contributed to their well-being. I'm a sucker for big doe eyes that look to me for help. I love nothing more than cuddling a cat or dog close to my chest and hearing them purr or meow their relief at my kindness.

I smile fondly now when I lift out a photograph album that Josie had put together of us. I feel guilty that our relationship has fallen away to birthday and Christmas cards to Bondi Beach where she is happily ensconced. On the bottom of the trunk lies a parcel in black tissue paper and I frown in puzzlement. What's this? And then, from somewhere in my distant memory on my twenty-first birthday, I remember Josie telling me that the trunk held a few bits and pieces of my mother's jewellery in a bag.

Until now, I've harboured no interest in my mother's life and had quite simply forgotten it was there. I sit back on my hunkers and take a deep breath. The rational side of my brain kicks-in and I know the jewellery cannot have any monetary value. If it had the jewellery would have been on father's paperwork when he died. I remember his will which had no mention of jewellery.

I rake my fingers through my hair. Is this something I really want to do now? Maybe I should leave it until later.

But natural curiosity takes over and I peel open the black tissue. A musty smell fills my nose with a whiff of old face powder, and I remember my mother's smell. My throat is dry when I pick up a set of pearls and pearl-drop earrings. I remember her wearing them when father took her out dancing and swallow hard at the early memories. Underneath the jewellery, however, is a flat soft-backed diary with a green ribbon tied around it. Her name is written on the front with the year 1984.

I slump back down onto the floorboards and stifle a small cry from my throat. I re-work the calculation because I will turn thirty-nine in October. I nod with clarity. She must have written this during the year she committed suicide. Gingerly I open the first page not knowing what to expect and begin to read.

Chapter Twelve

My first week at work has been amazing. I can't think of another word to describe it all. Everyone on site has been so welcoming it has staggered me and has eliminated my previous misgivings about southerners not being friendly. I know without a doubt that I've made the right decision to come here.

I suppose without realising it I had become quite staid in my old job, which is perfectly understandable after all the years I'd worked there. It would be impossible for anyone, no matter how good they are at their job, not to be. The atmosphere here couldn't be more different and most days the development team are buzzing.

Everyone is optimistic and encouraging to each other almost as though it is game to see who can achieve the most impressive cake. There's a lot of high fiving going on between the team and I can't help getting caught up with it all. The technologists are all working on different projects and we are delving into new areas which are so exciting my head is spinning with it all.

'Gone are the days of two-tone square Battenberg cakes,' Jessie Brown tells me on my first afternoon. 'We are now placing five and six different coloured sponges in the centres of cakes!'

I could tell within hours of being here that my senior technologist is the main stay of the department and invaluable to everyone. Jessie is fiftyish and lives in Bexley not far from the house we are renting.

I knew within minutes of being in her company she is going to be a good friend to me, and hopefully to Erin too. At nearly six-foot-tall with a large matronly chest and shiny chestnut hair, which she told me is out of a bottle and made me laugh, Jessie has worked in the bakery for thirty years and loves her job.

I know I'm going to be relying heavily upon her over the next few weeks because I've been thrown in at the deep end, as it were. The manager I'm replacing, has left earlier than expected therefore I'm going to have to get to grips with everything quicker than I'd originally thought. Yet, this doesn't faze me because I've always loved a challenge and am more than ready to dive straight into the work.

Home life, however, has caused me a few niggles of concern. Erin, which is totally unexpected, seems a little out of sorts with herself. I thought she'd be running around the new house and village excited as a kitten, but not so. She certainly isn't cock-a-hoop, in fact, if I had to use a word to describe the look on her face since we arrived it would be morose.

Last night, when I asked her if she was okay, or if there were any problems, I'd received a nod and then a shake of her head. We had just finished dinner and were watching a travel show on TV. I'd pursued her with more questions.

'Do you like the house?'

I received the short reply. 'It's lovely.'

'Do you think we'll settle in Bexley? Have you met with any of the neighbours?'

I'd received equally blunt replies. 'I'll be fine. No, not yet.'

I'd got up and wandered around the house from room to room looking at all the boxes in the hall and kitchen. Then I'd made my way upstairs and stared uncomprehendingly at the unpacked suitcases in the bedroom. It was almost as though she didn't want to unpack and settle into the house. The most I'd unpacked was the necessary clothes and toiletries that I'd needed to go to work, but she hadn't even unpacked her own necessities.

I'd sighed remembering the conversation we'd had two days before leaving Kibblesworth when Erin had asked me to leave all the unpacking to her. She didn't plan to look for a job straight away and wanted to explore the area first. Financially, because we are renting and have spent some of her father's money on our deposit, I'd readily agreed.

I'd then wandered into the spare room which she'd commandeered for her studio. This was the only room where she had unpacked her art stuff. Her old trunk from Australia was in the corner of the room with a rug over it and she had her easel up and canvases strewn around the walls and floor.

Returning to our room I'd perched on the edge of the bed trying to understand why she was acting like this. Didn't she like the house? But that didn't make sense because she chose the house out of the three rental properties that were available. Maybe it didn't live up to the photographs and itinerary on the details we received.

I'd stretched my hand out and stroked the silky bedspread whilst working out that we hadn't made love

for three nights. Which is a rarity. Not that I was
chomping at the bit, you'll understand because it had
been a tiring few days for me, but I was missing our
togetherness.

I also made excuses for us remembering the long
drive down on the Saturday with road works and an
accident on the motorway. Therefore, when we'd
arrived with the keys and the removal men had placed
the large pieces of furniture into all the rooms, we'd
been knackered. All we'd done was make up the bed
with clean linen and collapse into it at midnight. The
next morning Erin had been up before me, so we
hadn't had our usual Sunday morning love making
session.

Lying flat on top of the bedspread I'd stared at the
ceiling rose which hadn't been painted fully into all the
corners of the leaf design. I'd then decided she seemed
a little distant and cut-off from me which was a bit
scary. I'd racked my brains wondering if I'd said
something out of turn in all the upheaval. Although I'm
still getting my good morning and good night kisses
when we are together, she seems tense in my arms. The
other weird thing that happened was during our last
night in the Kibblesworth cottage.

I'd gone straight off to sleep but then after an hour I'd
woken when she got out of bed. Often when she has
painful period nights, I rub her stomach and back
gently, or make her a hot water bottle and a warm
cocoa. But when I looked to see if she was okay, she
was propped up on one elbow staring at my face.

'Erin,' I'd murmured. But she didn't answer. She just stared at me. So much so that I wondered if she was still asleep. Then with a shrug of her shoulders she turned onto her side away from me.

The next morning I'd decided that I'd imagined it all because I was uptight with the move and the fact that my lunch with Sally had been tense. Our final farewells had been awkward, to say the least.

I'd hugged my daughter tightly, but she'd been rigid in my arms and it was nothing like our usual dad and daughter cuddles. I know Sally often gets sullen and defensive when she is upset or worried. I also know that now she is technically a young woman, there's very little I can do. I promised repeatedly to ring every weekend and come to see her as often as I could in my cheerful encouraging voice, but I could almost see the accusations in her eyes when she'd muttered, 'Yeah, whatever.'

When I'd dropped her off back home Beth had been waiting at the front door and had called out, good luck, then waved. But Sally had stomped towards the door and brushed past Beth with her head down. I'd driven away with my shoulders down feeling that even though it has been two years since I'd left, I was abandoning them all over again. Beth had looked tiny standing in the doorway, and I'd noticed for the first time how much weight she'd lost. I'd comforted myself with the fact that when you see someone regularly you stop noticing these things.

However, now it's Friday evening, I've just left work and am determined to sort out what is troubling Erin and have a great weekend in the new house. I hadn't noticed how hot it was whilst at work because the bakery is a modern air-conditioned building. Now I'm outside I can tell by air that it has been a very hot sunny day and is now a sultry evening. I roll my shirt sleeves up after I park the car in the garage on the side of the house.

It's an attractive house standing on the corner of a quiet street that runs down into the centre of the old village and its amenities. I'm not sure if I should call Bexley a village because it is more of a small town. Erin tells me from her google search that it had once been a tiny village but has grown extensively during the last ten years. The front of the house is built with a light beige stone and has cream stone trims around the windows and doorway. I hurry through the side door from the garden into the hall and practically bump into Erin who is placing a vase onto our polished bureau.

'Hey, there,' I say and wrap my arms around her waist from behind. I let out a breath of relief that she is dressed and unpacking some of our belongings. She looks more like her normal self and doesn't stiffen in my embrace.

She wriggles away from my cuddle. 'David,' she mumbles. 'I've got loads to get through.'

Wanting to stay upbeat I follow her into the lounge and see two opened boxes on the floor with piles of rumpled-up newspapers. The lounge is a large square-shaped room and we know the landlord has renovated the house before placing it up for rental. In my opinion, although I haven't said this to Erin, he has lost some of the character in the house by using new skirting boards and cheap doors.

However, it's nice to see our stuff in the room and I inhale the vanilla smell from a large half-burned candle Erin has placed on the deep windowsill. The photograph of me and my mates in the pub, and our Venice wedding photograph are on the fireplace. Our orange throw and cushions are on the settee and I smile. This is what's called a woman's touch.

I notice she has changed the place of our furniture and the settee is now facing the large front window.

Knowing she wanted to do the unpacking I waver. But then decide to offer. 'Hey, the settee looks much better over there. Shall I give you a hand?'

'No, I'm fine,' she answers but does at least smile at me. 'You won't know where to put things.'

I nod and try another tack. 'Okay,' I say. 'Jessie at work has suggested we try the Italian restaurant down the road. She said the food is good at a reasonable price. What do you think?'

Erin turns to look at me. 'Sounds good. Why don't I finish here while you shower, and we can walk down later?'

Her small eyes have a misty sad expression and are a little puffy underneath. I wonder if she's been crying. My insides twist with pain because she looks so unhappy but I'm at a loss not knowing how to help her.

I'm not used to feeling helpless. If I have a problem, I try my hardest to sort it out. That's just the type of guy I am. But because Erin won't tell me what's wrong, I can't try to put it right. I decide it is like Chinese torture because I don't know what to do and I love her so much. I can't bear anything to hurt her.

I give her my lop-sided grin and put my head on the side. Without speaking she knows I'm asking her again what's wrong. I open my hands palm upwards and lift a shoulder.

'I'm fine,' she states with an obvious false bravado. 'It's just taking me a while to adjust, that's all.'

'Okay,' I mutter. 'But it'll be okay, Erin, you'll see,' I say optimistically, and try to hold her empty hand. She takes her hand away and picks up a roll of bubble-wrap.

'I know. Of course, it will,' she says unwrapping another ornament.

I head upstairs towards the bathroom deep in thought.

***

'Tell me what's wrong,' I say holding her securely in my arms when we lie in bed later that night. I'm determined she is not going to turn away from me again because I'm desperate to know what is troubling her. I want whatever it is out in the open, so we can talk about it. I don't think it ever does any good to bottle things up.

Although, she'd looked great in the restaurant with her hair piled up, her make-up glowing and wearing a little black dress, I could tell her conversation was too animated. It was as if she was making a monumental effort to enjoy herself. Throughout the meal she kept shaking her head as if she'd wandered off somewhere in her mind and needed to come back to the here and now.

Now, I wrap my arms around her tighter and squeeze. 'Please talk to me, Erin.'

'It's nothing, I've told you. I'm fine,' she mutters shaking her head defiantly. She covers my lips with hers and kisses me hard pushing her tongue into my mouth. It's not the gentle tease that she usually does. This is forceful and I worry that I'm going to gag.

Her hands roughly rub my skin while she starts to make love to me. It feels as though she is striving against something that she can't get out of her mind. Or in a race and is determined to prove she is the winner.

It's fast and furious. Of course, I rise to the challenge and join in because I feel desperate for release after three nights of abstinence. At one stage I see her grinding her back teeth while she pounds onto me. I sincerely hope I can withstand the ferocious pressure. It's not that I always like our love making to be soft and gentle, but now my head is reeling with the rapid aggressive movements she is forcing us into. One of the positions hurts the top of my right thigh and I try to move her slightly to relieve the pressure for a few seconds. But she has a vice-like grip on me and groans her refusal.

'Erin,' I mutter into her hair. 'Can I just move…'

But she shakes the mane of her hair so violently that it whips my face and stings my left eye.

'Erin, please, just a minute,' I try again but she throws her head back and screams aloud in her release.

I know she has finished when she collapses spent on me and I'm able to move my right thigh that has been cramped. It is now in pins and needles and I work my toes and foot until the feeling comes back. I feel as though my body has just been used as a battering ram in a fight against unknown elements.

She turns onto her side and I can hear her breathing change. She is instantly asleep. I lie staring at the Victorian ceiling rose and wonder what the hell just happened.

Chapter Thirteen

Mummy did love me. I read it in her diary and now I remember the feelings. The feel of her body close to mine, her smell, her cuddles, and her laughter. Her tears of mostly joy, but sometimes, and for no reason that I could figure, her tears of sadness. Now I know the reason why and can remember everything about her.

It feels like having a chunk of my memory restored to me that has been hidden away in the same trunk where her diary had been. Or maybe a shrink would say, now you don't hate her any more you can remember all the good things about her that you'd pushed aside in your mind. I sigh knowing this psychoanalysis is way above my level of understanding but remembering her now is a good feeling.

I've read mothers diary from start to finish three times and understand the happenings and circumstances that were behind her tragic actions. It's appalling what she went through and I'm berating myself for not questioning my father more when he was alive.

I wonder for the umpteenth time since I found the diary if he had read it. Did he know the reason why she'd done it? And if so, why didn't he do anything about it. Not wanting to think ill of my father for anything I console myself with the hope that he hadn't read her explanation and lived in ignorance of what she'd suffered.

I've gone over countless conversations we'd had in my teens. 'Erin, there were obviously circumstances beyond your mother's control,' he'd stressed. Of course, I didn't want to listen to his explanations.

Now, I sorely wish I'd let him. I shouldn't have been so dogmatic and tried to at least understand mother's actions then I wouldn't have hated her for years.

Josie had said at the time, 'Hatred is a wasteful emotion and it uses up too much energy. Life is easier if you can learn to forgive.' Being too young and headstrong I'd shrugged it off. Josie was also keen on saying, 'You can't put an old head on young shoulders.'

And boy, I think, how right she was. At thirty-eight I can see that now but couldn't in my teens and twenties. If only, I sigh wistfully, if only.

Knowing what was in the diary years ago would have saved me a lot of grief and anguish. The outstanding realisation from her writings was that she did love me. If she hadn't suffered from poor mental health, she would never have done what she did.

The sun streaming through the lounge window is in my eyes and I hold my hand level above my eyebrows because it is making me squint. We've just moved here to Bexley and I know I should be unpacking the boxes littered around the room but cannot drag myself away from my thoughts. My sense of time seems completely out of sync. I look around the disorder in the room and feel a little lost in my mind which seems full of sludge.

The rattle of the letterbox when a leaflet is pushed through startles me back to the here and now. I give myself a shake. I must try to concentrate and be normal. I force myself once more to look around the room. It's quite a nice lounge area. Not the open plan living space we had in the small cottage, but because we've a separate dining room there's plenty of room for us and our belongings.

The hours since we got here have flown and I've done very little except drink coffee, forget to eat, and wish I hadn't stopped smoking.

I try to shake myself into action and start sorting out the house in the hope that it will make me feel better. The house, I remind myself, that I've been longing to move into for weeks now. I'm still in my pyjamas and ordinarily the lovely sunshine would draw me outside like a magnet. I should be eager to explore the area and do all the things I'd dreamed of doing. But still I can't stir myself into any action. Every time I determine to do something constructive another small memory tumbles into my mind and I must think it through.

My mind is constantly transported back to Brankstone and the words that mother wrote which are now securely fixed in my mind. I'm wallowing in memories and fitting her words into the months prior to her taking their lives and trying to understand. I think of her on the long flight out to Australia and how pale and distracted she'd been.

'It's just because I'm carrying the baby in here, Erin,' she'd told me and placed my small hand gently over her bump. 'But we'll both be fine once we get there.' She'd smiled reassuringly and I'd settled myself back to read my book.

Now, of course, I can understand how awful she must have felt having another man's baby grow inside her.

A baby that she couldn't possibly have wanted. A baby conceived against her will through an act of sexual assault. A baby that must have reminded her constantly of something she'd wanted to blot out of her mind. But, more than anything else, a baby who my father naturally thought was his. My mind screams knowing what she'd suffered at the hands of that swine.

When I look back at my sexual experiences with men, I class myself as lucky that I've never been in the awful position. All the sex I've had in relationships over the years was consensual.

I remember a couple of semi-enjoyable fumbling sessions with younger boys which I think all women have until they learn the rudimentary act of sex and what it involves. This had progressed until I reached my twenties and then had a fling with an older man in his mid-thirties. He had been from New Zealand, was worldly-wise and a master at technique. He'd said, 'I'm going to teach you to get as much pleasure out of your own body that I take from it, Erin.'

However, the fling had ended after a few months when I found videos of what looked like sixteen-year-old girls in Thailand. Even as a young woman I'd known this was a dark area and I shudder now at the memories.

I tuck my legs up underneath me in the big chair and sigh looking out of the window again. Of course, I've read about rape and sexual assault. I can't begin to imagine how horrid it must be to have a man take over your body against your will and endure the assault through fear for your life.

Certain words mother wrote in her diary are emblazoned in my mind.

His hand was squeezing my throat as his other dirty hand pulled at my knickers and tore them off me. His drunken breath was in my face, and his slobbering wet lips sucked down my neck.

I feel bile rise in my throat thinking of the agony she'd gone through and tremble with disgust at how despicable the man's behaviour was.

I forcibly shake myself and head towards the shower knowing I cannot re-wind the clock and there's absolutely nothing I can do that will change what happened. I can only use the facts that I know to move forwards with my own life.

Dressed in dungarees, I start to tackle the pile of boxes sitting in the middle of the lounge and begin to unwrap. I hurry from room to room depositing our belongings from the dining room to the bathroom and to the bedrooms. I have set up my paints and materials in the largest south facing bedroom with my Australian trunk in the corner with a shawl over the top.

I place the diary carefully back inside the wrapper in the top of the trunk. I was contemplating putting it in my bedside drawer but then worried that David might find it. To my knowledge he has never gone through my personal things, but I can't take the risk of him ever finding the diary. He must never read the contents. Not now. Not ever.

I turn on the radio and find the local station hoping a little music will keep my thoughts from straying back to mother again. Hurrying around the rooms I make a list of things we will need. A filing cabinet for David's office and work necessities which he will use in the third bedroom. A full-length mirror for our bedroom and another standalone wardrobe plus a set of drawers.

Our wardrobes were built-in at the cottage and David has a lot of suits and clothes for work. As I'm emptying the suitcases, I calculate that he has more clothes than I have. Usually when I put his clean underwear into a drawer, I stroke his boxers feeling the softness of the fabric conditioner. Now, I hurriedly push them into the drawer. I don't like these changing thoughts about him, and I dismiss them quickly then hurry back into the lounge.

The one and only bookcase we possess is standing by the wall empty. I kneel and open one of the large boxes full of David's recipe books and begin to unpack. Cakes, cakes, and more cakes, I sigh, not knowing exactly how to place the books. Some are old from the seventies and eighties, but many more are from the last five years. All the celebrity chefs are here, Delia Smith, Mary Berry, and Gordon Ramsay, and I wonder how David will want them grouped. I decide to put the older books on the bottom shelf and newest on the top shelf. Or, should it be the tallest books on the top and shortest on the bottom? Or, I sigh, maybe I stop fussing and let him do it himself.

Even the simplest of decisions seems to send me into a whirl. I bite down on my lip and look across the lounge then frown. From the moment the removal men had placed the settee up against the long wall in the lounge I've disliked the position. I drag and manage to push it into the window space then manoeuvre the coffee table and standard lamps into different positions until I'm satisfied that I've made the best of the rooms natural light.

I push the small oak bureau through into the hallway and place my Venetian vase into prime position just as David arrives home.

***

I'm sitting opposite David in the Italian restaurant forcing seafood risotto into my mouth while he raves about the fabulous parmesan sauce and flavours. I have no appetite and it all seems tasteless. My mouth is dry with anxiety and it feels as though there is a ball of tension lodged in my gut. I'm hoping the risotto will rectify this, but so far, it's not working. I gulp at the water in my glass.

There are photographs on the walls of Rome, Florence, and Tuscany, and we've already reminisced about our holiday in the villa, and our plans to retire there.

It had been such a glorious holiday where we'd both been totally relaxed and carefree for fourteen whole days in the hot sun. We'd swam in the pool, wandered around the local markets and art galleries in our shorts and vests. I'd been amazed at how much knowledge David had gained about The Italian Masters in just over the two years we've been together. Whether that is because he really likes the paintings or because he loves me and wants to be interested in my activities, I'm not sure. But it had been idyllic. While I painted, David cooked and read.

I try to hold onto these lovely memories to make myself feel more normal and drive out the anxious feelings. But it doesn't make much difference. I give myself a shake and look at David. He is smiling and entertaining me with his tales from work and the people he's met. I try to appear interested and join in his relentless banter but all the while my feelings towards him are so mixed-up now it's frightening me.

I take a large gulp of red wine and glance around the small room filled with people enjoying their evening. My mind is filling with dislike and disgust at all the men sitting at the tables. I know this is an irrational reaction to my mother's ordeal. I stare across the room at a group of loud rugby players sitting in the corner. I can't help wondering if any of them have ever forced themselves upon a woman.

I lay my fork down. 'I'm full now. I couldn't eat another mouthful,' I say. I've wound my hair up into a knot in the back of my head and it seems to be shooting daggers into my scalp.

My kind thoughtful husband asks, 'Have you got a headache?'

I rub my temple and nod. I'm longing to set the weight of my hair free. He caresses my hand across the table while he asks for the bill.

Suddenly I wonder what my father would have thought of David. Would he have liked him? I decide he would have done because there's nothing remotely to dislike about my husband. And I know father would have appreciated David's work ethic and kind nature.

While David reaches into the back pocket of his trousers for his wallet and chats to the waiter, I think how well I know the man I promised to love, honour, and obey on our wedding day.

His appendix scar to the right of his belly button and the small strawberry birth mark on his left shoulder. Even if I was blindfolded, I would know where they were and every inch of his body. But do I really know what's in his mind? There's never been an occasion, up until now that I've not wanted to make love to him. So, I suppose the issue hasn't been put to the test. Can I categorically put my hand on my heart and know David would never ever force himself onto me? Or any other woman for that matter.

David tried a few times last night to instigate making love. I just felt cold, unyielding, with no sex drive at all. He knows something is amiss and I know it's not fair on him, but I can't talk about it. Not yet. I will eventually. And I've every confidence that my never-failing hormones will kick-in again and I will feel sexy at some stage. However, now, the word, No, No, and, No, is what I want to use for my mother's sake, if nothing else.

Chapter Fourteen

The slapping of my skin started the night after our meal in the Italian restaurant. We'd spent a pleasant day sorting stuff out in the house and garage. Later in bed Erin had started to make love to me slowly and tenderly. I'd been delighted thinking we were back on course until we both heightened towards our ending when she had slapped my buttocks hard. So much so, that the pain had ruined my pleasure and I was left feeling stunned and depleted.

Obviously, the episode had a different effect on her. 'That was amazing', she'd moaned into my shoulder.

I'd shaken my head in disbelief once more and spent the rest of the weekend too scared to ask her about it.

Now that I'm away from her and driving to work I'm trying to rationalise the situation. Technically, I suppose it's not the first time she's slapped my bare buttocks when we are making love. The first time had been in the London hotel when the gentle slap had intensified my pleasure to another level. I'd found the whole experience totally exhilarating. However, on Saturday night when she'd slapped me it had been very hard, and it had hurt. I didn't like it at all.

Being the type of guy who usually wanders through life with my cup half-full as opposed to half-empty, I'm trying to find an upbeat reason or happy solution to this. But right now, I can't.

I pull into the large car park and turn off the engine. What is the matter with her? I try to make excuses for her behaviour last week but am puzzled to say the least. The sullen mood swings, the aggression in bed, the slapping, it's as though I've done something awful and she is getting her own back on me. But what? I shake my head and tut. Now, I'm getting paranoid.

I lift my briefcase from the passenger seat and determine to keep it from my mind for the day.

***

'I just can't get the chocolate to cut without it cracking into huge pieces,' Jessie says frowning.

I smile at her and nod. We are in the light and airy test bakery with three chocolate cakes on the bench in front of us. It's a relatively new area with space for three lengths of work benches where the technologists can work easily within their dedicated space. Jessie's space is just in front of the oven area at the back of the kitchen and I can feel the warmth from the three large ovens.

I've chosen to spend my day working with Jessie today for two reasons. First, out of my team Jessie is the friendliest person I have working for me. Second, after the worrying weekend I've spent with Erin, I need today to be easy.

'I might just be able to help with that,' I offer and hurry through to the large washroom. Retrieving a large jug, I fill it with hot water and return to the bench. Jessie raises an eyebrow when I pick up a large cake knife from the bench and place it into the jug.

'Let's just give it a few minutes while I explain about Vienna,' I say.

She grins. 'Okay, so we're going to talk about your latest holidays?'

I laugh knowing we share the same light sarcastic humour. Today, she has covered her eyelids in a bright violet-blue eyeshadow which I think Erin might say clashes badly with her brown eyes. But I think it brightens her face and her eyes are dancing with amusement.

'Nooo, but I'm going to tell you about the TV program I saw featuring the famous Sacher Torte chocolate cake. It was made in Vienna by the royal pastry chef for the king in the 18th Century. Don't quote me on that date in case it's wrong,' I say. 'Basically, it's a rich moist chocolate cake with a thin layer of apricot jam in the middle then coated top and sides in liquid dark chocolate.'

I can see Jessie is rapt now and my junior technologist, Jakub, has moved further along the bench towards us and is also listening.

I lick my dry lips and remove the knife from the jug. 'On the program, I saw the chefs in the café in Vienna cutting the chocolate with a warm damp knife, which they reckon is the best way to cut enrobed chocolate,' I say then usher a little prayer. I slide the knife easily through the chocolate and down through the cake with only the tiniest sliver of a crack in the chocolate.

Jessie cheers and Jakub whistles through his teeth in appreciation. I swell with pride that at least something is going right for me. My shoulders relax and I realise how refreshing it is to talk to about things I know will work and that I am confident about. To be somewhere I don't feel out of my depth like I do at home with Erin.

'Neat job, boss,' Jakub mutters and sidles back along the bench while Jessie takes the knife eagerly.

'Let me try this cake,' she says joyously sliding the knife through the cake. 'Ah, that's great, David. We can put this information onto the serving suggestions on the back of the cake box for the customer to do this at home.'

I nod in agreement and congratulate her on a job well done.

We head back to our desks in the office area and talk through Jessie's other three projects. With my stomach grumbling and Jessie stating she could eat a horse; we head off to the canteen for lunch.

**

The canteen is a large bright room with a TV and numerous hard-plastic tables and chairs. Jessie tells me it was all done out and modernised last year. One long serving counter fills the back of the room and there are two fridges in the corner for staff to use at other shift times.

By the end of lunch, I feel as though I've known her all my life. She tells me about her husband, Mike, who is a big jovial taxi driver. And how her son, Luke is studying medicine at Edinburgh university. The pride in her eyes shines in abundance while she talks about them both and I can tell from what she says that they adore her too.

I tell Jessie everything about myself and cannot believe how easy it is to talk to her. She sits opposite me stirring sugar into her coffee and then rests her large dimply arms on the table in front of us. Every now and then she clasps her chubby hands together and plays with her wedding ring while she smiles with understanding. I cannot believe I'm doing this.

Me, the man who is usually reserved, and doesn't open-up until someone has gained my trust. I tell her about mam dying, not knowing my father, living with Uncle Geoff, meeting Beth and having Sally, then years later falling in love with Erin.

She listens quietly and considerately nodding every now and then as though she knows I need to talk. I didn't realise until then that I did need to talk, but out it pours from me.

'So,' Jessie says. 'From what I can tell, the north's loss, is our gain.'

I grin back at her knowing I've found a true friend.

When we are leaving the canteen area and I have an invitation to dinner at Jessie's house, a colleague from the factory approaches. Jessie introduces me to her, and I shake her hand.

This friend is just back from honeymoon and Jessie congratulates her on an amazing wedding day then opens her big arms and hugs her tightly. In a large flowery silk tunic, I can tell how soft and warm Jessie's embrace feels. The women are chatting about her beautiful wedding dress and I instantly think of how sensational Erin looked in her dress at our wedding. Then I feel the weekend's sadness loom back upon me and sigh. For one split second, I wish I was in Jessie's embrace and could put my face into her big soft chest for comfort.

***

By the end of the following week the slapping has become a routine every time we make love. In fact, I'm going to stop calling it making love and start calling it having sex. Because that's what it feels like. There's no caring warmth in the act; it feels too fierce to be called loving. Erin will near her release and yell aloud or even growl. Yes, she growls like an animal in pain. She smacks me hard and not only on my buttocks, but on my arms, back or any part of my body that she is clinging onto.

I've challenged her of course and said, 'Please stop hitting me, Erin. I really don't like it.'

But she just laughs. It's almost a cruel laugh which is right in my face. 'I'm just enjoying herself and having a bit of fun, David. And, I don't know what you're moaning about because any other man would be glad to have a bit of rough sex!'

'Well, I don't think it's funny or enjoyable at all,' I'd said and tried to go to sleep.

I'd tossed and turned wondering if she was right. I suppose other men might like rough sex and have secret dreams of a woman being rowdy in bed. However, I've never been the type of man to talk about my sexual exploits with a woman, so I don't know anyone who is into this type of thing. It would be beyond me to open-up and confess the intimate nature of this problem to anyone. And for the first time since moving down here I long for home and its normality. Or should I say, the fact that Erin was her normal self when we were at home.

When I had managed to fall asleep, I'd dreamt I was with my pals in the pub telling them about the slapping and rough sex. I'd got the typical macho man's response to the problem: they'd howled with laughter.

***

We've been invited to Jessie's house for a BBQ. I am in the bathroom having just stepped out of the shower while Erin is dressing in the bedroom.

It's been a pleasant day so far. Erin has been painting and I've tackled the old lawn mower in the garage and managed to cut the grass. I took her tea and a sandwich at lunch time to which I received a loving hug and kiss on my cheek. Her mood does seem to be more upbeat and normal.

I dry my hair with a small towel and try to push last night's memory out of my mind. I'm determined to enjoy my new friends' company this evening. There are another two of my team going with their partners to Jessie's BBQ and I know this is a great chance to meet everyone socially.

'I'm really looking forward to meeting Mike,' I say when Erin comes into the bathroom. 'I've heard so much about him from Jessie, he sounds like quite a character.'

It is a large bathroom with a long powerful radiator on the wall under the window and a walk-in shower cubicle beside the roll top bath. On the opposite wall is a full-length mirror and I glance through the steam at Erin who looks stunning.

Her hair is plaited into one long plait that she has curled around her ear and down her shoulder. She is wearing a white gypsy top which is off-the-shoulder and a pair of lemon shorts showing off her long slim legs. She already has a slight tan and is glowing with only a minimum amount of make-up.

'Yes,' she says. 'And I'm looking forward to meeting Jessie, too.'

I frown. Was there the slightest hint of a smirk when she said the name Jessie? I give myself a shake deciding I'm looking for things that aren't there.

I bend forwards and down to dry my feet with a large towel. Suddenly, I feel a sharp sting along the back of my legs, and I yelp. Erin has picked up the small wet towel from the floor and swiped it across my legs.

'Hey, that hurt!' I shout and swing around. She twists the wet towel around her fist again getting ready to take another swipe at me.

'Stop it!' I yell and put my hand up in front of her.

She cackles at me. It's not a laugh. I know the difference. She chucks the towel into the open linen basket before sauntering out of the bathroom. I stare after her and let out the breath I didn't realise I was holding in. I rub the back of my left leg which is still stinging and shake my head. What the hell is going on? This isn't just fun and games anymore. I grimace and look in the small shaving mirror. This has gone way beyond normal teasing and messing around.

I see my pale face in the mirror and with a trembling hand I try to shave the stubble from my chin. I rinse the shaver under the cold water tap and bite my lip with apprehension. It's not even the swipe with the towel that is worrying me, but more the look on her face when she did it. Almost as though she enjoyed hurting me. I hurry into the bedroom determined to tackle her, but she has gone downstairs. I dress in my shirt and a pair of long chino shorts.

Erin is waiting for me downstairs in the hall and I touch the side of her arm. 'Hey, what was that all about? Why did you swipe at me like that?'

'Don't be such a cry-baby I was only messing around,' she says, and shrugs her shoulders. 'When you were bent over, I couldn't resist it. I thought you'd laugh and join in with the fun?'

I draw my eyebrows together and swallow hard. 'But it wasn't funny, Erin,' I say.

She pulls away from me. 'I think you've left your sense of humour in Kibblesworth,' she smirks. 'Loosen up a bit why don't you!'

At this she flounces out of the front door leaving me to follow and lock the door. I frown. I wouldn't have laughed at what she's just done whether we were here or at home.

We walk down the path in silence. I marvel at the peace and quiet under the large oak trees lining the street. I side-step the bumps in the pavement caused by the huge tree roots growing underneath.

The street is quiet at seven on a Saturday evening. We pass a couple walking their dog and then a single lad. Although I give them a slight nod and smile, neither look nor acknowledge us in any way. I couldn't do this at home.

In our village I couldn't walk a hundred yards without seeing someone I know. Or someone that knows me and my family. The sense of loss and longing for my familiar surroundings makes me catch my breath.

Is it the village community I'm missing, or the sense of belonging? I take a sidelong glance at Erin and wonder if she is feeling the slightest bit homesick. Maybe she hasn't thought of the village at all since we arrived here. I suppose, even if she was, she wouldn't admit to it because she was the one who was longing to escape. Erin could walk three miles at home without anyone stopping to speak to her or pass the time of day.

I shake my thoughts back to the here and now. I wonder if she is right. Am I turning into a grumpy old man? I think of the TV program where older male celebrities moan and complain about tiny things in life which aggravate them, and I cringe. I determine, at least for tonight, to forget the issue and enjoy myself.

***

Jessie's small semi-detached house is only a short distance at the bottom of the street nearer the village centre. I'm sitting in her back garden in an old-fashioned stripy deck chair drinking a bottle of larger. Their garden is larger than ours because it is on a corner plot and has decking in the centre surrounded by plants in colourful pots. Small tea-lights are dotted around the three wood tables and the BBQ is in the opposite corner. The smell of meat cooking wafts through the air mixed with happy chatter from all her guests and music is playing in the background.

I've circulated around everyone from work especially my little team and have met their partners. I've joked and laughed with Jakub and Mike and have accepted their invitation to join the local cricket team.

'I'm just putting it out here now, that although I love to watch cricket my abysmal batting skills are legendary in the Kibblesworth cricket club. And to be honest, I'm not much better at catching a ball in the field either!'

They'd both roared with laughter and I could tell they thought I was exaggerating. But I'm not.

Jessie is sitting next to me on this balmy evening sipping a glass of wine. She is dressed flamboyantly in a bright turquoise sundress with huge white drop earrings and a beaded necklace. We are both looking at our work colleagues milling around chatting and drinking. Erin is talking animatedly to Mike at the BBQ while he cooks seabream wrapped in foil.

As if to prove that I've imagined the moods and strange aggressive behaviour of the last two weeks, Erin is the life and soul of the party. She is friendly and engaging towards all my new friends and their partners from work. She has danced with Jessie and the other women and agreed to a shopping trip into London. She's told everyone, as soon as we have sorted our back garden, we'll buy a BBQ set and they must all come to us for a party. I am gob smacked. I have never, other than when we are on holiday, seen her appear so carefree and appealing.

Our holiday in Italy last year springs to mind. We'd stayed in an old farmhouse in Tuscany and loved every minute. Sitting in the late evening sun we'd dreamt of buying a rundown property with her father's money and doing it up over the years. It would be to rent out initially and then we'd retire to live permanently in Tuscany. I'd imagined Erin painting in an outside studio in the sunshine surrounded by the amazing views while I'd cook pasta with sun-ripened tomatoes.

These are some of our plans and now with my increase to a manager's salary the Italian dream looks like a distinct possibility. The sooner, the better, I think smiling at her.

After two bottles of larger, I decide that I've probably been so anxious over the move and start of my new job that I've blown everything up out of all proportion. My face blushes and I feel somewhat ashamed of the misgivings I've had towards my wife.

Jessie murmurs, 'Well, your Erin seems to be enjoying herself?'

I turn towards her and nod. I like the term, my Erin, because she is. My chest swells with pride when I look at her. 'She is, isn't she?' I say. 'I've been a little worried as she didn't seem to be settling in as well as I have.'

Jessie gently squeezes my arm. 'Well, it's different for her being at home on her own whereas you've been with us every day with your mind occupied.'

I listen to Jessie and hope she doesn't think that I've been neglecting Erin. 'Yeah, but Erin is more than used to her own company. Usually it's what she loves. It's where she is at her happiest,' I say looking into Jessie's big eyes.

Jessie folds her arms across her chest and smiles. 'Well, maybe she is missing home more than she thought she would and feels a little spooked by it all?'

I take a slug of the larger and feel the alcohol loosen my limbs. I explain how Erin hated Kibblesworth, how the villagers reacted to my split from Beth and Sally, and how desperate she was to leave it all behind. Jessie nods in understanding.

At the mention of Beth and Sally, I sigh slightly. Although I've tried Sally's mobile on numerous occasions, I've only managed to talk to my daughter twice since arriving here. Both conversations have been very one-sided.

I've told her all about the house, the village, and my new job, while she has non-committedly muttered just enough to let me know she is still on the line.

If it wasn't for Facebook however, I'd be more worried. I don't do much social media, but I do log into Facebook every couple of days because I am friended with Sally. I can see her posts and photographs of what she's been up to with her boyfriend, Ian. I make a mental note to talk to Beth about him and make sure he's an all-right type of lad.

I cross my long legs that are cramping sitting low down in the deck chair. I follow Jessie's gaze towards Erin and re-join the conversation. 'Whatever the reasons Erin's had for not being herself since we got here, I'm so pleased to see her like this and enjoying herself.'

Erin walks towards us now carrying two plates of fish and salad and I scramble up out of the deck chair. I sit at the small table with her while Jessie wanders off to talk to her guests.

Chapter Fifteen

Although I'd left the Italian restaurant saying no to any thoughts of making love my hormones suddenly rose to the occasion when David had pulled me into his arms. I'd felt charged and desperate to get rid of the tension and stress from my body. I'd wanted him. So, I took him.

I find now that I don't like namby-pamby love making. I want hard gritty sex. I don't want David caressing me and whispering soothing endearments into my ear. I don't want to caress him. I want to hurt him, so that he feels as wounded and angry as I do. I know he's not really enjoying the discomfort and smacking but I can't seem to stop myself. His body seems to cry out to be slapped. I've decided that it will be like everything else in life, he will get used to the change in us. After a while he'll forget our previous lovemaking and will throw himself into our new and exciting sex life.

It's Monday morning and I'm on the train going into The National Gallery in London. I'd begun the day promising David, 'I'll definitely look for a job today.'

I must admit this promise is half-hearted because I'm now engrossed in my painting again. He seems to think that if I'm out and about mixing with people instead of staying home alone, I will revert to my kind and loving old self. I know this won't work because being on my own isn't the reason for the change. I dread the very thought of getting stuck in some boring meaningless job when I could be painting and engrossed in my craft.

It's just after ten in the morning and although the train is busy, I've managed to get a seat in the first carriage.

I saw the advert for the Australian impressionist's exhibition in the newspaper and within the hour I was showered, dressed and on my way to the station.

It seems apt because my mind is trapped back in Brankstone now that I should look at Australian paintings. I'm expecting to see the works of Tom Roberts and John Russell. I'm tingling with excitement imagining the scenic Australian outback.

I rest my head gently against the train window watching our green countryside whiz past and feel my eyes dazzle with sun streaming onto the glass. The train has some form of air-conditioning and I settle back in the cool atmosphere. I know it's going to be hot in the city today, so I've bundled my hair up with a large grip and am wearing a pink cotton vest and shorts. It's taking a while to get used to the heat, which is so very different to Kibblesworth summers, but as I've always loved the sun it isn't an issue. I plan to go shopping after the exhibition. I only have two pairs of shorts and the other pair is in the wash basket from the BBQ on Saturday.

I think of how much I'd enjoyed the BBQ evening at Jessie's house. I'd felt a little guilty after swiping David with the wet towel and had wanted to make some type of amends. He is my husband after all. I know in my rational moments, what my mother suffered, is not David's fault. But when he'd been naked and bent over in such a vulnerable position with his tight bottom sticking out, I'd felt it was begging to be smacked. I couldn't stop myself. And as the trendy speak goes, it was there, and I had to go for it.

I'd started the evening determined to show David that I was fine. That I'm normal and not going loopy. I knew if I'd tried to be nice to his work colleagues it would make him happy.

It turned out that when I did make an enormous effort to look as though I was enjoying myself, I found that I was.

David has rattled on about Jessie since his first week at work, so I'd been interested to meet her. I admit to having a few niggles in the back of my mind, not exact feelings of jealousy, but more curiosity to know if I had anything to worry about.

Hugging my handbag into my side and smiling to myself, I decide, she's no comparison to me. She is a Beth look-a-like. Grossly over-weight, with big soppy eyes, hideous dress sense and if I had to choose a word to describe her, it would be inoffensive. I grin with the knowledge that this is not the type of woman David likes. He likes a woman to have a bit of something about her. An interesting personality. A go out and get what she wants type of woman. Just like me, I think happily and hop off the train.

***

Walking up to Trafalgar Square I smile at the sight before me. People are milling around the lion statues and children are laughing and climbing on them. I stand still for a few minutes soaking up the atmosphere. From the grand steps leading up to the massive pillars and the sun glittering on the small dome at the top of the double storey building, I smile. It is such a beautiful structure and I watch people drinking coffee and snacking while sitting on the benches in the square.

A council man wanders from one litter bin to another emptying the rubbish and replenishing them with clean plastic sacks. A little old lady is sitting with her face held up to the sunshine smiling with pleasure. I think of the history over the years and how people have used the square. It has been a major tourist attraction for all generations.

Slowly I mount the steps to the entrance to buy a ticket and regret that I will be leaving the glorious sunshine for a while. But thinking of the paintings I'm about to see makes me hurry up the steps quicker in anticipation.

I've been inside the gallery a few times and am confident at finding the room where the exhibition is held. I gasp in awe at the first painting. It is an oil on canvas named, A holiday at Mentone, by Charles Conder, 1888. I don't know this artist and stand in front of the painting against the short rope railing that is placed in front of the painting. I marvel at the colours in the sand and blue sea. It is a simple scene of a woman sitting in a deckchair and a man standing behind her looking out to sea. The artist has captured the essence of the seaside and I can almost smell the sea and hear the seagulls squawking above them.

I stand back to take in the scene from a distance and tread on a man's foot.

'Oh, sorry,' I mutter quickly.

He steps back from me. 'No problem.'

I look at the man aged around fifty in a grey raincoat with a bald head and a goatee-beard. He seems to leer at me with his beady brown eyes travelling up and down my shorts. Feeling slightly apprehensive I step around him and carry on to the next group of paintings.

There's a small cluster of people looking at these paintings and I instantly feel more assured. I try to shake the previous incident from my mind but know for me to tread on his foot he must have been very close. Almost too close behind me. I shiver and look over my shoulder to see if he is still in the room. He is nowhere to be seen and I settle myself back into the atmosphere of life in the cities of Melbourne and Sydney.

In the next room with dark green walls and lights above each painting I take my time studying the use of colours by each artist in dazzling landscapes of the coast and bushland. I walk towards the back-to-back chesterfield settees strategically placed in the middle of the room. These are for people to make the most of the viewings and I sink back into the comfort of the soft leather. I can't quite decide whether I feel a little home-sick for Australia. Although I spent more years of my life living there than I did here in England, but because my father had done, I always class this as home.

I tilt my head back and instantly tense when I feel someone's arm at the back of my shoulder. I turn around to see the same man sitting directly behind me with his arm along the back of both settees. He seems to smirk at me, and my heart begins to thump. I grab my handbag from the settee and scramble to my feet.

My canvas sandals make a squeaky noise on the polished wood floor when I jump back and look frantically around to see if there are any other people. We are alone in the huge room and I'm scared. Why is he wearing a raincoat in this sunny weather? He is rubbing his hand across his beard. His heavy eyebrows are drawn together in an intimidating manner.

My mouth is dry, but I know I must say something. I find my voice, 'A…are you following me?'

His eyes stare at my shorts and then up to my vest. He is ogling my breasts.

'No, I'm simply admiring the view,' he whispers. He sweeps his arm around the room as if his answer could be construed to mean he was enjoying looking at me and the paintings.

The hairs on the back of my neck are tingling.

My heart is pumping much faster now as though it is fit to burst out of my chest. A fleeting image of my mother springs to mind and how terrified she must have felt being accosted by a strange man. I must get away and find someone to help. I hurry along the short corridor into the next room and breathe a sigh of relief with the sight of a gallery attendant in his uniform.

Gabbling quickly, I tell the attendant about the man who has been following me. The attendant is a

youngish man in his early twenties with a kind face
and looks eager to help.

'We'll soon sort this out,' he says strutting across the
room with me hurrying along behind him. My heart
rate has slowed down and annoyance has replaced my
fear. The attendant is talking all the while stating how
everyone should have the right to view the paintings in
a congenial atmosphere. We hurry back along the
corridor and enter the room.

Quite a few people are now in the room and the man
is still sitting on the settee. I point him out to the
attendant. The man has removed his raincoat, and has it
folded neatly over his arm. A stylish woman in her
forties is standing in front of him giggling at something
he has said. When we approach the couple, I can see
now that the man is dressed in a grey expensive shirt
and designer jeans. He does appear perfectly normal.
Or maybe not as disturbing as I first thought.

While the attendant explains how I felt that he had
been following me around the exhibition, the heavily
made-up blonde woman raises a pencilled eyebrow at
me. She stares down at my canvas sandals. 'Are you
joking?' she says in a clipped dismissive voice.
'You're accusing my husband of following you!'

I slink back slightly behind the attendant.

I can tell by the look on the blonde woman's face that
if he was going to stalk a woman, he'd certainly pick
someone with a little more refinement than I obviously
have.

'The young lady simply trod on my foot in the other
room,' he explains to the attendant. He looks relaxed

and unperturbed by the whole incident. 'I just sat down behind her here on this settee.'

I try to explain about the close contact and how he'd brushed his arm against mine and know that I'm gabbling. My cheeks flush and my throat dries.

The blonde tuts loudly and rounds on the attendant. 'I think it's disgraceful how this gallery allows these lone neurotic women into the exhibition!'

I feel myself deflate like a balloon that has been popped. The couple look at me as though I am crazy. The attendant turns to me opening his hands as though he isn't sure what to do next. I feel tears well up in my eyes and turn quickly then hurry away from the couple. I hear the blonde woman call out, 'Bloody weirdo.'

***

I'm back at home now. I'd managed to stem my emotional outburst on the journey back to Bexley. Now that I've run through the front door, I'm letting the torrent of tears cascade down my face.

I'm standing with my back against the front door feeling scared. My mind is changing, and I know I'm not coping like I usually do. I cannot see anything in the hall because my eyes are full of tears which makes me panicky. I stifle a choking sob in my throat and drag a tissue out of my jacket pocket to blow my nose.

I'm usually not one for crying. I have never been a tearful person but when I do cry the floodgates open. The actual physical act of crying almost hurts. My chest is racked with harsh sobbing. My throat constricts and feels ragged. My eyes sting and swell. Crying seems to exhaust my body.

I want to slump down the tiles because I feel so alone. I start gasping for breath. My heart begins to race. Sweat forms on my top lip. I tug the damp vest over my head and remember an article in a magazine about hot flushes and how they can be exacerbated by stress. The writer had advised blowing into a paper bag to alleviate the panic.

I push myself away from the door then scamper through to the kitchen. On the counter is a paper bag with apples that David has left. I empty the apples out of the bag then breathe deeply in and out. I count five, six, seven times. My heart rate slows down.

Feeling a little cooler and calmer, I head upstairs slowly and roll onto our bed under my favourite grey throw. I wrap it around me for comfort. I wonder if the man in the gallery had really been coming on to me. Or was he just a normal man and I'd built up his manner and smarmy look out of all proportion. I snatch a tissue from the box on my bedside table and dry my tear stained face.

I know I would have coped with this so much better if I'd been my usual self and not upset about my mother. I remember the fear when I'd jumped up from the chesterfield settee and how vulnerable he'd made me feel. This isn't like me. Ordinarily, I would have told him to piss-off and stuck up for myself more. But today, all I've done is make a complete fool of myself.

Maybe from now on I should think of my life as before the diary and after the diary.

I know my thought processes are not what they were. I'm not being rational at times but there again, I suppose I've always been a bit like this.

My father used to say, 'You can jump from rational to irrational at the drop of a hat, my little bonzer.'

I sigh in confusion. Maybe, I'm allowing myself to feel locked in this irrational chain of thought and can't distance myself from mother's writings. Is my mind becoming obsessed with what I've learnt about her? I dwell on the words she'd written the day she'd walked down to the river.

I can't live with the shame! When I realised, I was pregnant after the rape I knew I'd have to let my husband believe the baby was his. I've also had to lie to my beautiful daughter, Erin and prepare her for accepting a baby brother into her life. But this isn't fair on either of them. I love them both so dearly. Every time I look at Neil I am filled with mixed emotions. I love him because I carried him inside of me and gave birth to him. Then I see his big blue eyes which remind me of his real father glaring and towering above me as he nearly tore my body apart. And, I cannot bear it any longer. Even in years to come I don't think I will ever feel any different to this. Neil deserves a proper mother. A mother who would idolise and love him without reservation. Therefore, it's best I take him with me...

'But it wasn't fair,' I rage into the silence of the bedroom. 'It was more hurtful when you took Neil with you!'

I start to cry again. Big wet tears that roll down my cheeks. I don't wipe them away. I let them drip off the end of my chin. I know without a doubt that my father would have loved Neil and raised him as his own son. Even if he had known he wasn't his real father. That's just the type of man he was.

And if mother had told me that Neil had a different father, I wouldn't have loved him any less. He would still have been my little brother. I seethe with annoyance. If I know this about me and father how come my mother couldn't figure it out.

I sigh heavily and roll over to look at David's alarm clock knowing he will soon be home from work. I've thrown the cover aside and stripped off my shorts because it is hot and stuffy even with the windows open. I fiddle with the lace on my red bra. It's a matching set that David bought me at Christmas. I can't help comparing my feelings from back then to what they are now. I remember Christmas night lying in front of the fire in this underwear wrapped in David's arms making love to him. I'd been in seventh heaven. So, why can't I feel like that now. I've got to admit that it feels like a love-hate relationship with him now.

I love him because I always have. But I hate him because he's a man and makes me feel sexy. Which on behalf of my mother I really don't want to feel anymore.

Chapter Sixteen

The good mood at the BBQ didn't last for long. Erin has begun to slap me even when we aren't having sex. She will often reach out when I pass by her and slap my arm. Or if she is behind me, she will slap the top of my head.

And I'm not just talking an affectionate slap in a teasing manner. This is a hard slap that she uses force behind. I'm beginning to feel on edge whenever she is within a few feet from me. This seems a ludicrous situation for a husband to be in that loves his wife so much.

Twice last week when I turned on my side in bed away from her, she hit my shoulder blade hard. At first, I'd thought she wanted something. Groggily in my sleep I'd half-turned towards her and said, 'What did you do that for?'

Now, I may have this wrong because I was half asleep but I'm sure she'd snarled, 'Because it's all you deserve!'

I'd gone back to sleep dreaming of the nasty look in her eyes when she'd made the weird comment.

I've tried to talk about it and delve deeper but emotionally she is becoming more of a closed book than she's ever been. Especially about her life in Australia. I can't seem to get through to her at all.

In the past when I've probed the subject it has always been strictly taboo. If I've asked about her mother or father's deaths, she'd purse her lips tight shut. She'd shake her long curls and refuse to even mention their names. 'Don't want to talk about it,' she'd mutter between clenched teeth. I'd try to hug and soothe her, but nothing had made any difference.

It's not as if I don't understand this because sometimes when you talk about upsetting memories it brings them back into focus in your mind.

They can linger, and I suppose upsetting images are something none of us willingly want to confront. But there again, I know that talking can often help as a release valve. And if it is early memories that are tormenting her then it might prove to be a better release than slapping me.

The only person Erin has ever talked freely about is Josie. I've gathered she was like a substitute mother to Erin and from the little things she has told me, I rather like Josie and would love the chance to meet her.

However, when I'd said this to Erin, she'd huffed, 'Well, you'd have to go to Bondi Beach if you want to meet her because Josie wouldn't fly over to England.'

I'd smiled. 'She might come if it was to see you?' I'd said. But Erin had got up and walked away from me, and the conversation.

***

I'm back at work today, as is Jessie who has had a week's annual leave. I have chosen to spend the day with Jakub. At only twenty-five and from Prague, Jakub is our ideas and new concept man. His ideas are often wacky and unworkable, but his enthusiasm and drive make listening to his proposals irresistible. Jessie has already warned me that sometimes he needs bringing back down to planet earth a little, but I've already figured this out for myself.

Years ago, although I was never totally off the map when it came to my new ideas, I can see the same drive and initiative in Jakub that I had. Which automatically likens me to him.

I relax in the warm friendly atmosphere around our desks where most of the conversation this morning has been about the BBQ at Jessie's house.

Jakub says, 'Hey, thanks for being the incomparable hostess, Jessie.'

We all smile at his words. Although not technically wrong he often uses words from a dictionary, which I presume is how he learnt to speak English at home in Prague.

Jessie grins. 'And thanks for coming everyone,' she says.

Discussions take place about who danced with who and the amazing food Mike cooked. Jessie mentions Erin a couple of times which I know is for my benefit, and I'm pleased to be included.

Later, I stand next to Jakub at the bench. He is tall and long-limbed with his white tunic stretched across his broad chest.

'I read this article at the weekend, boss,' Jakub says.

He offers me the magazine and I scan-read the article. I nod in agreement with many of the comments that cakes in the new Instagram era are enjoying a global growth. From the cupcake frenzy in 2000 and all the TV cookery shows, the baking market is certainly thriving.

I look at Jakub while he is busy filling two layers of a cake with buttercream.

'First, Jakub,' I say. 'Just call me David. And yes, the article is right in many ways. We're lucky to be working with cakes now.'

His work area is littered with sprinkles, chocolate shavings, and decorations of all colours, shapes, and sizes. I know Jessie would say it was a complete mess because she works tidily, and her area is always well organised. But I've learned over the years that everyone has a different method to their working practices and there's no rule book to say one is right and the other is not.

So, I wait patiently looking forward to the outcome.

Jakub looks at me and grins. Unfortunately, his skin is still marked from the acne he'd obviously suffered in his teens, but he has piercing big brown eyes that sparkle now as he grabs a handful of orange jellybeans and dolly mixtures.

I notice one layer of his cake has a banked-up mould of buttercream on the edge and shake my head slightly wondering where he is going with this.

I raise my eyebrow at him, and he smiles. 'Just bear with me and I'll show you what I want to do.'

One side of the layered cake is wide open where he places the sweets into the mass of buttercream. The cream is slightly sloppy in the layers and the sweets look as though they're about to tumble out. Kindly, I try to tell him this.

He claps his hands in glee. 'You've got it, boss. That's what they're supposed to look like. This way it looks fun. It looks like a home-baked cake that someone with very little experience has put together.

It's not…' he says drawing his eyebrows together. I can tell he is thinking of a suitable word. 'It's not meticulous or accurate, but it's trending on twitter and people are photographing on Instagram!'

Obviously, he isn't going to call me David but that doesn't matter. Now he is mixing a bright pink royal icing and piles bright orange round balls in the centre as a finished decoration. The whole cake looks lopsided to me. I must admit though with the wide expanse of cream and sweets with the pile of balls on top it does look crazy and lots of fun especially for children.

I place me hand on his shoulder. 'Well, Jakub, it certainly looks very entertaining. Very different to our usual portfolio and I agree, you're bang on trend.'

I jerk my head for him to follow me back to the desk with the cake and we sit down to discuss his ideas. 'We might have to adjust them somewhat, so we can produce them in the factory, Jakub,' I say softly not wanting to dampen his enthusiasm. 'But well done, I think we've got some great ideas here.'

Jakub grins and I see his shoulders lift with pride before he hurries off back into the kitchen area.

I'm sitting at my desk alone now because all the technologists, except Jessie, have gone on a training course for the afternoon. Moving Jakub's lopsided cake to the end of my desk I sit back in the chair, clasp my hands behind my head and stretch out my legs looking around the big room. I'm pleased I'm located in the same area as my team and not in a separate managers office because I love feeling a part of the hub.

With no meetings until later I gaze around the office space. My desk is the largest and at the back of the room and the technologist's desk are placed side-by-side down the room. If I was a stranger entering the department, I could still guess which desk belongs to which technologist simply by the state of their desk areas. Jessie's is tidy and neat while Jakub's looks like a bomb has dropped. The other three have designated areas and are a mixture of packaging and Christmas décor.

I cast my mind back to our office in Kibblesworth and smile. I've come a long way in such a short space of time. Although I'm having short periods of homesickness, I think I'm bearing up rather well. Much better than I thought I would. I remember our last few days at home and I recall my visit with Uncle Geoff. I can't stop thinking about his words, 'Your father was shagging the local barmaid!'

Mam never mentioned this, but she wouldn't, would she?

I wonder if it was true and if my father a womaniser who cheated on mam. Or was this just a figment of imagination from a confused old man.

Even as a seven-year-old I knew mam had had a difficult time bringing me up on her own. It hadn't been easy for her. She'd often have a strained look on her face and her eyes would wash with tears at the mere mention of any upset in our lives. So, I'd determined not to cause any. Uncle Geoff used to call me the little man in the house. A teacher at school had once said on parents evening, 'David is a serious little boy but an asset to have in the classroom.'

I'd spent all my childhood staying within the boundaries set by mam because I'd known stepping outside them would cause the upset in her eyes which I couldn't bear. 'I want to see your best behaviour and be respectful to your elders, David,' she'd say.

When I met and married Beth I became the big man in my own house. I stayed within a different set of boundaries which came along with my family. Beth looked to me and my wage to pay the mortgage, insurance, energy bills and to provide for Sally's future.

I sigh. Meeting Erin was the first time in my life I'd felt like I could step outside these boundaries and have some fun. I didn't have to be myself. I could be another man or at least another type of man.

I had been known as a private cautious type of guy who didn't find it easy to show my feelings. But Erin had brought out my fun-loving side. She'd made me want to throw my caution and these boundaries aside, let myself go, and enjoy my life more. I'd felt free being with Erin. She'd make me laugh until I felt quite giddy. She'd excite me until I thought my chest would burst. She'd make me feel melancholy over a sad film.

Then instead of sloping off to the bathroom as I'd done with Beth and Sally, she'd encourage me to shed a few tears with her.

I'm snapped out of my reverie and sit forward abruptly in my chair when Jessie breezes into the office. She calls out a greeting and comes to perch on the end of my desk. Her large thighs in cream slacks hanging precariously over the edge so I lift a pile of books from a chair and push it towards her.

She sits down and raises her eyebrow looking at Jakub's sloppy fun-filled cake. I explain his idea and she giggles. I can tell it is light-hearted and friendly. Jessie doesn't have the meanness to be catty about another colleague's work. I smile in agreement with her.

'It's nice to see the sparkle back in your face,' she says quietly. 'I was a little concerned a few weeks ago. You looked as though you had the weight of the world on your shoulders.'

The one thing I've learned about Jessie is that she is interested in us all. I know amongst the team she is thought of as a good friend to everyone. She certainly has been to me. She is sensitive to my moods almost like Beth was, and Erin used to be.

'Yeah, I did feel a bit like that with worrying about Erin,' I say then shrug my shoulders.

Jessie smiles and rubs the side of my arm. 'Well, she seemed fine at the BBQ. Surely she's settled in a little better now?'

I want to tell her about the slapping but know I can't. I'd feel such an idiot and be totally embarrassed. It would look like I don't know how to manage my own marriage.

I side-track. 'Oh yes, she is. She's been into London a couple of times to art galleries and is painting every day.

And she's ordered pieces of furniture for the house. So…' I say purposively avoiding Jessie's eyes and look down at my desk. 'It just seems to be me she has the problem with now. I've racked my brains to think if I've said or done something to upset her but can't think of a thing.'

I fiddle with the potholder full of my pencils and pens that I brought from my desk at the Kibblesworth factory. Suddenly I feel such a longing for home that it makes me sigh at my previous thoughts of homesickness and how well I've done.

I think of us back in the cottage when we were normal together. Where I know she wouldn't have dreamt of slapping or hurting me in any way.

'Maybe, it's nothing you've done and more about something that's happened to her. And because there is no one else down here she's taking it out on you,' Jessie says. 'I sometimes do that with Mike and pick at him like a scab. But we've been married for so long now he just ignores me until I'm ready to tell him what's bothering me.'

I look up at Jessie who has put her head on one side. I can see real compassion shinning in her big eyes. I listen carefully to what she is saying. After all she is a woman and may be able to understand more than I can about what is troubling Erin. And let's face it, I need all the help I can get.

'But what?' I say. 'I've asked her repeatedly, but she won't talk to me, let alone tell me if anything has happened.'

'Be patient and give her time,' Jessie recommends.

I nod and place my hands flat on top of the desk. I stare down at them. 'It's just so unusual for us to be like this. We've been together for over two years now and up until we moved down here, I knew every thought in her gorgeous head. Now I haven't a clue what's going on in there.'

Jessie takes one of my hands and squeezes it tightly. 'And she is gorgeous. All that fabulous hair! I'd give anything to have hair like that,' she says running her hand through her own chestnut bob. 'Just remember anytime you want to talk I'm always here,' she says.

I smile knowing she is helping to alleviate my worries. She seems like my own release valve and I nod at her.

'And if you want to bring Erin around to ours maybe the four of us can have supper. Although I don't know Erin very well, I could try talking to her.'

My hopes rise. Maybe Erin would bare her soul and talk to Jessie. Anything is worth a shot, I suppose. 'Look, why not come to us for supper at the weekend?'

Jessie agrees and meanders back to her desk. I decide she has become a close ally in just a few short weeks.

***

The dining room table is laden with food because Jessie and Mike have joined us for dinner. They call it supper down here for some reason and the night before I'd mistakenly used the word. Erin had laughed and teased.

Although the house is rented as part-furnished the landlord has included a long oak dining table that will comfortably sit six people. It's nearly eight o'clock and although the sun hasn't set, I've turned on the dimmer lights which is creating a warm glow around the table. Even though Erin is not being unfriendly to our guests, I'm wishing she could offer a little more of a welcoming glow towards them. She seems distracted and is certainly not as enamoured as she was at their BBQ.

However, when I think back to Kibblesworth this is no different to how she'd been on the odd occasion we'd had people to dinner.

It was almost as if she resented the intrusion in our lives. In those days, I'd often wondered what people thought of us as a couple. Did they think we were the perfect twosome because we looked good together? As I look at my wife now, I figure that might not be true anymore and I wonder if the cracks in our relationship are beginning to show.

I've cooked red snapper, tossed salads with dressings and warmed walnut bread with unsalted butter. Mike has brought two good bottles of Australian wine which I thought was a lovely gesture. And although my wife thanked him, she didn't expand on their virtues compared to other wines.

Erin has made an amazing cheese board with different chutneys, grapes, and figs. It is placed in readiness on the old sideboard in the corner of the room. With our glasses filled we toast the summer sunshine and begin to eat.

'How's the gardening going?' Mike asks looking out of the window into the garden. He is sitting directly opposite me and is dressed casually in jeans and a white shirt. His jovial face is red tonight because he's been outside gardening and has caught the sun.

'Well, we didn't have outside space in our cottage at home,' I say. 'But I'm getting used to cutting the grass with an old lawnmower the landlord has left in the garage for us to use.'

'Ah. I can look at that after supper, if you'd like?'

I see a tiny twitch of amusement pull at Erin's lips which helps me relax slightly on the hard-back dining chair.

Jessie is sitting to my right and is chatting to Erin about the curtains she has hung.

'We brought all of the curtains from home and these are the only pair that don't fit. They're too long, but I've always loved this burnt orange colour...' Erin says wistfully looking at the windows. 'Maybe I will try to get them taken up.'

Jessie, dressed in a simple white dress which looks toned down somewhat to her usual attire, smiles and explains where Erin can take the curtains.

Conversation flows easier now then Erin steps into the kitchen to make coffee while I place the cheese board onto the table.

I'm more relaxed after my second glass of wine and Erin glides easily in and out of the room with cups and side plates.

'Well, I've had a little good news from home this morning,' I say. 'My daughter Sally is to be married soon.'

Jessie immediately looks from me to Erin then raises her glass. 'A toast to the happy couple,' she says.

We all join in the toast sipping from our glasses. Except Erin, who drains half of her wine in two large mouthfuls. It looks as though she will need sustenance to get through the rest of the conversation.

She isn't exactly glaring at me, but I can tell she's not happy that I've told our guests. I could kick myself for being careless. I should have thought about her feelings before telling them and know this may well put a dampener on my wife's mood. It could spoil the rest of our first dinner party.

Erin raises an eyebrow at me. 'And I've told David to ask if it's going to be a shotgun wedding.'

We all look at her and she shrugs her shoulders then pours more red wine into her glass.

Mike looks at Erin and laughs. 'Shotgun? That's a very old-fashioned term to use now-a-days. Unless of course, David does have a gun hidden away and intends to use it.'

Nervously, I chortle.

As ever, Jessie comes to my rescue. 'I don't think it matters these days,' she says. 'Just because young people seem to do things in a different order to what we did it doesn't really matter as long as they're happy.'

Jessie then proceeds to tell us all about their son at university which takes the onus from me and Erin. I relax once more.

After dessert, Jessie asks Erin if she could have a look at her paintings. Although I know it is a ruse for Jessie to talk to my wife on her own, I sincerely hope Erin agrees. Erin usually hides her talents and is not forthcoming about showing her paintings, but to my surprise she takes Jessie by the arm and heads upstairs to her art room.

Mike and I wander into the garage and I feign enthusiasm and interest when he looks over the old lawnmower.

Later, while we stand together on the front doorstep and wave goodbye to Mike and Jessie, I squeeze Erin's arm into my side. Apart from my small faux pas, it has gone surprisingly well. Although I'm not entirely sure if Erin has enjoyed the evening, I'm pleased that she was at least kind to our guests. I really want Erin to like and get along with Jessie because I know she'd be as good a friend to her as she is to everyone at work. As Jakub would say, it's simply in her DNA.

Chapter Seventeen

Yesterday, when I saw the thin blue line on the testing kit and realised, I was pregnant I bordered on the edge of hysteria. My overwhelming feelings had been of horror at the thought of an alien invader inside my body. It had been in the morning when I realised, I'd not had a period since the move. As we are into the fifth week of living here, I'd known something was amiss.

I'd consoled myself hurrying down to the village chemist that I'd been stressed to an all-time high after reading the diary and the move to a new area. And this could have delayed my natural cycle. However, I'm never late with periods and when I'd left the chemist with the small paper bag, my walk home had been slow and deliberate. I'd dreaded the outcome with every step I'd taken.

When I'd done the test and stared at the blue line my mind went into some type of melt-down. I'd shaken my head and looked once, twice, and three times more but still couldn't believe the line was blue. I'd left the stick lying on the top of the toilet cistern and scattered from room to room. I made coffee that I didn't drink and then hurried into my art room where I'd paced around and around my easel like a panther stalking its prey.

'Noooo,' I screamed aloud then ran back into the bathroom to take another look. There it was like my sky-blue paint in the palette. I'd sank to my knees on the bathroom floor and howled in terror.

When David had arrived home, I was in bed in my pyjamas and told him I had a migraine. He left me alone for the whole evening and by the time he came up to bed I feigned sleep. I lay very still until I was convinced, he was asleep.

***

This morning I'm sitting in the leather armchair in the lounge lost in thought. The sun is streaming through the window onto my face and I rub my hand gently over my belly. I think of me, the woman I am inside this body and don't feel as though there is room for another person.

Some days I can hardly cope with myself let alone a dependant. I know that's what a baby is, totally and utterly dependant on its mother. Since meeting David I've had little fantasies about having children and have often thought with him by my side, I might just be able to cope. But that was before the diary, of course.

Now my feelings and thoughts are so very different. I know categorically that I wouldn't be able to raise a child. I would lose control of my life and have to change my daily schedules to prioritise around the baby.

He or she would be in control, not me. It would demand my time, and although all maternal women are more than willing for this change to take place, I'm not. I know I would resent these changes.

I get up out of the chair determined to have a shower and start to paint. But my stomach seems to twist as if it is pained and I slump back down trying to come to terms with it all.

I suppose, if I wanted to, I could now call myself a mother. I sigh knowing the term, mother, holds a mixture of feelings. I've thought for most of my adult life that my own mother couldn't wait to get away from me, but now at least I know that she did love me.

I frown and pick at the skin around my thumb. What if I feel nothing for this baby when it is born? What if I can't love the child. Will I spend the rest of my life trying to love someone because life dictates to me, as a mother I must do this?

My mind spins and I sigh heavily watching a young girl pass the window pushing her baby in a buggy. I can see the baby is red in the face and crying. The girl stops and leans over the buggy to push the dummy back into its mouth. It looks like she is making little cooing noises which obviously soothe the baby. It snuggles back under the blanket.

I cringe. What if my baby isn't soothed by my voice? And if there is no bonding between us will my child instantly know I don't want it. I start to tremble. It would be humiliating to have everyone notice that my child doesn't like me. I shudder.

The knowledge that I don't have to put myself through this and can have a termination slowly but surely creeps into my mind. The seed of a plan begins to form. I can feel myself begin to relax and feel more in control.

I wouldn't have to tell David anything about being pregnant and he would be none the wiser. It would be easy to check into a clinic in London and have the procedure done privately. No one, other than me and the doctor need ever know anything about it. The tension in my shoulders dissolves and I feel like I can breathe normally again. With this survival plan in place, I'm back in charge again and stride purposively upstairs to the shower.

***

By the following weekend I've come to terms with the pregnancy and have an appointment for a clinic on Harley Street. I've had to join a GP surgery in Bexley, and they've transferred our records down from Kibblesworth.

I'm setting the table outside in the garden with cutlery, glasses, and plates. The new black rattan garden furniture has arrived, and I've decided we should eat outside while basking in a glorious summer evening.

It's only a small garden with a strip of decking near the dining room window and I've chosen the furniture to fit perfectly into the space.

I wipe the glasses while mulling over things. Considering I've always classed myself as an honest person I've found it incredibly easy to make up a deliberate lie and deceive my husband. I'd read somewhere a nicer description of telling lies which I rather like. It stated, telling lies was a way for your brain to fill in holes in your life with plausible or likeable images.

I have convinced myself that this lie is only a trivial likeable image. It won't last forever. And, of course, I would never lie about anything major. A tiny voice in

my mind niggles, but this is major to everyone else.
However, to me, it's not.

I've decided that these are exceptional circumstances.
And in my own way, I'm saving David a lot of
heartache by not knowing he is going to be a father
again. This is one of my likeable images because I
know I'm helping him. David would be shocked at first
about the baby, but then he'd be delighted. That's just
the way he is. Also, we'd have to forget about our
Tuscany retirement dreams if we have a baby, and I
know he wouldn't want that.

I'm going to use my age for the main reason to
terminate the pregnancy. I'll stress at the clinic that
although many women do have children later in life,
it's just not for me. I will tell them about the
menopausal hot flushes and complain of feeling very
stressed following the move. I plan to make it obvious
that I won't be able to cope with a baby at this time in
my life.

I'm wearing David's favourite gypsy off the shoulder
top and a flowing pleated skirt.

Although I know there's nothing of the baby to show
yet, I figure if I wear loose garments from now
onwards David won't notice any difference in me.

I sigh with pleasure and sip my prosecco while David
serves the salmon fillets which are cooked to
perfection. He looks relaxed in his green shorts and
black T-Shirt while he tells me about his day at work.

'Now this is something we were never able to enjoy
in Kibblesworth,' he says looking around the garden.

I nod and sit forward in the chair to pick up my knife and fork. I tell him about enrolling us both at the doctors and the dentist and how they are transferring our records. He seems delighted.

Sipping his wine, he says, 'We're really settling in now, aren't we?'

I nod and pick at the salmon. The fish is lovely, but I just don't seem to have much of an appetite. 'Yes, of course, we are,' I say brightly. 'Before much longer we will be able to class ourselves as southerners!'

David laughs and I remember how good it is to see him so happy. It hasn't been an easy time since reading the diary. And I know if I didn't have my survival plan in place life would become even more difficult. I wait until David has finished eating and I lay my cutlery together on my plate. I clasp my hands together under the table and rub my knuckles.

'I had an email today from Vicky,' I say. 'She is coming to London next Friday to see an art exhibition and has asked me to join her.'

David grins. 'Hey, that's great! You'll hear all the news from the vet's surgery and how they're getting along without you.'

I take a deep breath knowing this is the tricky bit of the plan.

'Yeah, and because she is a little wary about staying in a London hotel on her own, I've said, well if you don't mind of course, that I will stay in the hotel overnight with her.'

Davis raises an eyebrow. I can tell he is surprised.

'Of course, I don't mind,' he says looking at me. 'But why not bring her here? There's loads of room and it will make us get that guest bedroom sorted. We can pick up another bed at a reasonable price and you can make the room look pretty with new curtains and accessories.'

Blast, I hadn't thought of this and I feel my cheeks flush. Quickly I rack my brains to think of another lie. 'We could, David,' I say. 'But Vicky has already said she will buy us tickets for a West End show as a treat and we won't want to travel out here late at night.'

He looks a little downcast. My palms are sweating, and I can hear the tension in my voice. I sit further back in the chair and sip my wine willing myself to relax.

I put my head on one side and smile coyly at him. 'Well, that's if you can manage without me for a night?'

David grins and stares into my eyes. It's one of our old searching looks that sadly has been a thing of the past lately. He runs a hand up my arm and towards my shoulder. I rest my head on his arm. We are together. We are latched into each other again. I feel a flood of happiness surge through me. This is how we used to be when I felt normal. This was before the diary and I'm determined to try and find my way back to us.

With the knowing looks and loving conversation, we've come up to bed early. My spirits have lifted, and I want us to become closer, not only in our minds but in our bodies. Most of the last few weeks problems are all my own fault.

Nevertheless, I'm determined to make it up to him now and love the very socks off him. I've left the cream silk curtains open to catch the moonlight and the window open. I smooth down the duvet cover then ruffle up our pillows.

David has such a great body. I've purposively left my bedside light on to admire him walking around the bedroom and getting ready to join me. A strong masculine chest with just a few hairs around his nipples and long lean legs. I can't wait to have him with me.

While he is in the bathroom, I can tell he is happy because he is whistling. If it wasn't for the pregnancy I would be feeling just as happy. I step out of my skirt and sit on the end of the bed. I wonder if this was how my mother felt trying to act normally with my father after she'd been raped. Did she tell him straight away that she was pregnant? Or did she wait a while until she'd come to term with her situation.

A darkness fills my mind. Am I living the same life as my mother did when she was pregnant? She didn't want Neil growing inside her and I don't want David's child growing inside me. The room spins ever so slightly.

I look at the temporary clothes rail and see two of my dresses on coat hangers waft precariously in front of the window. Maybe the wine has gone straight to my head and I fight against the sad mood settling upon me again. But mother's words sneak back into my mind. I squeeze my eyes shut trying to rid myself of her writings.

I'll never forget the stale smell of dirty sweat on him and beer on his breath. With his hand squeezing my throat I'd been terrified he was going to strangle me, so I'd lain still praying for the ordeal to be over.

He'd left teeth marks on my breasts and tore at my body, so much so, that even after two weeks of salt baths I was still sore and bruised.

I hear David plodding back to me and I shake away the reverie. I begin to chant softly to myself; I must be nice to him. I must not be aggressive.

He pulls the duvet back and climbs in next to me switching off the lamp on his side.

My mother's ordeal is often in my mind when we're having sex which is probably why I feel aggressive when he makes me peak. I blot her words from my mind.

Desire wells up inside me, it is curling its way around my gut like a snake from the out bush. I smile at my Australian comparison and feel quite giddy with delight.

I look at his neck and lick my lips. It's just so clean and tempting that I can't seem to stay away. Recently, I've taken to biting his neck and shoulders, but I've stopped now because he says he doesn't like it. I begin to kiss his throat and chest gently.

'Thank God I don't need to put the alarm on tomorrow, and can have a lie in,' he says while I curl into him and drape a leg over his.

I murmur my agreement. 'Yeah, we can have a slow start to the weekend and stay in bed until lunch time like we used to do.'

We begin to make love and it's going ever so well. He's kneeling at my shoulder and I see him strong and hard weaving in and out of my vision. I'm sweating and writhing with desire surging through my body. David is teasing me with his lips and tongue which ordinarily I would enjoy.

Now it's aggravating me. Why does he need to torment me like this? Is this how my mother felt?

I feel like my eyes are bulging out of my head as he squeezes my throat. He is so big and engorged that I close my eyes tight in dread of what's to come.

The hairs on the back of my neck stand up. I can feel my lip curl in disgust. Well, he's not going to demean me, I seethe. And before I realise what I'm doing, I smack his member hard away from my face.

David howls in pain and rolls across the bed pulling his legs up to his chest. He puffs and pants then moans. I smile in satisfaction knowing he'll never tease and get the better of me again.

He sits up and turns towards me then shouts, 'Why did you do that! It really hurt!'

He looks furious. His face is red and sweating.

With my face pushed into the pillow, I try desperately not to smirk. I've got my own back on him and feel cock-a-hoop. 'Sorry,' I mumble.

'You have to stop hitting me, Erin. It's not funny and I don't like it,' he says.

He grabs hold of my arm. 'Erin, look at me,' he snaps. 'What have I done? Are you punishing me for something? Just tell me what it is, and we can sort it out.'

I know my hair is a great smokescreen on the pillow and he won't be able to see my face. I want to holler at him. I want revenge. I want to see you suffer. This is pay-back time for my mother. But I don't.

I take a deep breath then push my hair aside like a curtain.

I smile. 'I was only messing around; I don't know why you're making such a fuss. I only tapped you,' I say. 'When I smacked your bottom in the Hilton Hotel you loved it?'

He draws his eyebrows together and groans. 'That was ages ago, and I've told you since then that I don't like it. And this wasn't a tap,' he says. 'This time, you've really hurt me.'

I shrug my shoulders, turn the pillow over and roll onto my side away from him. 'You're just a big softy,' I say and pretend to drift off to sleep.

I can hear him shuffle through into the bathroom. He's probably inspecting his weapon of mass destruction; I think and stifle a giggle.

Chapter Eighteen

The nipping and twisting of my skin began soon after the slapping, but this is mainly when we're having sex. She has become even more wild and most of the sexual act is done in a hostile manner. This is only on her behalf, not mine. There's nothing remotely loving or enticing about being with her in bed anymore.

She glares at me through gritted teeth when she reaches her release. Even though I know the intense pleasure is pulsating through her body it's as though she hates me for making her enjoy it so much. She twists and nips the skin on any part of my body savagely until I yelp in pain. Which strangely seems to satisfy her just as much.

Last night we'd had supper outside in the garden sitting at our new table eating salmon fillets in the lovely sunshine. And she'd seemed so normal. We were just like we'd been at home in the cottage. So together. So us. She'd even perked her tongue out at me. A little sign that only I have ever known. It reminded me of how we used to be.

But sadly, it hadn't lasted long. When we were in the throes of pleasing each other, she'd roughly hurt me again. I'd been furious and had taken her to task. Although she did apologise, she'd told me I was a big softy.

I'm standing in the shower cubicle now inspecting my body in the mirror. My member looks okay, and the assault, because let's face it that's what it was, doesn't appear to have caused any injury. It's not swollen but is still a little sore to touch. I sigh, was my reaction a little over the top? But all the same, I peeve, she shouldn't have done it.

I look at the rest of my body following this week's sessions.

I'm calling them sessions now because the demanding sex and pain she inflicts on me is like a form of torture. I've got to the stage that the fear of her assault, and the trauma I know I will suffer is more off-putting than the desire to be with her.

Whereas last week I'd felt edgy around her now I feel downright uncomfortable. I am tense most of the time that she's in the same room and flinch when she touches me. When she calls my name, my skin prickles and on a couple of occasions I've felt the hairs stand up on the back of my neck. I sigh heavily knowing this is not the right way to be with my wife. I shake my head unable to believe this crazy situation.

I turn around in front of the mirror and see the skin is bruised on my left buttock and lower back where she twisted her fingers hard into my flesh on Monday. My balls are red and tender after an earlier attack and I dry them carefully with a towel. I peer closer into the mirror and see three big purple love-bites on my neck and shoulder. These are still sore to touch, and her teeth marks are evident in one of them. There is a bleb on my bottom lip which she bit the day before. I wince in pain and feel tears fill my eyes.

I rest my forehead against the bathroom cabinet and groan. What am I going to do with her? She behaves like an animal in our bed, and I know this behaviour isn't normal not even for a passionate woman like Erin.

I can hear her pottering about in her art room where she's been since early morning. I've managed to have a lie in and haven't spoken to her yet. I had woken at six with the in-built work alarm, but realising she'd got out of bed I'd relaxed and dozed back off into a deep sleep.

I try to sort myself out and blow my nose then wipe my wet eyes and get dressed. I pull on my old baggy jeans hoping they won't be tight between my legs.

Christ, I think, this must stop. I pull on an old brown shirt and hope the collar will hide the bite-marks then run the comb through my hair. I wonder if she knows how much she is hurting me. Maybe she is so engrossed in her feelings that she doesn't realise how much pain she is causing. I grimace, here I am making excuses for her. But the biggest question that goes around and around in my mind, is why?

A memory enters my mind from when we'd been out walking one day last year. I'd trodden on an old tree branch and wrenched my ankle. 'Oh David, are you alright,' she'd asked with eyes full of concern.

'I…I think so,' I'd muttered holding onto a tree. I'd hobbled home leaning on her for support.

She'd sat on the floor in front of me and bathed the dirt from the scratch with antiseptic then applied a cold compress until the swelling went down. 'I wish I could do something to take the pain away for you,' she'd said, and had been in tears watching me hobble through to the bedroom.

That's how caring and loving she's usually been to me. That's the Erin I love. Swallowing a lump in my throat, I whimper, and that's the Erin I want back. Not this aggressive she-devil who wants to torture me. Giving myself a shake, I try to get a grip on my feelings and potter downstairs to make coffee.

I take my coffee and three slices of buttered toast outside into the garden. The hot strong coffee does wonders for my mood and I perk up somewhat listening to the birds tweeting.

I look around the garden and decide the new furniture looks great.

I wonder if I should hold a summer party here for the guys at work. I remember the conversation with Jakub and his offer to BBQ one night. But Jessie has told me that Jakub lives in a block of flats which doesn't sound feasible.

I look at the neat short cut of the grass and smile knowing I've done a reasonably good job with the old lawnmower. In the past I've had no interest in gardening, but I did quite enjoy doing this lawn. I sign, it's a shame we didn't use the outside space more in our cottage back in Kibblesworth.

With home in my mind, I think of Beth and Sally. Beth has emailed me twice now and we've exchanged long conversations which is the most contact we've had since I left. Up until now we've only exchanged stilted sentences on texts. But these two emails, as much as you can tell from an email, seem to be written in a warm tolerant voice. I scroll down and re-read her last email.

'Sally had been a little moody when you first left but is now like a different girl since things have progressed with Ian,' Beth writes. 'I like him a great deal and he is from a good family in Gateshead. Like you, I was a little concerned at the haste to marry, but apparently, Ian's grandfather has died and left him his run-down cottage three doors away from where Uncle Geoff lived. Understandably, Ian wants to move in quickly and start doing it up and of course, Sally wants to be with him.'

There is another break in the email, and I can imagine Beth's thoughtful face when she decides what to write next. 'In a way I'm quite proud of Sally because she doesn't just want to live with Ian. They both want to make a commitment to each other and spend the rest of their lives together.'

I sigh and close the email. My little girl seems so grown up. Memories of her as a baby fill my mind.

Learning to ride her bike without stabilisers while I stood behind frightened to let go in case she fell. Crying because she couldn't do her homework and understand logarithms While I sat next to her feeling equally frustrated because I couldn't understand them either.

I think of Sally living a few doors away from where I was raised and imagine her life being a replica of my own. She seems to be copying how quickly Beth and I got together. But I know she will live happily in Lamesley. It didn't do me any harm and when I think of all the terrible things that could happen to a naïve eighteen-year-old these days I feel happy she will be with a nice lad and settled close to Beth.

I put my phone back into the pocket of my shirt and try to imagine the future. She will have her own family and I will eventually become a grandfather. I sigh. The thought of that makes me feel old but know at the same time I will be very proud of Sally.

Tipping my head back to drain the coffee from the mug I catch sight of Erin at the bedroom window. She has her hair tied back with a bright red scarf and is in her dungarees. This means she will paint for most of the day.

At one time I'd feel a little peeved that she'd want to spend her day without me, but today I feel a surge of relief that I can be alone. I gaze up at her and as if by telepathy she sees me and opens the window.

'You've had a good sleep,' she calls. 'I'm just getting started with a painting if that's okay with you?'

I wave my hand at her in agreement. Obviously talking about the assault last night is the furthest thing on her mind.

Like all the other episodes this one will probably be brushed aside as though it's nothing. I settle myself into the chair to read yesterday's newspaper.

**

By lunch time, and after a good thirty-minute walk through the park, I'm restless. I decide to go down to the village and have a haircut. I wander down the leafy street looking at the large double-fronted houses and wonder what the sale values are. They are probably too far out of our price bracket. But I console myself with the fact that we won't have to make the decision until the cottage sells and our six-month tenancy ends. I smile looking up at the trees. It is a nice area and if we could find a smaller house I wouldn't object to staying here.

I pass Jessie's house and see her in the hallway with the front door wide open. She is hoovering the carpet and calls out to me. I hurry up to the door.

Within minutes we are sitting in her garden drinking tea and chatting easily about the busy week we've had at work.

'Mike is out train spotting with his friends for the day,' she says.

I grin and we settle down like old friends.

'You've made such a big difference to us all at work, David. Our last manager stayed in her office all day,' she says. 'Sometimes she didn't speak a word to us other than send emails asking, have you done this? Are these samples ready? It drove us mad.'

I tut and whistle between my teeth. 'Really?'

Jessie nods. 'We all felt she couldn't be bothered to walk down the corridor and speak to us. But you are really part of the team. Everyone loves having you as our manager.'

I smile at her compliments and feel a comfortable warmth flood my face. It makes me feel valued and even though I'd hoped I was doing a good job, it's nice to be appreciated. 'Well,' I say. 'Everyone has different ways of management, but I like to be in the thick of things.'

She nods. 'And we're all grateful for that.'

We sip our tea and talk about the evening in my house. I explain Erin's jealousy towards Beth and

Sally. 'So, that is why she made the snidely shotgun wedding comment.'

Jessie nods. 'Ah, that makes sense now,' she says. 'It's strange though. You'd think she'd want to make, well not exactly friends with your ex and daughter, but at least have some type of communication.'

I clasp my fingers around the mug of tea. 'I know. They've always been a taboo subject between us, and I've learned over years if I want a peaceful life then it's best not to mention them. Which is cowardly of me…' I say looking down at my tea. 'My daughter should at least be worth a few arguments.'

Jessie offers a deep and thoughtful sigh. 'It's not easy, David. You've got a new life now and as we all do, we move within our daily activities as peacefully as we can. Mike and I often skirt around arguments especially about his family who I've never really got along with. I suffer them at Christmases and birthdays because I have to, for him. But to be honest if I never saw this father again in my lifetime, it would be a blessing!'

'Yeah,' I say. 'Well, as they say, you can choose your friends, but there's nothing you can do about your family.'

I want Jessie to know that there's nothing wrong with Beth and Sally. I tell her all about them. She lets me talk and nods her head every now and then.

I know she's really listening to what I say which makes me feel good. And that is Jessie's major asset, I decide, she is a good listener.

'I was a little worried about Sally,' I say. 'Before we split up, she had quite a few friends and was very outgoing with lots of interests. But after I left, she seemed to spend hours alone in the bedroom on her computer. Beth told me she was fine and just being a typical teenager, but still I worried how our divorce had affected her. Now, with this news I can stop worrying because she seems to have found a nice lad.'

Jessie nods. 'Will Erin go with you to the wedding?'

Although I've reassured Beth that I will take Sally down the aisle and will pay for as much of the wedding as possible, I've never given the actual day much thought. 'I don't know,' I shrug. 'I suppose that depends on whether Sally invites her.'

Jessie smiles. 'Well, in Erin's defence, it couldn't have been easy for her living in that small village community with you. And being what is commonly known as the other woman.'

I sigh in agreement envisaging the wedding arguments there'll be with Erin.

The afternoon sun gets stronger. Jessie makes us cold drinks then takes off her cardigan revealing those big soft arms I'm often drawn towards. I feel so much better having a normal conversation with someone who is easy and kind-hearted than dancing around Erin's moods at home. It's not that Erin isn't kind because she can be. Although I often think my wife is kinder to animals than humans.

We are sitting on soft sun-lounger chairs and when I snuggle further back the discomfort from the bites on my shoulder catches me unawares. I grimace.

In an instant, Jessie is in front of me wanting to know what's wrong. I shake my head and try to pass it off as nothing.

'You might as well tell me, David. I can see you're upset about something. I've seen it in your face since you first sat down. And,' she warns raising her eyebrow. 'I'll not rest until you tell me what's really the matter. Ask Mike, he'll tell you, I'm like a long-playing record when I get going.'

I manage half a smile but feel my stomach lurch. I can't possibly tell her about Erin hurting me. I'd be a laughingstock. I don't think Jessie would tell anyone, but all the same, I'd feel like a wimp of the most idiotic kind. I mean, what type of a man would put up with this and I shudder with embarrassment.

She starts again. 'Come on, I can tell you're uncomfortable sitting in that chair and some part of your body is aching. You've got a bleb on your lip which looks like you've had a run in with somebody.' She sits forward in concern. 'It's no one at work, is it?'

'Nooo,' I say shaking my head. 'Everyone at work is great.'

I stand up with the intention of making an excuse to leave and pull my collar up over my neck. She is beside me quicker than I realise and eases my shirt collar aside. The gasp she makes proves to me that the bite marks aren't a figment of my imagination. They are real. And they hurt.

'Dear, God! What are those?'

She puts a hand on the middle of my back and gently begins to rub it up and down. Whether it's because I feel starved of affection from Erin or that Jessie has a special soothing action to her touch, I don't know. But I can feel myself weakening with her kindness and empathy. I slump back down in the chair.

My cheeks burn and I lean forwards with my elbows on my knees and cover my face with my hands.

To my horror, I feel tears trickle through my fingers. Breaking down in front of a woman is alien to me but something inside snaps. I can't carry on being brave and the macho-man that I think I should be.

'Hey, hey, come on, honey,' she says in a soothing manner which reminds me of my mam. I catch a sob in my throat.

'I…I just don't know what to do with her anymore.'

In between sobs, I tell Jessie about the slapping, twisting and now the biting of my skin.

Jessie is shocked. I can tell by the incredulous look on her face. Her mouth is open, and her big eyes are bulging, but she keeps on rubbing my back. She makes encouraging noises until I tell her the whole story from arriving in Bexley and what has happened with Erin.

I'm still muttering from behind my fingers because I can't bear to look at Jessie. I feel mortified at my break-down and know she'll think I'm pathetic. But gently she prizes my fingers away and hands me the tea towel to dry my face. I do so and take big deep breaths of air to gain control.

'Christ, I'm sorry,' I say shaking my head. 'I can't remember the last time I cried like that.'

Jessie grins. 'Well then, it's a long time coming. Mike often has a weep on my shoulder and tells me the next day he feels relieved. He says it's okay because he's one of these new men who can show their feelings.'

I blubber with short bursts of laughter then rest back in the chair. And she's right. The relief of letting it all out is enormous. I feel my shoulders totally slump for the first time in weeks. I cross my legs and turn towards her. 'Thanks, Jessie,' I say. 'But I think I've snotted into your tea towel.'

She giggles and gives my arm a gentle punch with her hand. 'Don't worry, anytime you want to do that feel free. There are loads more of them inside. I get tea-towels every Christmas from the in-laws because they think I need them working in a kitchen!'

We talk at length about Erin and Jessie is sure that whatever is making her behave in this manner is to do with sex.

'But what?' I ask. 'I'm not doing anything different.'

Jessie takes a deep breath and folds her arms across her chest. 'You might not want to hear this, but…' she pauses and raises an eyebrow. 'Could she be seeing someone else?'

The suggestion takes me completely by surprise. The thought hadn't entered my head and I try to imagine Erin with another man. I can't. I think of the deep relationship between us and then Erin's insecurities. No, I dismiss the idea. I don't think Erin would be brave enough to go with someone else, and more than anything, I can't imagine Erin lying to me. We've always been too close.

I look earnestly into Jessie's eyes and she tilts her head onto one side.

'To be honest that's never occurred to me. Erin doesn't know anyone down here. The only people she has been with socially is you guys. And, I mean…' I wring my hands together, 'well surely if she is seeing another guy, she would be avoiding sex with me!'

Jessie shrugs. 'Maybe it was just a one-night fling and she is wrestling with the guilt. She could be doing to you what she had done to her because she enjoyed it,' she says. 'But David, whatever it is, something other than your usual sex pattern has changed for her, without a doubt.'

I know Jessie is right. Not about the affair, but the fact that something for Erin has changed. I think about her whereabouts since we moved here. The only place she has been without me is the art galleries in London, and I wonder if she has met someone there.

I don't know what she's up to when I'm at work, so it is possible. Eight hours a day is ample time to meet another man. And when she says she's spent the day painting what's to say she hasn't been to another man's home. I have never checked up on her. I've never felt the need. As a couple, Erin is the one who wants to know where I am most of the day and checks up on me.

'Hmm,' I mutter deep in thought.

Was Jessie right. Has Erin met a man who has shown her how to be aggressive to get what she wants. The memory of last night looms large again in my mind. I shuffle on the seat trying to rearrange things in my jeans.

I'm so comfortable with Jessie now and feel like I can tell her most things but draw the line at talking about my nether regions.

I nod miserably. 'The worst thing is that I've had no one to talk to since I moved down here because my friends are all at home. God knows what the lads would think of it. I'd be a laughingstock because us northern guys are supposed to be real hard macho-men, you know.'

Jessie smiles. 'Don't beat yourself up, David. They'd probably do the same if they were in your place,' she says. I relax back in the chair at her kind words.

Chapter Nineteen

It's Friday morning and I'm sitting in the reception of the clinic on Harley Street. It's a large airy room with tall windows and a circle of chairs around a coffee table. I feel physically sick to my stomach. Whether this is due to nerves at what I'm about to do or morning sickness beginning, I don't know. I'm not even sure if it's too early to feel these symptoms with a baby which confirms my gross lack of knowledge.

The slight clinical smell had hit me the minute I'd walked through the door into this alien atmosphere and situation. Other than an overnight hospital stay when I was twelve with severe tonsillitis, I've never suffered from any illness. I've always praised myself that to get to my age without having an illness is a major achievement.

However, the sickly feeling could also be because of what I did to David last night. I still can't believe that I punched him in the eye when he wouldn't have sex with me. I hadn't meant to, of course, it was simply a knee-jerk reaction to my mother's words raging through my mind. I'd wanted him to feel as vulnerable and scared as she had done at the hands of a brutish thug. Which was wrong of me, I know.

When I left at seven this morning, I'd looked at his gorgeous face and felt tearful because I'd injured him. I do feel remorse after I lash out at him but can't seem to stop myself when I fly into a rage.

I'm perched on the edge of a red tub-chair in the waiting room looking out of the Georgian windows that have long gold drapes hanging to the floor. My white handbag is on my knees and I'm clutching the handle even though my knuckles are still sore from hitting David. I've rammed my knees together to control the tremor in my legs.

I know the aggression is because of my upside-down state of mind. I can almost hear Josie saying, 'Maybe this isn't the right time to make such a monumental decision and terminate a pregnancy.'

But I'm convinced it's the fact that I am pregnant which is making me feel even more unbalanced.

My overnight holdall is on the polished wood floor next to my feet and I notice the well-used clasp isn't closed properly. The receptionist has placed a glass of water onto the coffee table in front of me. I lick my lips relishing the thought of the cold water in the back of my dry throat but cannot move a muscle to bend forward and pick up the glass. I feel rigid and rooted to the spot noticing all the tiny things around me but unable to concentrate upon the major action I'm about to take.

There's a pleasant breeze blowing through the top of the open window and I think back to last night. The ending had been disastrous which was a such a shame because it had all started off so well.

When David had got into bed, he'd put his arm around my shoulders and happily sighed. He'd pulled me in closer and I'd been tingling with desire right down to my toes. Usually he started by running his hands up my body, but he didn't and had lain completely still.

Hmm, I'd mused, maybe he wanted me to make the first move. I'd let my hand wander down over his stomach, but he'd taken my hand and moved it aside.

'I'm absolutely bushed tonight, sweetheart. I just want to drift off to sleep,' he'd said. 'Can we catch up tomorrow?'

I'd felt the anger build up in my chest and I'd sucked in a deep breath. He'd not wanted me to make love to him.

Dear God, I'd thought, this was the first time since we met that he'd ever declined my advances. His blatant refusal had staggered me. The hairs had bristled along the back of my scalp. I'd been going to turn on my side to ignore him but of course, the minute someone tells me I can't have something, I want it even more.

'Oh, David, once I get you going, you'll soon liven up,' I'd said and shook his hand free to let mine roam across his thigh.

'Not tonight I won't, Erin,' he'd whispered. 'Let me cuddle you until we both doze off.'

Cuddle, I'd raged. I'd wanted him to shag me. My temper had reached boiling point. Who the hell did he think he was saying no to me?

I'd thrown the cover back and glared at him. The dim light from my lamp had been just enough to see his face. I'd searched his eyes and expression for an explanation. What I saw was a look of exasperation.

'I don't want to be bloody cuddled,' I'd shrieked. He'd tried to placate me like a small child. 'Please, Erin, not tonight.'

I'd shaken my head dumbfounded. 'What do you mean not tonight, what's wrong with you?'

I'd been livid. I'd wanted to lash out at him. The need to hurt him had filled all my senses. My fingers had tingled, and my heart had raced with adrenalin pumping. I'd ground my back teeth and felt a cord in my neck throb. I'd climbed above him straddling his legs with my thighs then shouted, 'How dare you come to our bed not wanting me!'

We'd already done it three times this week, but tiredness had never stopped us before. Unless, I'd seethed, he was getting it somewhere else.

With my hands on my hips, I'd demanded, 'Who have you been shagging at work?'

'Erin, please,' he'd replied shaking his head. 'I'm not, and never have been with anyone else, but you.'

He'd looked bewildered and shocked at my rantings. I'd thought this could be just a ploy. I'd craned my head forward, so my face had been right in front of his. 'It couldn't possibly be that Jessie, could it?'

'Of course, it's not,' he'd said.

I'd seen how embarrassed he looked when he tried to ease me from his legs. I'd wedged my knees hard into his sides and insisted, 'David, you will put it in me right now!'

He'd pushed my knees further down his body to expose himself. 'I can't,' he'd mumbled, 'look…'

He'd been limp. Even in my rage I'd known there was no way he would rise to the occasion. 'No, no, no,' I'd yelled, and knew I'd not achieve my release. My eyes had filled with red flashing lights and I'd heard mother's words.

I saw his hand raised and knew he was going to strike me, so I scrunched my eyes waiting for the blow. My cheek stings and the pain blasts into my eye socket.

Let's see how he likes it, I'd thought. My heart had pumped so fast I could hardly catch my breath. I'd scrunched my hand into a fist and punched him as hard as I could in the eye.

***

I've had the treatment and have made my way in a taxi to the hotel room now. I'm sitting on the end of the bed looking around the room with its uninspiring terracotta carpet and striped curtains. I've chosen the same hotel David and I used when we came down for his interview because at least I'm familiar with the location and the lay out.

Now, however, I'm questioning this decision and trying hard not to remember our day and night of passionate lovemaking in room 401.

Which of course, was before the diary. I remember how happily optimistic I'd felt back then and sigh. That was only a couple of months ago, but it seems like a different lifetime now.

I could have gone home straight after the tablet, but I figured if there were any repercussions, I'd have to tell David more lies, and that I didn't want to do. I wasn't sure how I was going to feel about the termination and figured it was best to play safe.

'I'm doing the right thing for me,' I mutter and place my overnight bag on the case stand.

I try to rationalise my actions to make me feel better. After all, it is my body. And if I do feel more emotional than expected I'll be on my own to deal with it.

The sun is shining outside but I don't pull back the curtains. I leave them drawn and the air con turned up high while I make a cup of tea using the kettle and milk pots on the tray.

I stare at the two modern art paintings on the wall. I remember Vicky commenting last year, 'We should be able to appreciate all forms of artwork, or, you at least should, being an artist.'

I tut. I can't feel moved by the geometrical grey stripes on a white background. I lie on the bed propped up with all the pillows and wait for the crampy pains to start. I have the sanitary pads ready and hope that it gets under way quickly. The doctor had said, 'Every woman is different and there is no set time to when it will happen.'

I sip my tea and place my hand on my abdomen. It can't come quick enough for me now. I hate the thought of another person invading my body. I'm thinking of it like an unwelcome intruder that I want rid of as quickly as possible.

I keep thinking about Vicky which is probably because I'm supposed to be with her. I remember what she'd told me about her sister last year. 'My sister is desperately trying to get pregnant. They've been trying for ten years and the first shot of IVF has failed,' she'd said. 'I feel so sorry for her because she'd make a

lovely mum. She'd be happy and fulfilled, and
motherhood would come so naturally to her.'

Hmm, I think, and here am I getting rid of my baby.
But I know I wouldn't be like those fantastic mothers. I
haven't got it in me to be maternal like Vicky's sister. I
gulp down a lump of sadness. I'm convinced that at
this moment in time, I'm doing the right thing. It's
hard enough for me to cope with myself in the
aftermath of mother's diary. So, there's no way I
would survive being pregnant.

I open my handbag to distract myself from the
negative thoughts. I've brought my own notebook with
me which I started to write the week after reading
mothers diary. I read what I've written so far.

I think of the similar words and phrases mother wrote
as a young woman and can see the likeness. I decide
that if she had lived, we could have been close and
would have had that special mother-daughter
relationship. I sigh, maybe this was just wishful
thinking, as the saying goes. But the thought comforts
me.

In the beginning of the diary she writes about my
father. '*John has been so tender and caring towards
me especially after Neil was born. He's the best
husband anyone could wish for, and I love him so
much.*'

I swallow a lump in my throat knowing that was just
like my father.

I feel a little envious that she shared those precious
moments with him because I remember how special he
could make you feel.

I dunk a biscuit into my sweet tea and feel a crampy ache in my abdomen. It reminds me what is about to happen. At least I've had options about dealing with my unwanted pregnancy. Mother might not have had any choice in the 1960's because women had fewer rights of their own. Maybe she had no other alternative but to go through with the pregnancy because I'm not sure whether termination was readily available back then.

The soggy biscuit drops into the bottom of the mug and I frown trying to retrieve it with a spoon. I wonder, if the option had been readily available whether mother would have still wanted my brother. Or, given the choice, would she have aborted her child like I've just done. Maybe she'd thought she would get over the rape and love baby Neil no matter what happened. But obviously, she hadn't. And, I don't think I could have either.

Therefore, in one way, I'm saving myself a year of heartache and trauma. And, in the long run, I'm doing David a big favour, too.

I know if I did talk this through with David his reasoning would be more sensible than mine. He'd say that by the time the baby is born I will have come to terms with the words from mother's diary and be able to move forward.

I can just imagine his cheery little face. 'Erin, the baby will be the making of you,' he'd soothe. 'I know you're going to do an amazing job with our child.'

I smile. David always seems to have so much confidence in me.

I'd be lying if I didn't feel the tiniest smidgen of guilt. David is my husband and I know I shouldn't be hiding this from him. He is, or was, my child's father and had a right to know.

I feel another crampy ache and sip my tea. I read the last page of my notebook again. When I'd started this, I'd thought it might help to sort out my feelings if they were written down. Each morning I've got into the habit of reading through what I've written the day before and how I felt. I'd hoped it would make me see that I've made progress.

But now I shudder while I read. My words sound obsessional with red bold underlining's and highlighted sentences. Feeling sad I close the notebook and know I've made very little progress. In fact, my state of mind seems worse now, not better. And I know to other people these words sound like fantasies, but to me they are real.

While I drink the rest of my tea and mushed up biscuit Josie comes into my mind. I remember her once saying, 'Everyone has good and bad traits in their character.'

I place the mug on the bedside table, turn the overhead light off, and sigh heavily. Maybe I've lost my good traits now and have an abundance of bad ones. I mean, where has being good ever got me in the past. Nowhere, is the answer. I grimace and snuggle down under the duvet feeling confused.

David's a man, right? He hasn't got the cells growing inside him. So where is the rule book that states he has the right to know just because he's a man. Moral rights, I think they're called. But I don't feel very moral at this moment. My poor mother had all her rights beaten out of her.

Stress and upset has always made me feel tired. It seems to seep the energy out of my body. My eyelids are droopy, and I can feel myself drifting off to sleep. The last thought in my mind is that David mustn't know anything about my findings in the diary. It would finish us.

Chapter Twenty

My right eye is blood-shod and swollen. Erin hit me last night when I refused her advances in bed. Not being able to rise to the challenge, which was a first for me, she scrunched her hand into a fist and punched me hard in the eye. I'd jumped from the bed in total shock and ran to the bathroom to splash cold water on my eye. When I'd stormed back into the bedroom she was sleeping soundly.

I've tossed and turned most of the night because my mind is working overtime. I know Erin is getting worse and her aggressive behaviour is escalating. I also know it's time to act now. But what do I do?

I'm in my car outside work looking at my swollen eye in the rear-view mirror. Can I go into work like this? If I was a woman, I could hide the swelling with make-up, but as a man that option isn't open to me. I tut and sigh heavily wondering exactly what type of man I really am. Am I the namby-pamby type who lets a woman do this to him, I sigh. What other choice do I have?

My confidence is at an all-time low and I try hard not to think that I'm to blame for what's happened between us. Jessie has said that victims blame themselves which makes me cringe. Is that what I've become in all of this. A victim.

My insides feel upside down with the shock. My guts are churning and I've no appetite because I feel sick with acid indigestion. This reaction isn't new for me. I was like this for weeks when mam was in the hospice. 'You've chewed enough antacids to fill a beer keg,'

Beth had said looking worried. 'Please go and see the doctor.'

'No, Beth, I'll be okay,' I'd reassured her. 'Once I come to terms with the shock my stomach will settle.'

And it had. I'd also felt in some weird way that I should be suffering because mam had been in torment with the cancer. The day she'd collapsed on the bathroom floor and was rushed into hospital fills my mind. I'd been distraught when the medical staff told me about her prognosis and how the breast cancer had spread. 'But why didn't you tell me?' I'd raged at mam with Beth clasping my hand and urging caution.

'Well, there was no point, David,' she'd muttered sleepily with the medication. 'There's nothing you could do, and I didn't want you to worry. You and Beth are always so busy at work.'

'But, mam,' I'd implored feeling sick to my stomach with the knowledge that I was going to lose her. 'Neither of us are ever too busy to help you. Surely, you know that.'

She'd smiled and taken my hand. 'And I didn't want little Sally to fret.'

Mam had adored Sally from the day she was born. She'd babysat in the school holidays and weekends to give Beth and I time to ourselves. When she did die, Sally at thirteen years old had been inconsolable.

The beeping of a car shakes me back to the here and now. I frown at the thought of going inside to work while feeling so wretched. When I'd first woken this morning and saw Erin had already left, I'd staggered into the bathroom. Looking in the mirror, I'd wondered if I should call in sick. But then had decided work would be a blessed relief. It would distract my mind. I grimace knowing I'd rather go inside and face the taunts from work colleagues than stay at home and worry about the mess in my marriage.

I swing my legs out of the car remembering all the preparation I need to get through for a major presentation next week.

If I'm behind it will look bad especially being a newcomer to the business.

Climbing out of the car I pull my shoulders back determined to get through the day as best I can then hurry through the main doors. The jibes start at the reception desk and carry on when I walk through the office to my desk.

'I walked into the bathroom cabinet,' I say. Jakub roars with laughter and the other technologists join in the light-hearted banter.

Apparently, in Newcastle we have a reputation for being aggressive and fighting. Not that me or any of my friends have ever been like this. If someone was to pick on me, I'd stand up for myself, but I'd never be the first to cause trouble and strike the initial blow.

Uncle Geoff taught me how to box when I was a little lad. 'Are you a man or a mouse,' he'd shout. 'Put your fists up.' He'd taught me how to punch using a cushion.

However, I've never had reason to use these skills in a fight. I've never been hit before either. Not until now. I sit down in the chair and boot up my laptop. It's ludicrous to think that I've reached the age of forty for this to happen, and at the hands of my loving wife.

It's Friday morning and we are all in dress-down clothes. With the end of the working week approaching there's an optimistic atmosphere in the office. Everyone will race through the jobs to get finished in time for the weekend. I open a new power-point document to prepare. I've asked all the technologists to come to me with their ideas at various time slots during the day. But I've left Jessie until last because she is at the dentist this morning.

Jakub pulls up a chair next to me and grins while we begin to discuss his new cakes that we will present next week.

'TGIF, boss,' Jakub says.

I smile. 'Thank, God, It's, Friday.'

I nod in agreement typing onto his slide in the document. I'm in jeans and blue shirt but Jakub is wearing a black vest with chinos. I look at the taut muscles in his arms and wonder if I should spend some time in the gym with him.

Jakub's huge hands with black hairs on his knuckles are lying flat on the desk and I stare at them wondering if he is handy with his fists.

I shake myself to concentrate. 'I don't have to ask if you have everything ready for next week, Jakub, because I know you'll work like a tornado,' I say. 'But if you do need help you only have to ask.'

Jakub nods. 'Thanks, boss. I'll be fine.'

He gathers his papers together and I know he is getting up to leave. He cocks an eyebrow. 'So, how did you really get the black eye,' he asks. 'Did someone take a swing at you.'

'Nooo, really,' I stress trying to sound as convincing as possible, 'I did bash it on the corner of the bathroom cabinet.'

Jakub runs a hand through his coal-black hair and draws together his thick eyebrows in consternation. He leans further towards my face. 'Well, if that bathroom cabinet gives you any more trouble, just give me a shout, boss,' he says. 'Because I've always got your back, right?'

I feel humbled at his concern and kindness. A lump is gathering in my throat while he walks back to his desk. I head off to the toilet and try to pull myself together. I take deep breaths to steady myself which had helped when I'd gone back to work after mam died.

Back then, I'd had some terrible days.

On top of the normal feelings of grief, I'd felt riddled with guilt that mam couldn't talk to me about the breast disease until it was too late. I'd always thought we were very close, but apparently not. Although Beth had thought differently and told me this every day until I finally stopped racking myself to bits over her death.

I put my cheek against the cold tiles and sigh. What would mam think of me now and the mess I've got myself into.

When I left Beth and Sally, I'd known mam would have been disappointed. At the same time, she would have still loved and supported me. In her eyes I could do no wrong. She would have been in torment for Beth

and Sally and would have felt tugged between us. Mam
had often said, 'Beth is like the daughter I never had.'

They'd done girly things together. Beth took her into
Newcastle to a hairdresser and they'd treat themselves
to beauty pampering sessions. It was the first time in
my life that I'd seen mam with nail polish on her
fingernails. She'd loved the female company. She'd
played for hours with Sally and the doll's house that
Uncle Geoff made.

I blow my nose into some toilet roll then wash my
hands and return to my desk. I force myself to think
about Christmas and make the appropriate slide on the
presentation document. I use green mistletoe, red
berries and white silvery snowflakes to set the theme.
Christmas words in stencils of Joy, and Glad Tidings
play major roles in the presentation and I go through
our samples with the technologist. When we've
finished and I'm alone again I make a coffee and sit
back in my chair.

Memories of last Christmas with Erin when we were
newly married fill my mind.

We'd rented a small cottage in Northumberland for
three days and had spent most of the time lying in front
of the log fire making love, drinking red wine, and
unwrapping silly little surprise presents.

I'd been rather proud of myself that I'd made our
Christmas together totally different to the previous year
which had been dismal. Being the first one that Beth
and Sally were alone I'd left Erin on Christmas
morning to see Sally. We'd opened her presents in the
pub lounge and then we'd gone to visit Uncle Geoff in

the home. Although Erin had said, 'Look, it's okay, I don't mind. I'll probably talk to Josie in Australia for ages.'

I'd still felt like a heel. But at the time it had seemed no matter which way I tried to limit the damage and not hurt anyone; I'd still felt guilty.

With Sally in mind now, I smile remembering happy Christmas mornings when she was a little girl. How we'd unwrap presents from under the tree with mam and Uncle Geoff. I'd danced Sally around the lounge in her new princess outfit and she'd squealed with delight. Beth and I always made Christmas lunch together. She makes the most amazing gravy with her mother's recipe. I sigh with pleasure at the memories.

Jessie sweeps through the office just before midday joking with Jakub in-passing and gives him a gentle cuff on his ear. When she approaches her desk and calls out a greeting to me, she stops dead in her tracks.

'Can I see you in here a minute,' she says tugging my arm.

I get up and follow her into the small packaging cupboard behind our desks. I know by the look of alarm on her face that she is worryingly sizing up the swelling on my eye.

She closes the door quietly behind us and I flick on the light then take a deep breath. I've just pulled myself together in the toilets and the thought of breaking down at work is mortifying.

I strive to stay in control. 'I …I know,' I mumble. 'I know what you're going to say.'

Jessie looks closer at my eye. 'What in God's name has she done to you?'

A whiff of Jessie's flowery perfume fills the space between us. I step back and perch on the top of a pile of boxes. I tell Jessie how Erin hit me but that I've told the others I bashed my eye on the bathroom cabinet.

Jessie stares at my face. 'Did you hit her back?'

'Me!' I retort. 'Hit a woman!' I feel horrified that she could even ask the question. I fold my arms across my chest. 'Jessie, I've never hit a woman in my life and I'm not about to start now.'

Jessie tuts and shakes her head until her hooped earrings tinkle together. 'She doesn't know how lucky she is to have a decent loving husband like you. She should be ashamed of herself!'

I hang my head in misery and then feel Jessie rub the side of my arm.

'Oh David, your eye looks really sore,' she soothes. 'You do realise this situation with Erin is getting worse not better.'

I look up into her big eyes which are wide with concern. I know what she is trying to tell me. I bite down on my bottom lip. 'I know. But what the hell am I going to do with her?'

Jessie wrinkles her brow and runs her hand gently over the side of her jaw. She explains how the dentist had trouble filling her back tooth.

'If it's hurting you can go home,' I offer.

But she poo-poo's the suggestion. 'I've taken painkillers and it'll be okay until I get through this prep for next week. It looks like you could do with some too.'

I nod while she rummages in her handbag and pulls out a packet of paracetamol. I take two tablets from the pack and look at them lying in the palm of my hand. I wish these tablets would make all my problems with Erin disappear and we could be back to normal.

'If only I knew why,' I sigh. 'If she would tell me what is making her behave like this then I could take it on board. At least I'd know the reason why she wants to lash out at me.'

'You have to get help,' Jessie urges pulling the strap of her handbag back onto her shoulder. 'Erin needs counselling or medical help of some kind because this has gone way beyond a little slap-stick humour. This is serious now, David,' she says in her soft voice then strokes my arm. 'If I was you, I'd start with your GP.'

I imagine the conversation trying to get Erin to talk to a doctor. Christ, I'm the closest person in her life and she won't even talk to me. I shake my head. 'She'll never agree, Jessie.'

She smiles gently at me. 'Then you'll have to threaten to leave if she doesn't go to the doctors. Stress to her that you won't tolerate any more abuse. Because that's what it is, David. It's domestic abuse,' she says. 'Usually it's from a man to a woman but in this case it's the other way around.'

Chapter Twenty-One

Erin is staying in London tonight. Although I never ever thought I'd hear myself say this, I'm glad. I'm so pleased to be alone to try and assess the situation. I've cheerily said goodbye to everyone at work and have driven home. The house feels cool because the temperatures have dropped a little today and I drop my briefcase in the hall deciding to eat later. I make a cup of tea and carry it through to the lounge along with a cold wet cloth.

Sitting on the edge of the settee I sip the hot sweet tea. I can feel my chin trembling with sadness knowing that what we had is broken. Erin has broken us. There's a huge wedge between us and I don't know how to fix it. Or if I even want to.

Erin wants to brush the problems aside as though there's nothing wrong between us which, even for her, is strange behaviour. Ordinarily her response to a problem is like mine. We talk it through and sort it out. But I sigh, when I can't even get her to admit we have a problem, how do we do that.

I relish the warm comfort of the tea. I just can't understand how we've got into this mess in just a short time. In the past when I've spent a day at work, I'm usually longing to see Erin. But now I'm grateful she's not here. How has that happened. Probably, I moan, because my body is aching with her continual assaults and I need some time to heal. It's not so much the physical pain from my eye, but the hurt I feel that she dislikes me enough to hit me.

Erin has sent a text which I read. 'I'm so soooo sorry!! I don't know what came over me, David. But rest assured I'm going to make it up to you as soon as I get home. We are enjoying the art gallery then will be heading to the west end for the show. See you tomorrow.'

I reply with a simple, 'Okay.'

Why do I feel sick at the thought of what her making up will entail? A shiver of apprehension runs down my spine as Jessie's words come to mind. Is this a ruse and is Erin meeting another man in London? I suppose it would be easy enough to find out. I could ring Vicky's husband in Gateshead. If she is at home, then I'd know Erin is lying to me. But if Vicky isn't there, I'd feel stupid knowing she is with Erin at the art exhibition.

I sigh heavily. I should be in a jealous rage that my wife could possibly be with another man. But I'm not. And that, in another way, is even more scary.

I lift my legs up onto the settee. If there was another man involved at least there'd be an excuse. A reason why she's behaving like this. I'd have someone to blame other than myself. However, as I'm almost convinced there isn't a third party involved, I know it's my lovely wife's fault. Erin has destroyed what we had. I feel bereft at this thought, almost as though I've lost something precious. Which of course I have.

I lie full length on the settee looking up at the hideous trendy lamp shade the landlord has hung from the old ceiling rose. I lay the cold cloth over my eye. The bloodshot in my eye has begun to subside since this morning but it's covered in purple bruising is now. The quiet stillness in the room sweeps over me. I feel peaceful with the cool pad soothing the swelling. I drift off into a light doze.

My mobile ringing wakes me with a jolt. I sit up and rescue the cloth which falls onto my shirt. I see Beth's name on the screen and smile. Perfect timing. I can at least talk freely to her without Erin continually looking over my shoulder.

'Hey, there,' I say forcing a cheerful note into my voice.

'Hi, Dave, how you are doing?' Beth asks.

I can hear her take a deep breath. Knowing Beth so well, I can tell she has something difficult to say. I'm not mistaken when she just comes straight out with it.

'Dave, I've tried as hard as I can, but Sally won't budge. I…I'm really sorry if this causes problems for you, but Erin is not invited to the wedding.'

Even though Beth is telling me disappointing news her comforting gentle voice floats over me like soft treacle. After such an awful day, I relax my shoulders and let her voice transport me back home to Kibblesworth. I swallow a lump of longing to be there. I could never in my wildest dreams ever imagine Beth hitting me or anyone else.

'That's okay, Beth,' I tell her. 'I didn't think Sally would change her mind.'

The news isn't a surprise because I know as well as Beth does how stubborn Sally can be. While I drove back from work, I'd already decided that if Erin wasn't to be invited then so be it. But I am not missing my daughter's wedding and will go alone.

I can visibly hear the relief in Beth's voice. 'I'm sorry if it's going to be awkward for you, Dave, but it's her special day and I want her to be happy and have everything she wants.'

I smile imagining Beth's face. I know there will be a slight crease of concern on her forehead while she wrestles with the problem. I also know how hard she will have tried to change Sally's mind.

'Me too, Beth,' I say wanting to alleviate her worries. 'So, don't worry it'll be fine, and Sally will have a wonderful wedding day. We'll make sure of that. I'll come up for the weekend on my own and I'll meet the lads in the pub. Then go to visit Uncle Geoff.'

I feel a quick burst of adrenaline around my body at the thought of going home. 'I'm so looking forward to coming back and seeing you all.'

Beth tells me more detailed plans for the venue at Blackfriars in Newcastle. While I listen, I imagine our old lounge décor and my fireside chair. Our closeness. Memories crowd in from all our years together when she talks about flowers, cars, and wedding photographs.

She pauses for breath. 'Dave, are you okay?'

I shake myself knowing I've drifted away. I wonder if Beth can tell I've got something lying heavy on my mind. Will she be able to hear in my voice that everything isn't the same with Erin and I'm having problems? In the past she could always tell what I was thinking. She was inside my head with me for years. As I was with her.

I reassure her. 'Yeah, I'm fine Beth. I'm just listening to the details.'

Since we split up, and maybe because for years she was close to mam I think of Beth entirely differently now. She is old family who stood by me through everything for many years. She sat on the opposite side to me at my mams bed in the hospice when she took her final breaths and died. She cried as hard as I did because Beth loved mam as much as her own mother.

Beth starts to tell me about Sally's wedding dress and how much weight she has lost. My overwhelming love for Sally floods through me. I remember her tiny hand in mine wanting to come everywhere with me. She had doted on me. And for some reason, it suddenly hits me how devastated she must have been when I left.

When I think back to the first few months after I left them, I'd been too full of Erin and our love for each other. I can see now I failed to be as focused on Sally as I should have been. Erin had used consoling words. 'Sally isn't a little girl any longer. She's sixteen and if she won't speak to you there's not much you can do about it.' To which, I'd readily agreed.

I cringe now at how easily I'd allowed myself those excuses and listened to Erin. After all, she is my daughter and I love her dearly. My stomach knots with tension. I should have been relentless and knocked the door down if necessary, to make her talk to me. And, I should never have left the breakup of our family for Beth to cope with alone.

Sweat forms along the back of my neck and my cheeks flush thinking about my past behaviour. Why

I'm thinking about this now and not two years ago, I can't explain.

Is it too late to make amends? It's never too late, I can hear mam saying. I shake myself back into the conversation with Beth. 'Well, it all sounds marvellous, Beth.'

'And, Dave,' she says. 'Ian has invited you to his stag party on the Friday night. He is having a few drinks with his father, brother, and his pals in town.'

I feel a lump in my throat at this generosity. I don't think I deserve their kindness. I clear my throat. 'W…well, that's great,' I say managing to lift my voice. 'It'll give me time to get to know him a little before the big day itself. I'll see what work is like that day, but I'm sure I will be able to leave early to travel up in the morning.'

We end the call in a friendly upbeat atmosphere with Beth promising to email me the venue details and costs.

Chapter Twenty-Two
Beth Henderson, Kibblesworth, Gateshead, Tyne & Wear. August 2018

I know there's something not quite right with Dave. I can hear it in his voice. Sally had mentioned that her dad sounded weird and distracted when she'd spoken to him last week. Now, I agree with her. Something is amiss. When you've known and loved someone for over twenty years it comes naturally to sense when something is wrong.

I'm sitting on our brown settee in the lounge with my feet tucked up under the throw. I stare at Dave's empty fireside chair. It's strange but neither of us have ever sat there since he left. We haven't mentioned it and I haven't moved its position or anything else in the room. Even when we have company it stands empty for some reason. Like a shrine.

I look around the room knowing it needs decorating. The gold curtains hang thin and lifeless at the windows. The old beige carpet in practically threadbare in places and the whole room seems dark and depressing. This is in contrast with the other rooms in the house which have had a makeover.

Four months after he'd left, I had the bedroom stripped and decorated. I'd bought a new bed and white French furniture with a fabulous dressing table. A sumptuous cream carpet and glass chandelier completed the updated décor. At the time, I'd hoped it would shred all my memories of him being in our bedroom. I sigh. Fat chance of that happening. It hadn't worked then, and it doesn't work now.

However, the lounge remains exactly as it's always been. When we'd first moved in, I'd gone along with everything my mother suggested. We had brown, beige and gold colours.

I'd been very close to my mother and I still miss her terribly. But I can see now that when I was younger, I'd behaved as though I didn't have a mind of my own. I never made any decisions for myself.

I've made a cup of tea and resist opening the biscuit tin on the sideboard. Sally and I both agreed when she met Ian and wanted to lose weight that we'd start to eat more healthily. Not diet as such but change our eating habits. Which I know, eyeing the tin, means cutting out cake, biscuits, and pastries. It's been amazing. In just three short months we've both lost over a stone each. I feel much fitter with so much more energy than I used to have.

Sipping my tea, I unwind from work and look at a photograph on the fireplace of Sally and Ian taken a few weeks ago. Her eyes are shinning with happiness. Ian has an arm draped around her shoulders hugging her tight. I like Ian. He is steady, reliable and I'll be glad to have him as a son-in-law.

When Ian was here last night for dinner, he asked me about our family history and previous generations. Although I know my side of the family, I couldn't tell him much about Dave's side. Mainly because Dave himself doesn't know. Apart from his mam, who I loved like my own, and his dear uncle Geoff, there's no additional information about them.

Ian had said, 'My sister has done our family tree on the ancestry website and we've found out back stories about our great grandparents.'

As far as I'm aware Dave knows nothing about his father. Other than the fact that he moved up to Scotland with another woman and years later was killed in a road accident. Well, that was all he knew when he was here with us. When he was married to me.

It still hurts, which is ridiculous after two years, but I can't help it. I'm still as much in love with him as I was the day we first met at university.

I'd been in the middle of my business studies degree when I met him in the student's union bar with his friend, also called, David.

'I'll call you Dave,' I'd said giggling. 'Just so I don't get you two mixed up.'

Not that I would of course, because Dave was so good looking. He'd drawn me into him like a magnet. From that day we'd been inseparable. I fell pregnant just when we graduated which was more out of ignorance than anything else. Dave is still the only man I have ever been with and I suppose I'll go to my grave feeling like this. Utterly Heartbroken.

The solicitor's office where I work is a large company and I do have some very good friends who have encouraged me to date online. I've had two dates with divorced men. And before these dates I'd really felt that at last I could finally move on and put Dave behind me in the past where he belongs.

However, both dates had been disasters. The men were tedious and seemed insignificant compared to Dave and his captivating personality. Sally reckons I've given up too easily and should keep trying but I feel weary at the very thought of more dates. I suppose, I've idolised Dave for so long now I just don't know how to stop.

I can feel the sadness sweep over me when my mind goes back to that night. The night he told me he was leaving and was in love with Erin. I eye the biscuit tin again. 'It's not the answer,' I can hear Sally say.

I remember the feeling of utter desolation while my life crumbled down around me.

For months afterwards I was numb. I couldn't feel anything. If I'd not had Sally to look after, God only knows where I would be today. It was the fact that I had to keep going for my daughter's sake that got me through it.

I knew the first time Dave said her name, Erin, that I was lost. I'd previously seen her in the village shop and knew that she was a stunningly beautiful woman. A woman I couldn't possibly compete with. She was in a different league to me. I couldn't really blame Dave for falling for her. She had her claws into him, and he obviously couldn't resist her.

My mother had been alive at the time in the nursing home and I'd cried to her like a little girl lost. She'd said, 'If you really love someone their happiness is paramount, and you must let them go.' And over time I began to agree with her.

When I did see Dave after the breakup, even at a distance I could see the happiness shinning out of every pore in his body. None more so than when he arrived home from Venice after his honeymoon. He simply glowed. I cannot remember a time, well, maybe when Sally was born that he ever looked as happy with us, as he did with Erin. So, I'm grateful that one of us is happy.

I've encouraged Sally to stay in touch with Dave because I still want her to have a good relationship with her father. Dave didn't have one with his father, therefore this is very important to me.

Sally has always maintained that Erin is infatuated with her dad. And the few times she was in their company Erin fawned over him in an obsessive type of manner. But I've dismissed these remarks as jealousy on Sally's behalf because she didn't want to share her dad on his weekend visits.

I hear Sally hurrying through the front door now laughing with Ian. 'Hi, Mam,' she calls out to me. I wipe the back of my hand over my damp eyes.

Sally bounds into the lounge and flops down onto the settee while Ian perches on the end next to her. She giggles and tells me about the joke they've shared in the car driving home.

I grin at my daughter in her white dental nurse tunic. Her dark hair is pulled back into a ponytail and although she wears very little make up, I can tell how much more prominent her cheek bones are now she's lost weight. The tunic and trousers are baggy on her figure and I know she has ordered smaller sizes from work.

I chat to Ian while she hurries upstairs to change. I'm hoping he will help and get Sally to change her mind about Erin's invitation. I know Sally is a grown woman and capable of making her own decisions. But I don't want her to regret not inviting Erin. I don't want to see David unhappy without his wife over the weekend celebrations. Maybe Ian's input will have a bearing on her decision.

Ian says, 'We're going to the cottage to do some measuring of floors and walls before my dad starts the structural work to move the bathroom upstairs.'

I smile knowing how fortunate they are. Ian's father is a builder and it is his wedding gift to the couple.

Sally flies back into the room in jeans and T-Shirt. I catch hold of her hand when she passes me. 'Sally, I know you're both busy tonight, but we do need to sit and write wedding invitations at the weekend,' I say. 'Your dad is ringing later this evening to discuss the arrangements.'

Sally stands still. 'Okay mam, but before you start, the answer is still no…' she says defiantly with her arms folded across her chest. 'I'm not having Erin at my wedding.'

'Oh, Sally,' I say trying to use my most persuasive voice. 'Think how awkward it will feel for your dad being at the wedding alone.'

Sally shakes her head and the pony-tail swishes from side to side. 'Dad won't be alone. You and all the family will be there with him.'

I shuffle towards the end of the settee and look at Ian for inspiration. But he simply gazes up at Sally and pushes the bridge of his gold-rimmed glasses further up his nose.

I try another approach. 'Sally, if you're doing this to safeguard my feelings then don't because it doesn't bother me one iota if Erin is there.'

Sally comes towards me and places her hand gently on my shoulder. 'Look, mam. I'm not refusing for your sake. It's just, apart from the fact Erin is the woman who took dad away from us, I simply don't like her as a person.'

And there it was. Plain and simple. What on earth could I say back to that comment. Nothing really, because although I've never said this to Sally, I totally agree with her. I don't like her either.

I shrug my shoulders and give one last searching look at Ian.

He mutters quietly, 'It's Sally's father, so ultimately it's her decision.'

Sally walks back across the room to Ian. I concede that there's no point in struggling any more.

'Mam, I want dad to walk me down the aisle,' she says pulling on her jacket. 'But I don't want her there.

It will spoil my day and I'll feel miserable every time she looks down her nose at me. And I'm not having it!'

I sigh in agreement and stand up to walk out into the hall with them. 'Okay, love, as you wish,' I say and peck her on the cheek.

'Oh, and Mam,' Sally says turning to give me a hug. 'Is dad going to stay here for the weekend?'

I try not to gasp with shock at my daughters next request. 'W…well, I'd never thought about that,' I pause stalling for time while my mind spins. 'I'll think about it later.'

Ian opens the door and Sally follows him outside. She turns to look at me. All I can see is Dave's mams face. She even sounds like her when she says, 'He is family, Mam. We can't have him staying in a hotel, can we?'

I close the door quietly and lean my forehead against the smooth wood. Good God, can I do it. Can I bear to have him here for three whole days feeling like this. I walk slowly back into the lounge thinking of being in his company which fills me full of joy. At the same time, I know these aren't healthy thoughts because he is married to another woman now. He is no longer mine.

I sigh in turmoil. I grip hold of the back of the settee and take deep breaths. I want Sally to have everything her heart desires on this special day. I give myself a shake and pull my shoulders back. Of course, I can do it.

Sally is right, I think, full of false bravado. I can't expect him to stay in a hotel. He is family after all, and it wouldn't be right. Also, if he did want to be pedantic, which I can't imagine he would, he still does own half of the house. Therefore, he may resent having to pay for hotel accommodation.

***

I was dreading the phone call to Dave, but as often in life, it was surprisingly easier than I thought. I apologised and told him I couldn't get Sally to change her mind.

He seemed accepting of the fact, almost as if he was relieved or pleased to be coming on his own. Surely not, I thought. Maybe I read more into his voice than was there. But he did sound very excited about his plans to spend the weekend back at home and was delighted to be asked to the stag night. He even said he longing to see us all.

He has insisted upon paying at least half of the cost although I've stressed that there's no need. My mother left money in her will. And although I've not lived frugally since Dave left, I've never been frivolous and can comfortably afford to give Sally her special day. I know Dave well enough not to argue because it will hurt him not to contribute. So, I've agreed and promised to email him the information about the wedding venue.

I'm sitting at the dining room table and boot up my laptop. I smile looking around at the brightness of the room. I've decorated this room in sage green with a beautiful forest wallpaper on one wall. The new chrome and glass four-seater table and chairs suit the modern décor so much better than the old wood table. It's rare that I have more than four people to dine now-a-days.

While I wait for the ancestry website to appear on the screen, I think of how Dave sounded on the phone. I frown. Underneath all the jovial wedding hype I could sense that he's not as happy as he was. Even though I haven't seen him I can tell there's no glow around him any longer. I could almost see the pensive look in his eyes.

I wonder why? Maybe it's the move south and he is homesick. Or maybe it's the job. Although he insists it's great, maybe it isn't working out as well as he thought it would.

After a while I manage to trace Dave's father. After finding more documents on other websites, my eyes are transfixed to the screen when I read how his father was in court years ago for assaulting a bar maid in their local pub.

Horrified at the old photograph, I gasp. I wonder if Dave knows about this. Did his mam tell him about it? I sigh heavily knowing that I'll have to show him what I've found at the wedding weekend.

Chapter Twenty-Three

Erin has sent me a text to say she will be home by three o'clock. I replied, 'Okay.'

It's Saturday afternoon and after sleeping for ten hours last night, and enjoying a lovely lunch with Jessie and Mike, I feel totally refreshed. When I woke this morning, I couldn't believe the length of time I'd slept.

Although, I've not been working long hours in my new job, I suppose the upheaval of getting used to a new place and different people could have worn me out. But I've never had much trouble sleeping. Even through the trials and tribulations of everyday life when Sally was little, and we had money worries, I'd always been able to switch off and sleep.

I'm sitting in the lounge waiting for Erin and watching the rain cascade down the window. I sigh remembering the last few weeks. Maybe I've been in such a state of apprehension sleeping next to Erin that when she wasn't there, I'd totally zonked out. Which is the way I should be able to sleep every night next to my wife.

I swallow deeply tasting the lingering flavour of garlic from Jessie's lasagne at lunch time. I feel bolstered-up by her pep-talk and know exactly what I'm going to say to Erin when she gets home. My plan is to be firm but fair. Kind but resolute. And if I flounder, then I'll follow my lead from work when I handle difficult situations.

Another glance at the clock tells me it's six o'clock and she still hasn't arrived. She is now three hours late and I'm beginning to worry. Maybe she has left me? Maybe she isn't coming back from the city and is going to stay there with her new man. If she has one. And maybe I'm letting my imagination run away with me.

I get up and pace around the room tutting to myself. If someone I knew was the victim of abuse, I'd talk the situation through and decide upon the best plan of action. I grimace, but how can I do this when she is the one causing the bloody anguish.

I sit back down and take a deep breath to calm myself. I lay the newspaper aside that I've tried but failed to read. I try to analyse my feelings but they're a mix of total confusion. On one hand, I have the usual feelings of love that I've always had for Erin. But these are mixed with hurt now because she hit me. There's also pent up frustration from weeks of suffering at her hands without an explanation. I feel a huge amount of trepidation for what to expect next.

Just as my finger hovers over the mobile to ring her number the front door opens, and bangs shut. She hurries through the hall then into the lounge. I can smell the damp atmosphere she has brought into the room with her. The heavy rain has plastered her hair to her face which is in red wet ringlets. Her white jeans are stuck to her legs and her blue linen jacket is soaking wet.

She drops the holdall to the floor. 'Sorry, I'm late,' she pants and puffs out of breath. 'I ran from the station because I didn't know if you were home and would pick me up.'

Normally, I would hurry and help remove wet clothes then find towels to dry her hair. But I remain seated and stare at her.

She stands in the doorway and I notice how tired she looks and how puffy her eyes are. She is white faced as though she's had a nasty shock. I wonder if she's been crying again.

'Vicky nearly missed her train at Kings Cross station,' she gabbles avoiding eye contact. 'And then I had to make my way back over to London Bridge, but I'd just missed a train. The traffic is a nightmare!'

Still I don't move or speak I just stare at her. This must be the first time since we met that she feels miles away from me. I don't know where she's been. What she's been doing. What she's had to eat or how she's slept. What money she has spent. I know absolutely nothing about the last forty-eight hours of her life.

Usually, she would drop down next to me on our leather settee, but the distance between us now feels like a huge gap. She perches on the edge of the armchair and pulls her jacket off laying it over the top of her holdall. Finally, she looks at my face for the first time.

I can see colour flush back into her cheeks when she looks at my eye. Obviously, she feels embarrassed. Well, I hope her red cheeks are due to remorse. But there again, I don't know what's going on in her mind anymore, so maybe it's not.

'Look, I'm truly sorry about your eye,' she says. She opens her hands with the palms uppermost. It's almost as though she is begging for forgiveness.

'Are you,' I ask staring back at her. The swelling in my eye has gone down a little and it's not half-closed any longer with using the ointment Jessie gave me. But it's still bright purple and blue.

'Of course, I am,' she says. 'I don't know what came over me. And I've tortured myself every minute I've been away because I should have been here to look after you.'

I shrug. 'I told everyone at work that I bashed it on the bathroom cabinet. Which they seem to think is hilarious. Apart from Jessie who gave me some ointment to put on.'

I can see her visibly take a sigh of relief. Maybe she is worried about what our new friends will think of us. But no, I frown, that wouldn't bother her. What people think about us has never been important.

She flops back into the seat and tries to change the subject. 'So, you didn't say on your texts what you've been doing last night or today?'

And that's it. That's all I'm to expect in a way of an apology for hitting me in the eye. Does she think we will just gloss over this like the other incidents? Obviously, she wants to talk about something else. Anything, it seems other than hitting me. So, I decide to take advantage of the fact that she is now in defensive mode and talk about Sally's wedding.

Erin knows as well as I do, that she's not in the position to complain and have a strop about the arrangements.

'Beth rang last night and unfortunately, I will be going to Sally's wedding on my own. I've also been invited to Ian's stag party. So, I'm figuring on going up home on the Friday and will come back Monday afternoon.'

She nods and I can see the old flash of jealousy in her eyes. She opens her mouth to say something derogatory, I suspect, but thinks better of it and clams up. Maybe she thinks I'm playing tit-for-tat because she left me for two days, so I will do the same. But I'm not.

'Great, I can book your ticket for you?'

'No, thanks,' I say. 'I can manage.'

A stilted uneasy atmosphere lingers between us. I can almost feel it hovering like a cloud above our heads.

She is looking down at her hands and twirling her wedding ring around her finger. I know she must be uncomfortable in the sodden wet jeans and, as if she has read my mind, she shuffles to the end of the seat to get up.

'I'm just going to have a hot bath and unpack this bag.'

I lean forward. 'Not yet, Erin, we can't skirt around this any longer,' I say. 'It needs to be sorted out. I know you'll probably feel better doing it when you're dry and warm but I'm not waiting any longer. And quite frankly I don't really care if you're wet and cold.'

She slumps back down in the seat like a petulant schoolgirl. 'Okay…' she says and calmly folds her hands together on her lap. 'But I have apologised. It was a mistake. I got carried away and it was stupid of me. I should never have done it.'

She raises her eyes to me which now seem full of hope waiting for forgiveness. I decide to come straight out with it. 'Are you seeing someone else? Or should I ask if you've been with another man in London?'

The look of horror and confusion on her face is my answer. I know she couldn't fake this which confirms to me that there isn't anyone else. She is not that good an actress and I like to think I'd still know if she was lying to me.

'What?' Her mouth drops open and she almost cries. 'Of course, I'm not! How could you even think such a thing!'

I shrug. 'Okay, then why do you dislike me enough to hit me.'

She shuffles to the end of the seat again. Her small eyes are wide in shock. There's a rim of make up on the neck of the pink T-Shirt which is unusual for her to wear something which is marked.

'But I don't, David. For God's sake, I adore you! Surely you can't think that?'

This should be when I relent and wrap her in my arms. But I can't. The need to know why and find answers to her behaviour is greater than the need to reconcile and make everything all right again. If I do give in, I know the reconciliation will be short-lived and within days, we'll be back to the assaults again. I take a deep breath knowing I must be strong.

The cat from next door slinks along the fence outside the lounge window and I stare at it. Erin often feeds and cuddles it so I can tell the cat is looking for her and not me.

My mouth dries and I swallow hard. 'Erin, I'm really struggling to believe that now,' I say, and bite my bottom lip. 'From the day we arrived here you have been different towards me. You've shut me out and refused to talk about what's bothering you. This has escalated to slapping me and twisting my skin even when we aren't making love. I know it's not a sexual thing. In fact, I don't even think we make love now, we just have aggressive sex. You've slapped my member so hard it brought tears to my eyes, and now, you've hit me in the eye. So…' I pause and look back at the cat through the window. 'I can't see how you can still love me. I can see the hate in your eyes when you hurt me.'

Suddenly she is on her knees at my feet in a begging position. I still can't look at her. The cat turns its head and looks as though it's smirking at me.

There's a catch in her voice, a small sob. 'B…but I do love you, David. You have to believe me.'

I shake my head mutely then look down on her mass of hair which is now starting to dry into frizzy ringlets.

'Well, if you won't talk to me then you will have to talk to someone else. Someone that may be able to help you because I can't take anymore,' I say. I lick my dry lips. 'You can't keep using me as a battering ram for your temper.'

I take a deep breath knowing what I have to say next will be the hardest. 'Erin, whatever is going on in your mind you need help to sort it out. You're obviously unhappy and maybe depressed. I don't know. But you're clearly struggling with something…' I say and swallow hard. 'I want you to go and see a doctor.'

I hear her gasp and I look down at her face. She looks even whiter than when she arrived home. I can tell the shock has drained all the colour from her and two big tears roll down her cheek. 'Nooo, no, I can't,' she splutters then covers her face with her hands.

Something inside me squeezes at my heart and I cannot bear to see her so unhappy. I lift my hand to my eyelid which is still sore and with Jessie's words in my mind I push on. My voice sounds strange and croaky with emotion, but I clear my throat. 'You either go to the doctor, Erin, or I'm leaving.'

Tears are streaming down her face now and she grabs hold of my knee. I flinch at her touch which must be an automatic defensive mechanism implanted in me now.

'Y…you can't just leave me. Please, please, don't leave,' she begs. 'I'll change. I won't do it again. I promise, David. Just please don't go.'

It's killing me to see her in such a state. I shake her hand from my knee then get up to stride around the room. I push my hands into the pockets of my jeans feeling emotionally drained.

Maybe I should give her another chance? She seems so contrite and sorry for what she's done.

But when I pass the mirror I glance at my eye and remember the aggressive force behind her fist when she hit me. I know I must stand firm and not weaken.

'No, Erin. However sorry you are, it's either the doctors or I will walk away.'

She has rolled over onto the orange rug in a foetal position. She is sobbing and when I look at her it is unbearable. I walk back towards her and crouch down on my knees next to her head. 'Then talk to me, Erin,' I plead. 'Tell me what's wrong and I will talk to the doctor for you. Or at least go with you.'

She looks up at me with a red blotchy face. I know in the two years we've been together I could never imagine seeing her in such a state. I've seen her tearful and sad but never distressed like this. Something must be seriously wrong.

She sobs and opens her mouth a few times to speak then shakes her head as though it is so awful, she can't say the words. She wipes her hand over her wet eyes and face. 'Oh God, I can't, David,' she blubbers.

'Tell, me,' I say, with my heart sinking. 'Please, just tell me!'

'I'm pregnant, David.'

'What!!!'

I rock back onto my heels. I feel the blood pumping through my chest with shock while my feeble little brain takes in what she's just said. This is shortly followed by a warm glow of relief which moves right through my body. Her reason is a good thing and nothing horrendous. My knees and heels are aching. I slump back down into a sitting position on the floor. I feel like I've been hit with a cricket bat and it's knocked all the stuffing clean out of me.

A baby. Another baby. I'm going to be a father again. I cannot help the smile that spreads across my face.

We'll have our own little family now and it will make such a big difference to her. And to me for that matter.

Erin raises her head and looks at me. She is still curled up on the floor and I put both my arms around her and pull her into my lap. She sobs quietly with her face in my groin. Forty minutes ago, I wouldn't have let her near that area again but now I know she's harmless.

'I'm s…sorry,' she sobs and hiccups. 'We've never planned to have a family and I'm truly sorry. I thought with the hot flushes starting I didn't have to worry about contraception.'

I cuddle her close and murmur into her hair. 'Of course, we haven't, but it's great news, Erin. I'm absolutely delighted. A baby is something to celebrate, we'll be our own little family.'

She pulls herself further up. She wraps her legs around mine and rests her head on my chest. 'I thought you'd be annoyed because of our age and, w…well, it ruins our dreams of living in Tuscany,' she whimpers. 'But I will go to the doctor with you because I know my mood swings have gotten out of hand. And, of course, we'll have to ask the doctor about special tests for women nearing their forties.'

I stroke her long hair away from her face and we look into each other's eyes. We're locked in. I feel like we used to.

The glow that fills my body makes me forget everything else in the world. 'Oh, Erin. Why didn't you tell me? You shouldn't have carried this worry around on your own. How long have you known?'

She looks tiny and vulnerable. She shrugs slightly. 'I did the test the day after we got here. And…I, well, I've been shell-shocked for weeks.'

I quickly do maths in my head and decide she must be two months pregnant.

***

We've lain in bed together wrapped up in each other but haven't made love. We've talked about her bizarre behaviour. She has gently touched my eye apologising repeatedly until I held up my hand. 'Stop apologising. It's over and done with now. The aggression was probably caused by the pregnancy hormones, darling.'

I've missed us being close together like this and feel as if the world has tilted back onto an even keel again. I make us breakfast in bed on Sunday morning and coax her to eat. She tells me she hasn't been sick but just has a queasy feeling most mornings.

I remember Beth suffering terrible morning sickness, but she'd taken it in her stride. However, that was Beth, easy going and accepting of most of what life threw at her. I know Erin will react differently to pregnancy because, after all she is a different type of woman to Beth.

Erin has agreed to make a doctor's appointment for us both to go along and discuss the pregnancy. She does have concerns with being nearly forty and I must agree. We need all the information this will entail. At the same time, she has reassured me that she will talk about the aggressive feelings with the doctor to discover if this is due to the hormones. We've decided not to tell anyone about the baby until after the twelve-week period and we've seen the doctor.

Chapter Twenty-Four

I wake feeling exhausted with the strain of the last few days. David has gone to work, and I stretch across the bed relishing in the luxuriousness of the quilt and soft mattress.

I back track over the two days in London and decide the overwhelming feeling in my mind and body is relief. Blessed relief that it is over and done with. And if I hadn't told David that I was pregnant I could blot out the fact that I was ever expecting a baby in the first place. But now I've lied, and he thinks I'm pregnant, I'm going to be stuck with the baby issue for a while longer. Until I can think of a way out of the situation. Which I will.

I throw back the quilt and plod through to the bathroom to brush my teeth and shower. The citrus shower gel wakens my senses while I lather my body. I'm so pleased I went to the clinic on Harley Street because I was well looked after. I had to use some of father's money to prevent David seeing the withdrawal on our bank account, but I know if father had still been alive, he wouldn't have minded. He would have understood and gladly given me the money to get rid of my unwanted baby. My father never refused me anything.

I still miss his company even now. I miss the time we spent together when I was in my thirties. Other than the couple of brief encounters with men, mostly I'd spent my evenings at home with him. I wasn't a party girl but was the typical single lady who made the numbers up around a dinner table. 'Do come along, Erin. You'll have a great night. I've got a lovely guy coming on his own. He's an arty type just like you.'

I'd been the single lady that wives eyed suspiciously whilst clinging onto their husband's arms in fear I was going to snatch them away.

I'd been the single lady, who at Christmas was placed next to their uncles or singles that they didn't know what to do with. None of this I'd minded though because when I reached home, I had father to entertain with the evening's funny stories.

We'd watch TV together, mainly anything to do with history or animals. Sometimes Josie would join us but mostly it was just us two. I imagine him now in his old herringbone dressing gown sitting in the big reclining chair with a box of his favourite Liquorice Allsorts. Happiness personified; I smile with tenderness at his memory.

Towelling myself dry I think of last night's awful scene with David when I'd returned home. I'd always thought he was a lot like my father, but I was wrong. He isn't.

He has turned into the type of man who wants to run away when the going gets tough. I'd got a huge shock when David was prepared to walk out of our marriage. There's a large part of me disgusted with him.

I think back to our wedding day in the registry office. Me, wearing a cream silk 1930's suit with blue heels and bag. Him in a dark grey suit. The words of the short ceremony come to mind and I fume. David had looked deep into my eyes and repeated the words. 'To have and to hold from this day forward. For better, for worse, for richer, for poorer, in sickness and in health, to love and to cherish, till death us do part.'

So, what happened to that, David. What happened to those wedding vows we'd so lovingly repeated to each other? I moisturise the dry skin on my legs remembering how I had stuck by him through all the troublesome times with the villagers. And Sally's stroppy moods. I sigh heavily, is this all the thanks I get. Obviously, it is because he's prepared to leave me since I bumped his eye.

Pulling on my underwear and jeans there's a tiny voice in the back of my mind saying you didn't bump his eye by accident, you hit him full on. I tut and ignore this. For goodness sake all this fuss over a black eye. Its peanuts compared to what my mother went through at the hands of that bully.

With a mug of hot coffee, I stride into my studio and sit on the stool in front of my easel. David had really caught me on the hop when I arrived home soaked to the skin. The shock of him demanding I see a doctor and, the fact that he was prepared to leave made me feel quite frantic. On the way home from the hotel, I'd felt reasonably in control of my feelings, but it was his cold blunt words and threats that had tipped me over the edge.

When I'd knelt in front of him sobbing and he didn't waver then was so unforgiving and cold towards me, I'd panicked. I knew I'd have to say something dramatic to keep him with me. Telling him I was pregnant was stupid and horribly wrong. I sigh. It's probably not the best decision I've ever made in my life. In fact, I can go as far to say, it was totally irresponsible and foolish. But it's done now. I feel perspiration form on my top lip and wipe it away. Of all the things I could have used as an excuse, why-oh-why, did I say that.

Of course, David is cock-a-hoop because he thinks he is going to be a father again and talked all day yesterday about the non-existent baby. I'd tried to explain my aggressive feelings without mentioning mother's diary which seemed to placate him. In the afternoon after he'd cooked lunch, he talked non-stop about the baby and our plans. I'd apologised again. 'This will stop our Tuscany retirement dreams,' I'd said raising my eyebrow to see his response. 'I can't see that happening now?'

But he'd laughed. 'Of course, it will happen,' he'd said. 'We'll just have a bilingual child, who will speak Italian as good as English.'

I'd shrugged and taken a deep breath.

Then, he'd mused, 'I wonder if it will be a girl or boy?'

I'd shrugged again and raised an eyebrow at him.

'I wonder if he or she will have your red hair?'

I'd shrugged once more willing him to be quiet.

'Maybe I can get paternity leave from work?'

I can't remember how many times he'd asked if I was as excited as him. He went on and on until I'd wanted to scream at him to shut up.

I'd bit my tongue of course. For us to get to this state in our marriage has really spooked me. I thought he was still as besotted with me as I am with him. That we were as close as ever. Obviously, for him, we're not.

He'd said magnanimously, 'I'm quite prepared to weather the storm now I know your fits of rage could be a factor of carrying our child. And I'm so pleased there's a genuine excuse for your past behaviour.'

Big of him, yeah? I spent yesterday being all innocent and kind but being sugary-sweet is grating on me now. I'm pleased he's gone to work so I can be myself.

I press my fingertips against my eyes so I can't see anything. The last time I felt as confused and upset as this was shortly after father died. When I wouldn't get out of bed for three days and couldn't stop my hands from shaking to paint, Josie had called in the doctor.

'It's a reaction to the grief,' the doctor had said. 'I'd like you to go into a clinic because I think you are totally out of kilter in your psyche and will benefit from rest and a controlled environment to recover.'

Josie had nodded her head in agreement. But I'd refused. 'No, No, No,' I'd stated emphatically. Instead he'd given me a course of anti-depressant drugs. They took a few weeks to start working but eventually they did numb the pain enough for me to carry on with daily activities. I worked through the grief and learned to knit which stopped my hands from trembling.

Maybe I should get some anti-depressants now? I remove my fingers from my eyes and let them adjust to the light. They might help with the hysterical outbursts. I give myself a good shake, loosen my shoulders and determine to paint something.

I focus on my memories from Australia and decide I'd love to take a trip back there sometime. In the past, before reading the diary, I wouldn't allow myself to do this. But now I know how much my mother did love me, I feel the need to remember it differently. I smile as an idea comes into my mind. Instead of just thinking about the house maybe I could try to put the image down on a canvas.

I find a couple of photographs from the trunk with Josie and father standing in front of the house. The familiar buzz of excitement fills me as I start the new painting.

I sketch our house in Brankstone from memory and the photograph. I try to capture how it was when we first moved there, and mother was with us. Then I make a rough outline of each room in the house on separate smaller canvasses.

The kitchen where mum cooked for us. My bedroom where she came to say goodnight and read me a story.

The small lounge where we sat together to watch TV and father had his bookcase in the corner. 'I'd love to have a study,' he'd joked. And mother had raised her eyebrow good-humouredly at him.

I'm so far entranced in my memories that I'm not sure what is real and what is happening now. I can smell mother and feel her thin wiry arms around me grasping me to her chest tightly: keeping me safe. I see her eyes. I hear her giggle at father when he says something funny. I'm surrounded with our old relaxed family atmosphere and it makes me swallow a huge lump of longing to be back there again as a little girl. Then finally, Neil's bedroom with his cot and changing table where mother used to let me help change his nappy.

Realising I'm back in my house in Bexley I look around the room in dismay. I could have been changing my own baby's nappy in months to come and I sob into my hand.

I take a deep breath and dry my face on an old paint cloth. What type of mother would I really have made? I haven't an inch of motherly intuition in me. I keep referring to the baby, as it, and not him or her? And that speaks volumes.

Pulling my shoulders back I determine to focus on my painting. Time deserts me while I work. It is only when my stomach groans with hunger I rummage around in the fridge and find cheese and crackers.

David sends a text. 'Are you all right?'

I answer him. 'I'm fine. And I've made us a doctor's appointment for tomorrow at three o'clock.'

'That's perfect,' he tells me. 'I'll leave work early to meet you.'

I have no intention of keeping the appointment, of course, but he won't know that. He will think I'm playing the game. His game.

I sit in front of my easel and eat hungrily. How I'm going to get out of the hole I've dug myself into. Now, there's no baby and I've lied to him I will have to think of a plan. My plan.

While I fill out the scenery on Neil's bedroom canvass by painting the walls baby blue, I start to conjure up scenarios. Maybe for a few weeks I could put some wadding inside my trousers to make my flat belly look more rounded. I rub my hand over it now and decide that won't work because he'll see my flat stomach in bed.

The one thing I do know is that I will have to dispel the myth of being pregnant quickly because I can't fake all the symptoms convincingly. Well, not enough to sway David. He has been through a pregnancy before having Sally and will have first-hand knowledge of what to expect and when. Whereas, I'm clueless.

Maybe I could tell him the doctor says there are complications with my age and the scan shows that baby is damaged, and I need to have a termination. But then he'd insist on coming with me and meeting the doctor, so that won't work.

Or, maybe I could have a miscarriage? However, I suppose that too, would involve a hospital admission and David would be there.

An idea sparkles in my mind. But if he's not here then he can't come with me to the hospital, can he? And his trip home to the wedding could prove to be the perfect time.

I lay the brush down and plan things out.

The moody little cow, Sally, hasn't invited me to her wedding in the hope that her and Beth will be able to fawn over David all weekend. Well, for once that might just work to my advantage in a few ways. I could pretend to have the miscarriage early on the Saturday morning and ring him in the evening to tell him what's happened.

I imagine the conversation and smirk. I practise my pathetic voice aloud into the empty room. 'I'm soooo sorry that I've lost our baby, David. But I went to the hospital to get checked over and the doctor reassures me that I'm fine because the foetus was only weeks old. I don't want you rushing back here to me. There's nothing you can do now it's over and you must stay in Kibblesworth with Sally on her special day!'

I know he will insist upon hurrying home to me on the Sunday. This will get him away from them both, and hopefully, spoil some of their weekend. I clench my back teeth and feel my stomach harden imagining him with them laughing and enjoying themselves while I'm stuck here on my own.

However, I decide, this small amount of self-sacrifice on my behalf will score me double brownie-points and put me right back in his good books again. Especially when I explain, 'I didn't ring earlier because I didn't want to spoil Sally's wedding.'

Oh, that's good. I smile knowing my rehearsal sounds great. And for me, I think happily, my new plan will solve the pregnancy issue within the next couple of weeks. Then I can get back to normal. I feel rather proud of myself coming up with this scheme while I pick up my brush to paint.

Chapter Twenty-Five

The following morning, I ring David at work. It's just after twelve and I figure he will be heading towards his lunch break. I'm quite calm and rational which is how I've learnt to be since the first time I told him the little white lie.

I press his name on the screen of my mobile and shake myself into focus mode.

'David,' I ask, 'Can you talk now?'

He assures me it's fine and I can hear concern creep into his voice. 'Are you okay?'

I smile and twirl my finger into a ringlet of hair trying to sound calm and reassuring. 'Yes, of course. I'm just ringing to let you know that apparently the computer at the doctor's surgery was down and our booked three o'clock appointment doesn't exist. We should have been given an appointment for eleven this morning.'

'Ah, damn,' he utters under his breath.

I push on trying not to gabble while I lie to him. 'So, when the receptionist told me I grabbed my jacket and ran down to the surgery so as not to miss out. She told me there were no more appointments again until the following Friday.'

'You did?' he asks. I can hear the disbelief in his question as though he's flabbergasted that I went on my own.

I try not to sound offended by his obvious lack of trust and his vote of no-confidence. I take a deep breath to calm myself and smile sweetly. 'Yeah, I saw the doctor and he told me that everything is fine. I'll tell you more tonight, but apparently pregnancy hormones can cause aggressive tendencies and terrible mood swings.'

'Oh, right,' he says.

I can imagine his shoulders sagging with relief.

I hope he thinks I'm being thoughtful. 'So, I just thought I'd let you know that you don't need to leave the office early today.'

I can hear the release of tension in his voice almost as if it is flowing through his mobile into mine. 'That's, great, thanks,' he says. 'I am busy. But you would have come first, sweetheart. You do, every time.'

I smile hoping he believes me. However, just in case, I suggest, 'Although, if you need to talk to the doctor then we can book that appointment for next Friday and go back together.'

I feel confident making this proposal because he will be on the train to Newcastle by Friday lunch time. We agree to talk it through properly again tonight when he's home and I end the call.

I played a blinder, and whoop for joy in front of my easel. Now it's time to play my game, David.

***

After dinner, I tell him snippets of information that I've read on the internet about older women and their pregnancies. In fact, I tell him what I think he wants to hear.

'Apparently, the doctors and midwives will take extra care and we'll have to attend every antenatal class. We can't afford to miss even one session,' I say. 'And there are different scans and tests to be done.'

He seems well satisfied with my knowledge and cuddles me lovingly into his chest which I manage to share in a good-hearted fashion. We are sitting on the sofa watching the news on TV.

His loving concern is irritating me now to a point where I want to scream.

When I look at his good-looking face, I think it looks smug and condescending towards me. Whereas before, his good looks used to make me swoon with delight.

Maybe all this loving is a smokescreen and he has hidden motives. I wonder if he is simply placating me, when all the time he is making plans to leave. I plump the cushion behind my head feeling on edge and resist the urge to pick the skin on my thumbnail.

Does he still want to be out of our marriage, or does he really want to stay with me? I sneak a look at his face and see him close his eyes. He looks tired. Once trust is broken in a relationship, and I do feel that he has broken ours, then I'm going to struggle to put my faith in him again.

When he ambles upstairs to shower, I decide to check his mobile which he's left lying on the coffee table. Maybe he's not being as loyal to me as I've always thought he was. I can see Beth has rung him this afternoon and he hasn't deleted the voice message.

Sitting in the armchair I listen to her words. 'Why not come and stay with us here, rather than pay for a hotel room for three nights, Dave.'

The bloody cheek of the woman, I seethe. Is it not enough that he is spending all the weekend with them? I can't tackle him about it because he will know I've been checking his mobile. I begin to pick at my thumbnail. He could simply avoid telling me where he is going to stay, I suppose.

I ring Beth, with-holding my own number. When she answers I don't say anything, I just leave her saying, 'Hello, hello.'

I hang up. I'm not exactly sure what I'm hoping to achieve by doing this, but in my way, I feel as though I'm letting her know that I'm onto her. However, I'd much rather scream at her to leave my husband alone.

The thought of her and David together makes my cheeks burn and I cringe. Although, I'm confident David wouldn't do anything, I can't be that sure about her. Later, I ring Beth another three times behind David's back. I hear her pathetic whimpering voice on the other end sounding more scared every time.

Being a nuisance caller is quite addictive, I decide, and smile with menace. Maybe I could find Sally's mobile number and treat her to a few calls. I tingle with pleasure at the thought that maybe, just maybe, I might rattle them both enough to mar their happy wedding plans. At one stage I'm even tempted to do some heavy breathing but then decide that really is quite beneath me.

***

It's the night before David is leaving to go home for the wedding. I feel quite rampant for sex again. In fact, every muscle in my body is aching for the chance to hurt him. However, I discipline myself into be loving and caring towards him. I've nearly lost him once through using him as a release valve and know I mustn't do it again. I need to keep him here with me for my plan to work.

I'm waiting for him to join me in bed and I wonder if I could punch the pillow instead. Or, I wonder if he would notice just one little nip. But I roll my fingers into the palms of my hands determined to be gentle and kind.

I don't think he is expecting sex tonight because we haven't done it since I bumped his eye.

Although he hasn't said as much, I know he must be desperate for me. I'd decided earlier to make love to him because I don't want him to leave for two nights without reminding him how good we are together. I'd also read in one of the glossy hotel magazines how many men go astray when their wives are pregnant and don't want to have sex.

I straighten down my silky slip I'm wearing for him. It's one of his favourites and he loves the feel of the material under his hands. I'm determined that I'm not going to lose my husband and let him stray during this phantom pregnancy. I've got more plans for him later.

I can see him zipping up his holdall ready for tomorrow morning then heading towards our bed. I squeeze my legs together with desire and excitement. He slides in next to me and I hear him gasp in pleasure when he runs his hands up and down the slip.

'Ah, Erin, you're wearing my favourite,' he whispers into my neck. I begin to kiss the side of his face.

He grins. 'I'm not sure I'm going to be able to contain myself lying here next to you in this.'

I laugh. It sounds deep and throaty as though it's coming from my very core. I roll on top of him. 'Well, the doctor hasn't said we're not to have sex, darling. And I know you'll be careful. You always are, David.'

He wraps his arms around me and then rolls me back onto the bed. I take a deep breath feeling confused. My insides sink with disappointment. Surely, he isn't going to refuse me again. It's been ages since the eye incident, and I thought I was forgiven.

'What?' I mutter, but he rolls me away from him and onto my side. I realise what he is doing when he pulls my slip up.

'This is the safest way, Erin,' he coos into my ear. 'When Beth was pregnant the nurses advised us at the ante-natal classes to do it this way.'

I can't believe what he's just said. Anger pulsates through me. I tug my slip from his hands and pull it back down. I snap back over to face him. 'So, you want to do it like you did with Beth, do you?'

He sighs heavily. 'Nooo, of course I don't. You're taking it the wrong way. I didn't mean that at all.'

He tries to pull me back into his arms, but I shuffle to the very end of the bed as far away from him as possible. The rage is bubbling up inside my stomach and within seconds I fly into a frenzy. I'm sick of playing, miss goody-two-shoes.

I yell at him. 'I don't want anything about our marriage to be likened to what you did with Beth. And in case you've forgotten, David. She is your ex-wife, and you are married to me now!'

He sits up in bed and looks down at me. 'Look, I'm sorry,' he apologises. 'I was only trying to help.'

I glare at him. Not only is he going to be with her all weekend now he's even thinking about her before he leaves me. I'm fuming. This is the last thing I wanted.

***

David will have left work by now and caught the train up to Newcastle. Although we kissed each other goodbye this morning, we are still very strained with each other. However, Sunday will be the turning point between us. I know once he is home again, he will soon learn how to play the game. My game. Not his.

I settle down to paint. I've decided to paint the beast who raped my mother.

When I painted the house and rooms yesterday it helped me with my memories. So, I figure this might help.

I fill the background colours of a field using green, black and grey colours. Already, it looks macabre and bleak. I'm using a vague old memory I have for the image of him. His build and stance from a distance is tall and stocky. I sketch his huge shoulders and chest wearing a dirty blue vest which show off the fair coarse hairs on his torso spreading up to his throat. Dirty jeans covered in cow's muck with his fat beer-belly hanging over a thick leather belt with studs on it.

The belt he struck my mother with. I've stared at the words in her diary so many times now I know them inside out. If you blindfolded me, I could still quote them word by word.

The studs on the belt rip the flesh on my bare buttocks and I scream in agony as he lashes me while groaning in pleasure.

He looks grotesque. Red veiny cheeks with a scar running down the side of his face near his ear. Saliva drips from his chin. Blond curly hair but receding from his forehead which is shiny with sweat. A twisted snarl on his rubbery coarse lips. Evil blue eyes with menace gloating from them.

I snarl and groan with the memory of what he looked like in his youth and see red flashes in front of my eyes. I can imagine what he will look like now that he's older, because I do know who he is.

I think of him as a revolting specimen of mankind and grunt with raspy loud breaths into the silence of the room. The thought of him abusing my mother fills me so full of hatred that I don't know how to cope with the feelings raging through me. How do I get the anger out of my body? I kick the skirting board and wish with everything I possess that David was here to torment. I want revenge.

I imagine mothers beautiful face and her slight thin body struggling underneath this monster and my temper reaches boiling point. Why did he have to do that to her? If he hadn't, she would be alive and well today, and we wouldn't have had the torturous life we were left with. I scowl at the foul likeness I have created. Someone is going to pay for our suffering.

I peer further towards the canvas and see David's face mingled in with the monster. He is grinning at me. I shake my head violently. Am I imagining it? It can't be David because he is on the train.

Then I know it's David because it's his voice that shouts, 'I've beat you into submission just like your whore of a mother!'

I hit my brush over and over against the canvass across his grotesque face. Blue paint splatters everywhere. I wipe the paint off my sweaty forehead with the back of my hand and scream. I grab the canvass from the easel and smash it over the back of a chair. There's a huge rip down his face in the centre of the painting. I drop to my knees and let the tears pour down my cheeks.

I throw myself flat onto the carpet and feel like I'm separating into two. One version of me is Erin. The other version is my mother. I throw my head back and howl in pain. The fury and temper engulf me. I can feel my mother's pain and every blow she suffered. I'm living her life now and I'm being raped.

Out of the corner of my eye I stare at my husband's grotesque face on the torn canvas. It's not the monster who is raping me, but David. He has pinned me down and then strikes me across my chest with the studded belt. I see droplets of blood on a welt on my breast and know I must escape. My heart is pounding against my rib cage and beating ferociously in my ears.

I feel breathless and gasp for air. But then I look over his shoulder and see Beth and Sally gloating and smirking behind my easel.

Chapter Twenty-Six

The train has slowed down to cross over the High-Level Bridge into Newcastle. I stare out of the window relishing in the old familiar sights. I glance over to The Tyne Bridge on the right and know I am home. We have seven bridges down the length of the River Tyne but only four are operational. I always think of The Tyne Bridge as our grand old lady.

I've been asleep for much of the three-hour journey. I'd gone into work at six this morning to make sure everything is in order before my three-day break. So, the moment I'd got onto the train and found my seat I'd instantly fallen asleep.

Things between me and Erin were a little tense this morning, but we did kiss goodbye when I left for work. I'm putting last night's upset about our different position in bed down to pregnancy hormones but can't help feeling a little peeved. I was only trying to be helpful because I don't want anything to harm the baby.

I can see now that mentioning making love with another woman wasn't the most considerate thing I've ever said. And the mere mention of Beth had sent her off at the deep end. I recall one night when we were first living together when Erin had asked, 'Was it like this when you made love to Beth?'

I'd cringed inside not wanting to even think of Beth when I was with Erin. It hadn't seemed right. 'Well,' I'd hedged. 'It was the way we'd always done it since we first met at Uni. We'd both been inexperienced and just sort of made out the best we could.'

I'd hoped this would suffice because I hadn't wanted to say any more. I didn't want to discuss the difference between making love to either woman. Thankfully, it had been enough.

While the train slowly heads into Newcastle Central Station, I sigh. Erin has been so much more like her old self since she told me about the baby. I thought we were back on course again, but last night's strop is concerning. In the future, I'll have to be very careful and think about things properly before opening my big mouth and upsetting her.

I don't do it intentionally and never have done. But like many other men sometimes I am clumsy with words and explanations. I don't find talking about feelings and intimate matters as easy as what women seem to do.

The train is heading onto platform one now and I smile grabbing my holdall and reaching up to get my dress-suit hanger from the rack above my head.

I suddenly think of work and especially the morning after Erin told me about the baby. I'd felt compelled to tell Jessie about the pregnancy hoping it would justify Erin's aggression. As it has done for me.

Surprisingly, Jessie had looked dubious and shuffled in her chair. 'I've never heard of any woman lashing out and hitting someone when they are pregnant,' she'd said. 'From my experience, in the first few weeks of pregnancy I was too knackered to raise an arm let alone hit anyone. I'd felt lousy with morning sickness.'

I'd defended Erin. 'Well, so far she hasn't actually been sick.'

Jessie had raised an eyebrow when I'd said, 'Well, the doctor confirmed the link between aggression and pregnancy hormones.'

Jessie had then smiled. It was one of her reassuring smiles that usually fill me with comfort but on this occasion, I didn't feel the smile quite reached her eyes. It had seemed forced in some way.

However, in her usual kindness, Jessie has offered to look in on Erin while I'm away. With that uplifting thought I head from the platform amongst throngs of people walking over the old walkway. I reach the concourse at the front of the station and then stride out onto the pavement. I hear everyone's Geordie accent talking all around me and feel happy. Whereas I'm the only one in Bexley with a northern accent, here I'm not alone. I grin. Home at last.

Memories crowd into my mind from the trips we've taken for football matches. I can see us all now shouting, laughing and clapping each other on our backs coming home elated because we'd won. Or sometimes, but not very often, deflated because we'd lost. Whichever way the match went we'd always eat a burger on the way home. I'm meeting the lads for a quick pint in the pub before I go to Ian's stag party tonight, I can't help but smile at the thought of seeing them all again.

There's not much of a queue at the taxi rank and I'm soon heading west out of Newcastle towards Kibblesworth. The taxi driver doesn't speak much English. I gaze at all the recognisable sights and look to the left at The Angel of the North. It's strange but when you're away from home you imagine things might be different when you get back. But they aren't, they're just the same and for this I'm glad.

I do however feel a little trepidation about staying at the house. Our House. It was great that Beth has invited me to stay and feel part of the celebrations. But when I pay the taxi driver then swing around to face the house, I take a deep breath.

Beth is waiting on her own at the doorway and is shielding her eyes from the sun because remarkably for the north east we are having a good summer too.

'Sally is out with her bridesmaid shopping for make-up and girly stuff to take on her honeymoon,' Beth says ushering me through to the lounge.

This is the first time since the night I left them that I've been back inside the house. Usually Sally would wait at the door for me and if she wasn't ready, I would sit in the car. Beth had never once asked me inside.

She is wearing a plain white summer skirt and a blue T-shirt. Now that I'm close to her I can see how much weight she has lost. I stand in the lounge and gaze around the room feeling quite strange. This was my home for years and as far as I can see very little has changed. Beth explains that she is going to re-decorate next month and I smile.

Without thinking I automatically sit in my chair while Beth hurries through to the kitchen to make tea. On her return she sits on the settee and we sip our tea from mugs. My mug is one Sally bought me years ago on Father's Day. I smile at the memory. Beth seems slightly on edge while she goes through the plans for the wedding. When she's finished, she takes a deep breath.

'I've been a little worried doing it on my own in case I've forgotten something important,' she says and then grins at me. 'But now you're here I'll settle down a bit.'

I smile at her. 'Beth, you've done a great job,' I tell her. 'I'm only sorry that I've been so busy and haven't got more involved.'

'Well,' she says. 'Starting a new job and organising the department on your own can't have been easy. It's no wonder you've been run off your feet.'

Nothing, it seems is ever my fault, which is how Beth has always been with me, whether I deserve it or not.

In these circumstances I don't think I warrant her thoughtfulness. We chat easily, and she tells me more about Ian and his family. 'I hope you will have time to look around the cottage with them and hear about the renovations they're planning,' she says.

'I'll make the time,' I say draining the tea from my mug.

If it's important to my daughter, then I'll make the viewing as important to me. Upon Beth's suggestion, I take my holdall and suit hanger upstairs to the spare room where more memories crowd into my mind. I remember painting the room a pale lemon colour because it was mams favourite colour and she slept in here when babysitting.

I can see Beth has re-decorated the bedroom and bought a new single bed with drawers and a wardrobe. I smile noting she has kept the same lemon colour scheme. Maybe it's Beth's tribute to mam, I think hanging my suit up in the wardrobe.

When mam had died, I'd been amazed how much money she'd left in her will. There is a trust fund for Sally to use when we feel she needs it most. Either at eighteen or twenty-one. Mam also left me and Beth enough money to pay off the mortgage on the house because she'd lived rent-free at Uncle Geoff's all her life. He would never take money from her and often said, 'It's enough to have my sister with me so that I don't have to live on my own.'

Erin has suggested a few times since the divorce papers arrived that I should ask for my share of the house value from Beth. So far, I haven't.

I remember that divorce day with great sadness and how I'd tried to hide my upset from Erin. I'd swallowed down tears sitting in my car sitting outside the cottage knowing my married life with Beth was over.

Erin, of course, had been delighted. 'At last, the moron's in this village can't call me names anymore because finally I'm not living with a married man!'

I'd nodded and given her the best smile I could muster. Erin had deserved this after the way she'd supported me, and I'd felt she'd looked upon the divorce as a prize for her loyalty. Which, I'd supposed in some respects, it was. I'd also known it wasn't fair to Erin to mourn over Beth. So, I hadn't. But when I'd been alone our divorce had felt like a waste of the years we'd spent together.

I know now that my thoughts back then were wrong. They weren't a waste because out of them came Sally. Our lovely daughter.

With the holdall emptied, I place it on top of the wardrobe. Erin had bought the holdall for one of our weekend trips and I think now of my pregnant wife. I suppose we will need to buy our own property in Bexley next year. I shrug, maybe I will need to ask for my value of this house. I shake the thought from my mind knowing this weekend isn't the time for money conversations.

I head through to the bathroom to shower. I look at the white tiles on the wall, and grin remembering how I'd tried DIY tiling myself. Beth had been so sick of my dismal attempt and slow progress that while I was at work, she'd got a tiler to finish the job.

Feeling refreshed, I hear Sally calling me from the bottom of the stairs and realise she's home. I can't wait to see my daughter and practically run down the stairs. Amidst laughter, shopping bags, hugs and kisses, we all settle down with more tea.

Sally keeps beaming at me sitting in my chair. I realise the sullen fifteen-year-old that I used to see on dad's weekends has gone. Instead she has blossomed into a lovely young woman who has her whole future ahead of her.

Beth starts to tell me about the strange phone calls on her mobile last week. 'When I answer and say hello, nobody speaks,' she says.

I frown. 'Have you given your number to anyone new lately?'

Beth shakes her head. 'No, well not that I can think of.'

Sally is unwrapping a small package of what looks like face powder and looks up at me. 'Em, how is Erin, Dad?'

My daughter purses her lips as if to say, I think it was your wife ringing mam. I stare down at my tea. I know Sally doesn't like Erin and never has which is understandable in a way. However, it is unfair that Erin gets the blame for everything. But I know if I accuse Sally of inferring that my wife was responsible it will cause an argument. This is the last thing I want on her wedding weekend. So, I bite my tongue and say nothing.

I nod my head. 'She's fine, Sally, thanks for asking. Busy settling into the house and has been into London to quite a few art galleries.'

Sally nods and then turns to Beth. 'Mam, did you tell Dad about Alfie at the bakery?'

Beth gasps. 'Oh, sorry, I forgot,' she says leaning forwards towards me. 'I was talking to the receptionist from the bakery a few weeks ago in town. Apparently, poor Alfie has prostate cancer and has been off sick for a month having treatment. But she did say, he hopes to recover enough to get back to work soon.'

I'm shocked. The image of Alfie beavering away at his desk and joking with me throughout our working years together preoccupies my mind.

I shake my head at the memories. 'God, that's awful news. I hope his wife is coping okay.'

Beth nods and lapses into silence obviously with her own thoughts. 'I hope so too. We met a few times at parties and she's a nice woman. Older than us, of course, but all the same, it's such a shame.'

Sally gathers her parcels and carrier bags together. 'So, Dad, what a pity you didn't stay in your old job because you might have been the temporary manager now.'

And she is right. I can see in her eyes she wants to say, if you hadn't moved you would have gotten what you wanted eventually. I smile and realise there will be many unsaid words between me and my daughter now while we try to keep the peace. Whereas in the past there's only ever been the two of us together but now Beth is in our company, we will have to remain guarded to save hurt feelings.

Sally wanders upstairs to her bedroom. Beth and I move through to sit at the table in the dining room and eat a light meal together. Whereas the lounge hasn't changed in its appearance this room has been altered dramatically. I love the subtle green colours Beth has used with a modern wallpaper. While we eat and discuss the plans for tonight with Ian's friends and family, I can tell Beth wants to say something.

I know her too well. The way she fidgets. The way she rubs the back of her neck. The way she avoids my eyes when I ask her what's up. And just like in the old days I pick at her until she agrees to tell me.

'But, Dave, I don't want to spoil your weekend with upsetting news,' she says. 'I'll tell you after the wedding.'

'No, tell me please,' I state emphatically. 'I want to know now.'

Beth explains about the ancestry website and what she found out about my father. How she did more digging and found a newspaper article about his court case. I'm gobsmacked. While she talks, I keep butting-in with what uncle Geoff had told me and how I'd thought it was merely an old man's ramblings.

'Show me,' I say.

She pulls her laptop across the dining table. I get up and stand behind Beth leaning over her shoulder in readiness to read the article. I inhale her well-known soapy smell. Everything about her is familiar. Her smooth bobbed hair that is such a stark contrast to Erin's wild abundance. Her controlled speech and voice. The way she wants to tell me the truth but tries to soften the blow with careful words.

While I wait, I glance around the dining room. Everything here is so bloody easy in comparison to being at home with Erin. Then I feel guilty for my thoughts. I love Erin and just because we've hit a rough patch in our marriage, I know I shouldn't be thinking this way. I really want to tell Beth about the baby, but I've already broken my promise to Erin once by telling Jessie. So, I keep quiet.

The sight of my father's ugly face appears on the screen. He is snarling. Yes, snarling at the camera man outside the old courthouse. This sweeps all other thoughts out of my mind. He looks foul. There's no other word I can think of to describe him, but foul.

There'd never been any photographs of him at mams when I was growing up so I've no idea what he looked like. And now I have, I don't like what I see.

'Can you zoom in?' I ask Beth and she fiddles with the mouse until his face is enlarged on the screen.

I have his eyes but other than that I can't see any other resemblance.

As if Beth knows what I'm thinking, she says. 'You look more like your mam than him.'

Chapter Twenty-Seven

I'd had a great night with my pals in the local laughing at old times. When I stood at the bar, I remember thinking how good it felt to laugh. I can't remember the last time I've truly laughed. Not just a titter or a grin, but a big raucous belly laugh. This good feeling had continued later in Newcastle with Ian, his family and friends. Beth is right. He is a nice lad and comes from a good family. I couldn't be happier for Sally and for us, knowing she will be well settled with him.

Arriving home just after eleven and with a final glass of wine, Beth and I discussed Sally's trust fund. We've agreed to give her the money now. I often have a live-for-today attitude when it comes to money, but Beth is very careful. Not frugal or a skinflint, just careful. Therefore, I welcomed her opinion. She reckons the youngsters will probably struggle on their two small wages to make all the alterations to the cottage. She also agreed that investing money into property now-a-days, is the best place for it. I know mam would have thought that too.

Now, it's the big day. After a couple of aspirins with two strong cups of coffee my slight hangover is lifting. I'm dressed in my suit, the flowers have arrived, and we are due to leave home for Blackfriars venue.

Beth asks, 'Please go up and chase Sally or we'll be late, Dave.'

When I reach the top of the stairs Beth's bedroom door is open and I can't resist a peek inside. I gasp at the beautiful décor. It is all white and there's a fantastic chandelier hanging dramatically from the centre of the ceiling. When I head towards Sally's room, I wonder who had advised Beth about the interior design.

I tap gently on Sally's bedroom door and walk in. 'Is the bride nearly ready?'

My chest feels like it will burst with pride. My little princess looks so beautiful when she swings around to face me. Happiness is pouring out from her. The long white dress is simple but elegant which is perfect with the short veil attached to something in the back of her hair. Her hair is fastened up and I gulp because I can see so much of mams face in hers. She has her big doleful eyes which are now darting around the room in case she has forgotten something.

I take her hands and hold them tightly in front of me. 'You look absolutely beautiful, princess,' I say, and swallow down a big lump in my dry throat.

'Oh, Dad, I'm so glad you're here,' she says. 'I'm a bit scared.'

Her hands are trembling slightly in mine. 'Will I spoil the dress if I give you a hug?'

She throws herself into my arms and I hug her tightly then rub her back. It feels as though she is ten years old again. Unashamedly, I choke back a little sob. 'You'll be fine, darling. Just hang onto my arm when we walk in and then we'll see Ian waiting for you.'

She nods and I feel her take a deep breath. I stare around her room and notice here too has been re-decorated. It's no longer girly pink and all her cuddly toys have gone. Although, I do notice she has kept one small teddy bear that Uncle Geoff had given her when she was a baby. It sits on a shelf on the wall looking old and tatty from when she carried it around for years by its ears.

I let her go from the embrace and hold her at arm's length. I know I should say something meaningful at this father-daughter special moment and lick my lips. 'I've been a little concerned that your wedding was a bit of a rush, Sally.

But after meeting Ian and his family last night, I'm confident you are going to be okay,' I say grinning. 'At the end of the day, me and your mam want you to be settled and happy.'

She tilts her head onto one side. 'Aw, Dad. I just want to be with Ian forever. I love him so much.'

I nod and grin back at her. 'Well,' I say. 'We think you should have the money from the trust fund to help with the cottage renovations.'

She giggles with delight. 'Oh, that will make such a big difference. Ian's parents are paying for the major alterations. So, even if there's enough money for me to buy the white goods in the kitchen and some of the flooring I'll feel that I'm contributing something to our new home.'

We both hear Beth calling up the stairs to say the cars are outside. With my arm carefully around Sally not to spoil her hair and dress, we leave the bedroom. 'Don't worry, Sally, there is more than enough money for what you need.'

I descend the stairs behind Sally where Beth is waiting at the bottom with the bridesmaid. Beth's eyes are misted over when she sees Sally and they have a brief hug when she tells her daughter how stunning she looks.

Beth also looks amazing. When I think back to Beth's wardrobe when we were married it was very casual although she always looked nice. Now she seems to be wearing trendier clothes and I notice her small petite figure which looks great. It reminds me of how she was when we were younger.

Her figure-hugging long lilac dress looks just the part for the mother of the bride. I grin at her. Her bobbed hair is glossy and swishes every time she moves her head to talk or laugh. She looks radiant. I sigh with pleasure and pride. She looks as special today as my daughter does.

I know I shouldn't be thinking along these lines. Not when I have Erin. Would I be thinking like this if Erin was standing next to me. I try to justify these feelings and convince myself that, yes, I would. Just because I love Erin doesn't mean I can't love any other women in my life. And Beth will always be very special to me.

I pull out my mobile to text Erin. 'Everything is going well so far. Hope you are okay? I love you, David. xx'

I don't get an answer to my text on the way over to Newcastle and shrug my shoulders. No doubt, she will be absorbed in her painting.

***

We arrive outside Blackfriars and I hurry around to open the door for Sally. Her bridesmaid and Beth arrive in the car behind us where a great deal of fuss is made over Sally's dress.

I look up to see the sun break through the clouds at exactly twelve midday and hope it's a good omen for them. We walk the short distance along the path to the chapel and Beth hurries in front of us to take her place inside.

I'm sweating a little and pull at the stiff collar of my new shirt which is rubbing on my neck. I reassure Sally with soothing words at the door of the chapel.

Fifty of our old friends and family are standing up when we walk down the narrow opening between the rows of people. We reach Ian with his best man at the front. I watch Sally's face light up when she sees Ian and feel the tension leave her shoulders. She'll be fine now, I think, and hand over my precious daughter to another man. I squeeze her hand tightly at this poignant moment and feel quite emotional when I take my place next to Beth.

The ceremony is lovely. Sun streams through the three long stained-glass windows in the old brick walls when Sally and Ian say their vows. Beth looks at me with eyes full of tears and I wonder if she is thinking how grown up our little girl seems.

The reception and my short, but well-meaning speech went okay. Time flew over until the night-time party in the local pub. Beth had hired the snug room in The Plough for the wedding which was perfect for Ian and Sally's friends.

By ten o'clock, Sally leaves and throws her bouquet backwards where funnily enough it lands at Beth's feet. We all laugh. The newlyweds have gone to the airport hotel for the wedding night to catch an early flight the next morning to Paris. It is a surprise honeymoon treat which I've given them.

Knowing a little about Ian I think he'll appreciate the old buildings and architecture. And I know my daughter will be in her element window-shopping on the Champs-Elysees.

My mobile rings just when we are loading the taxi with all their wedding presents. I step aside from Beth to take the call from Erin. The merry mood from the champagne leaves me in seconds. I listen miserably while Erin tells me about her miscarriage. A crushing blow of sadness settles in the middle of my chest. The baby has gone. We are not going to have our own family now. I listen to Erin sobbing and apologising to me.

I think rapidly longing to get to her. 'Look, Erin, there's no more trains tonight but I could hire a car and drive straight back to be with you!'

Erin snuffles and I hear her take a deep breath. 'But you'll have been drinking, David?'

I realise she is right. 'Ah, that's true. I've had quite a few glasses of champagne and will be well over the limit!'

'NO,' she shouts. 'I'm not having you drive down here tonight. You might have an accident and that I couldn't bear,' she says pausing to blow her nose. 'David, it's okay. It happened early this morning and I've been to the hospital for a check-up. They've told me I'm fine and that there shouldn't be any complications.'

I sigh listening to her voice and catch a small sob in the back of my throat. 'Oh, Erin, I'm so sorry I wasn't with you.'

'Don't fret, darling. I didn't want to ring earlier because I didn't want to spoil your happy day with Sally,' she whispers.

The shame for my previous unkind thought's curl around my gut and I feel my cheeks burn. I want to hold Erin tightly to help her through this loss but feel useless standing in the car park with two bottles of champagne tucked under my arm.

We say goodbye and I tell her that I will be home tomorrow as soon as I can. I won't listen to her protests about staying until Monday. Eventually she tells me that she will be glad to have me at home with her.

***

I climb into the taxi with Beth for the short journey down to the house. She looks at me out of the corner of her eye while we sit in silence. I can tell she knows there's something amiss. I pay the taxi driver while deep in thought about the baby and all the dreams I 'd had.

A large part of me had wished for a boy. A son who I could play football with and take to St. James Park. We could have done boyish things and I wouldn't have had to sit on the side-lines like I had done with some of Sally's girlie hobbies. As opposed to Erin's misgiving's the age difference wouldn't have mattered one iota to me.

I firmly believe that I could be an energetic father until my child reached his or her twenty first birthday.

Beth and I carry all the bags into the house dropping them in the hallway.

'What's happened,' she asks switching on the light then gently strokes my arm. 'You look like you've seen a ghost?'

I don't encourage nor brush her hand from my arm because I like it being there. I know there's no point in bluffing with Beth. I tell her about the baby and the sad news. My chin trembles a little and I take a deep breath. I manage to hold myself together. 'So, I'll have to get the first train back to London in the morning.'

Beth covers her cheeks with both hands. 'Oh my God. How awful for her. Well, for both of you,' she says. 'I'm very sorry.'

And I know she means it. She doesn't have a mean bone in her body, and I know her concern is heartfelt. Jealousy from one woman to another doesn't even come into the equation.

'Thanks, Beth. We only found out a couple of weeks ago,' I say. 'And at our age it came as a bit of a shock.'

Last week I'd rehearsed a conversation in my mind that I would have with Sally when I told her about the baby. How she would always be my special daughter and how I hoped she would welcome a half-brother or sister.

'Please don't tell Sally,' I say. 'I was going to tell her in a few months' time.'

'Okay, not a word,' Beth whispers even though we are alone in the house.

I sigh heavily and walk through to the dining room table to put the champagne bottles down. 'Although, I suppose there's no need to have the conversation now. Not now that the baby's gone.'

Beth nods and plods through behind me with a few of the bags. We stack the presents together on the table. 'Ah, damn. I was going to see Uncle Geoff tomorrow.'

Beth brightens. 'Well, don't worry about that. I can go for you,' she says. 'Although when I went three weeks ago, he didn't know me and slept for most of the visit.'

I feel another tug of remorse that I haven't been to see him. I weigh up the importance of my options. I can't do anything to help Uncle Geoff, but I can help Erin with our grief. Therefore, leaving on the first train must come first.

'You can always come up another weekend to see Uncle Geoff,' Beth says. 'I'll text you tomorrow to let you know how he is.'

Beth to the rescue again, I think after saying goodnight and climbing the stairs to bed. I lie in the single bed with sleep the furthest thing from my mind and worry how this blow is going to affect Erin.

Chapter Twenty-Eight

I am sitting on the settee holding Erin in my arms. The train was late with engineering works and a diversion, so I didn't get back until late in the afternoon.

I'd had a reassuring text from Jessie on the journey down. She had called on Erin over the weekend, but they'd only had a few words standing at the front door. I'd explained briefly to Jessie that I was on my way back to Bexley because Erin had a miscarriage. Jessie didn't answer the text, but I wasn't unduly concerned because I had a poor signal on the train.

Erin and I have been in tears. We are taking solace in a glass of red wine while she explains more of the happenings the day before. I keep apologising that she went through the trauma of losing our baby on her own.

'I should have been here to support you,' I say.

I hold her tightly in my arms and she snuggles into my chest. I can tell she is a little upset, but she does seem to be coping remarkably well. As opposed to me. I feel emotionally wrung out. The red wine is loosening the tension in my limbs, but my mind is still overly active.

I'm still in my jeans and t-shirt from travelling and know I need to shower and take my holdall upstairs. But I don't want to move and spoil our closeness. Erin looks delightful in a pink cotton dress and her hair is piled up into a top knot. Her pink thin cardigan is draped around her shoulders and I can smell her sweet deodorant spray.

I pull the band from her hair and run my fingers through it hoping to soothe her. I want to be near her. And there for her. Whether it be today, tomorrow or however long it takes.

'If I must take time off work then so be it, Erin. But I promise you this. You will come first on my list of priorities,' I say drawing my eyebrows together.

'I'll be fine, David. The doctors have checked me over and physically I'm okay with no lasting damage,' she says. 'Don't fret.'

But I'm still a little worried. I feel energy in my muscles and can't help tensing my biceps.

My mobile on the coffee table tinkles with a text. Keeping Erin enclosed in my arms I reach over to read it. 'Oh, it's from Beth,' I say. Deciding Erin might get a little tetchy, I read it aloud, so she'll know it's just a simple message.

'Beth has been to see Uncle Geoff for me because I didn't get time,' I say and squeeze Erin feeling pleased with the uplifting news. 'She says he looks much better than a few weeks ago and he had a little joke with her.'

I hear Erin huff and puff then pull away from my arms. I realise it was the wrong thing to do. I should have shrugged the text off as an advert or something, and not mentioned Beth at all.

Erin gets up from the settee and begins to pace around the room. I feel a quiver of apprehension in my stomach. Her face has reddened, and her hands are making little jerky movements. She stops still then turns to look at me. I can tell she is agitated and picks at the skin on her thumbnail.

'So now you've spent the weekend in your old home with Beth am I to expect regular contact from her,' she snaps. 'Is she going to be part of our lives now even though you've never seen her for over two years. Or at least that's what you've been telling me. Maybe that's a lie and you have been seeing her.'

I hate this jealous streak in Erin. Especially when I can't see any reason for it. I've never once given her cause for concern about other women. I'm too unassuming to flirt. Mainly because I don't know how to do it and I never look at other women when we're together. I've been obsessed with her from the first day we met.

'Please don't do this, Erin. You know how much I love you, and there's never been anyone else.'

She shrugs her shoulders and then looks past me towards the window. She fiddles with a button on her cardigan. I can see her lips twitching as though she is thinking of a response, but she doesn't speak.

After a long pause I decide this may be a good time to head upstairs. It will give her time to calm down. 'Look, I'm going upstairs to the loo and then shower,' I say. 'Why don't you have a nap on the settee, and then I'll make us something nice to eat.'

She doesn't answer me, but flops back down onto the settee.

I make my way upstairs. With hot water splashing on top of my head in the shower I re-think the last few minutes. I have just spent two nights with my ex-wife. Although I know nothing whatsoever happened between us, but maybe that's enough to make a woman feel insecure. And Erin must be feeling especially vulnerable after what's happened. I pull my shoulders back. I'm going to have to find a lot more patience and understanding during the next few weeks. And decide that reassurance is the best way forward.

Leaving the bathroom, I notice the bedroom door where Erin paints is ajar. I push it further open and look inside. I gasp at the sight in front of me. A large canvas is lying smashed in the corner and her paints and brushes are scattered around the room. There are paint splatter marks on the wall. I frown.

I hope the landlord doesn't charge us for this damage and know I'll have to tackle her about it.

What's happened? I shake my head slowly and whistle through my teeth. Erin is usually quite methodical and precious about her materials and equipment. This looks like she's run amok destroying her things and more worryingly, her work.

I remember the aggressive temper in bed over the last month and groan. The thought of going through her assaults again makes me cringe. My cheeks flush and it's not with the steam from the shower. I know I shouldn't be thinking this way about her. But, I determine, once we work our way through the loss of the baby, I'm sure I can get us back to our usual loving relationship.

I make my way back downstairs wondering what I can use to remove the paint from the walls. If it is like emulsion paint it may wipe off with a soapy cloth. But does that work with oil-based paint. I'm not sure. It's when I reach the bottom stair that I hear her raised voice on the mobile and hurry back into the lounge.

Erin is snarling accusations and shouting down the phone. She has her mobile in one hand and her other hand is flapping about wildly.

I glare at her. 'Who is that?'

She continues shouting, 'He is my husband now, not yours anymore. So, leave him alone!'

With a sickening realisation I know it's Beth. I think of the timid expression that will be on Beth's face and how apprehensive she will feel.

'Stop that now!' I yell.

I grab the phone from Erin's hand and apologise to Beth who sounds scared. Sally's insinuation comes straight to my mind and I know my daughter was right. It had been Erin making the weird phone calls last week because somehow, she has Beth's mobile number.

'For God's sake, Erin. What on earth has gotten into you.' I say but receive a shrug of her shoulders in reply.

I slump back down onto the edge of the settee and run my hands through my hair while she sits on the arm of the chair. Her eyes are wide and darting frantically around the room. I can feel waves of suppressed anger coming from her.

Maybe it's the shock and grief of losing the baby, I reason. But there again, she hadn't lost the baby last week when she was tormenting Beth with silent calls.

A knot of tension grips my stomach and I realise Erin looks a little unbalanced. I'm not sure if that is the right word to use for her state of mind. I don't want to seem harsh or cruel with my thoughts, but all I do know is that she doesn't seem normal.

Erin slumps down onto the other side of the settee and promptly curls up with her knees to her chest. She closes her eyes and seems to fall asleep. I look at her not knowing what to do. She looks so angelic when she sleeps. I remember when we were first together how I used to delight in watching her sleep.

Should I call a doctor and ask if this is normal behaviour after a miscarriage. But it's Sunday afternoon and the surgery will be closed. I could ring a walk-in centre, but I sigh heavily. The clue is in the name and I'd never get Erin to walk inside.

I head into the kitchen and decide to cook. When I'm rummaging around in the freezer looking for something to defrost, I hear my mobile ring.

Remembering it is on the coffee table I hurry back to the lounge hoping to answer before it wakes her up.

She has already answered. And this time I know straight away who has rang me.

'Jessie,' my wife snaps. 'I must insist that you leave David and me alone and stop interfering in our marriage. I didn't appreciate you coming around here and pestering me on Saturday morning and I certainly don't appreciate it now!'

I'm appalled at Erin's voice and manner. As opposed to Beth, Jessie is a totally different woman. I know she will stick up for herself with Erin, but I still flinch. It's embarrassing because she's a good friend. 'Don't speak to Jessie like that,' I shout. 'It's not fair!'

I grab my mobile from Erin's hand and she pushes me aside to run into the kitchen.

I apologise profusely to Jessie. While I'm talking it suddenly dawns upon me that if Jessie called to the house on Saturday morning how could Erin talk to her if she was having a miscarriage. A cold shiver runs down my back.

'Don't worry, David, there's no harm done,' Jessie soothes. 'She's bound to be upset after losing the baby.'

I nod. 'I just wish I'd been here instead of her going through it all on her own.'

'Of course, you do,' Jessie says. 'Are you all right?'

I'm just about to reassure her when Erin returns from the kitchen. She is standing in the doorway with the large bread knife in her right hand.

I gulp down a dry sob in the back of my throat. I'm in serious trouble. My mind panics. I feel stunned and rooted to the spot.

Erin is standing very still and looks quite mad. Her hair is flayed around her face. Her face is flushed, and she is clenching and unclenching her left hand.

Foolishly I think of Glen Close in the film, Fatal Attraction, when she lunges towards me. I drop my mobile and raise my arm to protect myself. My heart begins to pound against my ribcage and I'm breathing in short rasps. I stagger back from her.

'You're my husband! No one else is going to have you,' she shrieks.

She slashes feverously at my arms and I feel pain tear through me. I must fight to get the knife off her. Blood runs onto the carpet and I know she has cut me somewhere. I grab at her shoulder. We struggle, but I succeed in pinning her down on the settee. With my knee on the inside of her elbow and her arm straightened out I force her to drop the knife to the floor. She starts to scream and howl obscenities at me.

I gasp for breath dragging air into my lungs and my heartbeat bangs in my ears. She is still writhing underneath me. The blood from my arm is running down onto her dress and lying in a small pool on the settee. My eyes are wet. I can't see where the blood is coming from. I rub my eyes with the back of my hand and see a big gash on my arm. I keep her down by moving my knee onto her chest and grab her thin cardigan from the back of the settee. Tying the sleeve tightly around my biceps I hope to staunch the bleeding.

My breathing starts to slow, and I feel a little more in control. Not trusting her to fight back again I hold the back of her hair firmly down into the cushion. 'Look, Erin, I'm going to call a doctor because you've clearly had some type of reaction to losing the baby!'

Holding her hair tightly, I scramble down by her side and onto my knees. I try to reach for my mobile which is lying under the coffee table.

She starts to scream. 'I hate you! You're pathetic. You don't have the guts to tackle a real woman, like me,' she rants. 'You'd much rather mess around with your useless ex-wife, and that over-sized Jessie.'

I want to shout back that they are the real women and not her. Antagonising her at this stage won't help. I grit my teeth and protest, 'I'm not messing around with anyone, Erin. I wouldn't do that!'

'You're a liar,' she taunts. 'You're like Jekkel & Hyde. Nice guy one minute and then in another minute you're just like your disgusting father!'

At the mention of my father I slacken my hold and stare at her. 'What did you say?'

'You heard me,' she spits. 'Like father like son!'

I feel dazed. I remember what Beth had shown me at the weekend. 'What do you know about him?'

She curls her big lips and emphasises every word, 'He, was, the, savage, bastard, who, raped, my, mother!'

I gasp in shock and loosen my hold rocking back onto my heels. 'W…what?'

Erin jumps up again and grabs the knife from the floor. She threatens and aims the point towards my face. She is towering above me. Her hair is hanging like a curtain around her twisted face. Her nostrils are flared. Beads of sweat are standing on her forehead. I notice a cord standing up in her neck while she cracks her head from side to side.

'But he c…can't have,' I manage to mutter. 'How do you know that?'

Spittle forms in the corner of her mouth. She hisses, 'I read it in my mother's diary.' Her big lips are pulled back almost as though she is baring her teeth at me. 'She couldn't live with herself any longer. She'd had to deceive my father into thinking that Neil was his son,' she rambles on. 'So, carrying Neil she waded into the river and drowned them both.'

Stupidly, all I can focus on is the fact that she's lied to me. 'But you told me they were killed in a car accident?'

She throws her head back dramatically and gives a guttural roar. She looks possessed like a witch I saw in a play at the theatre. But I know this isn't a stage-show. This is real and I'm terrified.

I shake my head trying to take in what she's saying. My voice has a shaky-hysterical note and I hardly recognise it. 'B…but, it can't be, you were all in Australia!'

I can see the point of the knife wavering in front of my eyes and panic fills me. My heart begins to race again and I'm struggling to catch my breath. Sweat runs down the back of my t-shirt. I don't know what to do and cower away from her.

'Why do you think she took us to Australia,' she snarls. 'It was to get away from your dad!'

I remember his foul face on the lap top screen at Beth's. He does look like a man who could commit such an awful act. But I can only stammer, 'N…no, way. It couldn't have been him.'

Her hand is trembling holding the knife. She keeps making little stabbing movements towards my nose. She cries, 'Mum knew if she told my father it would shatter him. Neil had been conceived by your foul father when he dragged her into the barn then savagely raped her.'

Her usual small eyes look huge and are darting around the room again. They come back to rest on mine.

I can see revulsion in them when she glares at me. I know she wants to kill me.

I stare at Erin with my mouth open. I feel giddy and breathless. 'W…when did you find this out?'

Erin rubs a hand over her stomach. Her other hand wavers slightly holding the knife. 'I found mother's diary in the trunk the day before we moved down here.'

I shake my head vigorously trying to comprehend what she's said. Is it true? I figure it must be. She couldn't make up something as horrendous as this. And the timing is bang-on. That's when she started being weird.

Pulling myself up with my left arm onto the edge of the settee I manage to struggle up from the carpet and stand in front of her. 'Erin, please calm down,' I croak.

I try to clear my dry throat. 'L…look, if they gave you drugs at the hospital this could be a reaction to the miscarriage.'

She throws her hair back from her sweating face. She sniggers then looks over my shoulder. 'I didn't lose the baby. I got rid of it when I was away for the weekend in London. I had a termination on Harley Street.'

My mind is spinning. I feel dizzy as if I'm swirling in circles like water going down the plug hole. I don't know what she's going to say next and when it will all stop. I drop my arms to my sides feeling helpless. I don't have any fight left in me. The woman in front of me is a stranger. I shake my head not knowing who she is anymore. She's not my Erin. And I'm petrified of her.

She begins to stalk around in front of me in small circles. She's still waving the knife around but in more of a careless manner. It's almost as if her body is here in the room, but her mind is somewhere else.

'I didn't want any other person growing inside *me*,' she rages. 'Not like my poor mother had to endure. I don't want any of your rotten family genes in my body.'

I can't speak. I don't know what to say. I'm not thinking clearly any longer. I cannot grasp how or why this is happening to me.

My hand is covered in blood now. It feels cold and clammy. I grasp my hands together in front of me hoping to stop the trembling. The metallic smell of blood fills my nose.

'Don't you realise my brother, Neil, was actually your half-brother? No wonder we get along so well and are attracted to each other. We're practically bloody family!' She stops still in her tracks and stares down at the knife.

'God knows how our baby would have turned out. It would probably have had birth defects, and the thought of that makes me feel physically sick.'

Now I'm shaking from my shoulders to my feet. Pain rips through my arm. Bile rises into the back of my throat at the smell of my own blood. I think I'm going to vomit. I nod my head at her agreeing. Yes, I feel sick, too.

Suddenly, she jumps in front of my face again with the knife pointing at my mouth. I stagger backwards grabbing hold of the settee. 'Were you in on the secret,' she screams. 'Maybe you knew all about it. Did your father tell you to keep quiet about the rape? Or maybe you watched him thrash my mother with the belt and got a thrill out of it!'

I can tell in her warped and twisted mind she is blaming me for what my father did. Maybe she thinks I am him. All I can do is shake my head dumbly and stare down at my clasped hands. I whimper now. 'It's not my fault. We left the farm when I was only seven.'

I feel faint with black spots in front of my eyes. I fall backwards over the arm of the settee and slide onto the floor.

She pounces and stands over me. 'Well, you're going to pay for it now. You're going to pay for what you did to my family.'

Erin is straddled over me on her knees. She is aiming the knife high above my chest. I know she is getting ready to plunge it into me. I close my eyes tightly shut waiting for the pain. Maybe I will die straight away. I realise the old saying is true, and my life flashes before my eyes. I think of Beth, Sally, and my mam then feel a tear leak out of the corner of my eye. I feel like I'm drifting and floating upwards.

Suddenly, there is noise and shouting. I feel a lightness on either sides of my body and realise that Erin has been lifted from me. I snap my eyes open. Jakub is manhandling Erin while she kicks and screams at him. A policeman is telling us all to stay calm while he holds onto the knife. Jessie kneels next to me. She puts her cool hand on my damp forehead.

'You all right, boss?' Jakub shouts.

Chapter Twenty-Nine

I wake up in hospital with Jessie sitting on one side of my bed and Beth sitting on the other. My mind is blurred and I'm struggling to remember what's happened. I can remember being in the ambulance with Jessie and a paramedic dressing my arm. Then nothing else.

'What time is it?' I ask looking towards the small window with the blinds open. How can the sun be shinning at night? And how has Beth got here.

Beth leans forward and explains. 'You had an operation on your arm last night and you've slept right through after a blood transfusion.'

Her calm reassuring face is so familiar to me that I feel like bursting into tears. I gulp and swallow hard. My mouth and throat feel bone-dry. I look at the glass of water on top of the bedside locker. 'Can I have a drink,' I ask trying to ease my shoulders up.

My arm is heavily bandaged and is propped up on top of three pillows on the bed. I have a hospital gown on which is tied at the back of my neck. I pull it away from my throat feeling as though it is choking me.

Beth jumps up and holds the glass to my mouth while Jessie unties the knot at the back of the gown and loosens it. I can feel that I'm naked underneath. The clinical hospital smell fills my nose and I gulp gratefully at the water.

Erin crashes back into my mind. My heart starts to thump and sweat forms on my lip. My eyes scan the big room with another three men lying in their beds. Where is she? Where's the knife? Can she get in here?

'E...Erin?' I ask and look wildly to the door. 'She's not in here, is she?'

Jessie lays her hand on my shoulder and squeezes it firmly. 'The policewoman last night told me she has been sedated in a psychiatric hospital. Two consultants have agreed to section her because she is psychotic and will need months, if not years of treatment.'

I slump back onto the pillows. I'm about to ask Beth how she got here when a doctor appears at the bedside.

The old ward sister is behind and hands him a folder. 'Well, Mr. Henderson,' he says approaching me. 'You've certainly been very lucky.'

He's a guy in his thirties and has a trusting kind of smile. He inspects the dressing which is down the full length of my arm to my knuckles. I can see dark shadows under his green eyes. I wonder if he did my operation and has been here all night.

I clear my croaky throat. 'Well, my wife tried to kill me last night so, I'm not sure how you think that's lucky.'

I see the ward sister purse her lips. He smiles then nods. 'Sorry, I meant, the makeshift tourniquet around your arm saved your life. Even with it you've lost quite a lot of blood. But without it, well...' he says and takes my fingers in his. 'I've had to put twenty-three stitches inside the wound and nineteen on the outside.'

He asks me to try and squeeze his fingers which I do and feel a pull of pain up the inside of my arm. I wince.

'That's good,' he continues. 'Your fingers are warm, and you have movement with some strength in them. The injury was very close to a tendon and I'm not altogether sure whether it is damaged or not. Time will tell because it was a nasty injury.'

I nod at him when he removes his fingers from mine. 'Thank you,' I mumble and the sister smiles at me.

'Look, stay with us until this evening,' he says. 'Then all being well, you can go home later tonight. But you will need physiotherapy after the stitches are out.'

He walks away from me giving orders to the sister who scribbles down on a clipboard and they leave us.

I take a deep breath and look at Beth. 'How on earth did you get here?'

Jessie speaks first. 'Well, you'd given me your home details while you were away for the wedding so, I didn't think you'd mind me ringing Beth to let her know what had happened. Also, before you went to theatre, they asked me for your next of kin,' she says looking down at her hands which are folded calmly in her lap. 'And because Erin was, shall we say, indisposed I had to give them Beth's number. I figured if they rang her, she'd get a hell of a shock, so I did.'

I look at Jessie. For probably the hundredth time since I arrived in Bexley, I thank God for her friendship. She has helped me so much but this time she's saved my life.

Beth interrupts. 'When Jessie rang me, I couldn't settle. I was so worried I rang a taxi into Newcastle and jumped on the first train for London. I figured that even if you didn't want me here, I just had to know you were okay.'

I shake my head in wonderment at the two women sitting with me. Their kindness overwhelms me, and I take another big gulp of water.

'And,' Beth continues, 'Jessie and Mike met me at Kings Cross station last night and brought me here.'

I can see a small overnight bag beside the bedside locker. 'You've sat here all night?' I'm astounded and feel very humbled. After what I did to her, she obviously still cares enough about me to come here. It's remarkable.

I try to think if I would have done the same and decide I would. If Sally rang and told me Beth had been attacked and was going for an operation, I'd have jumped on a train too.

'Dave, I couldn't sit at home fretting. I didn't know where Erin was. Or if she was still after you?'

Beth smooths her hair down. 'But I did have a sleep in the big chair. The nurses were kind and brought me a pillow and blanket,' she says with her cheeks flushing. 'Gosh, I must look an awful sight.'

'I've never seen anyone look so good in all my life,' I murmur. I mean every word and know I'll have time to talk to Beth later, but for now, I say, 'It's great to have you here, thanks for coming and keeping watch over me.'

I turn to Jessie and don't know where to start. I feel overwhelmed with gratitude. 'Jessie, I don't know how to thank you. You've saved my life,' I say. My throat feels thick and I swallow hard. 'If it hadn't been for you…' I shake my head slowly.

Jessie interrupts, 'But it wasn't me, David. It was Jakub, really,' she says. Her cheeks are pink, and she fiddles with her big daisy earring. 'I'd been so worried when you left me hanging on the end of the mobile. I could hear noises then a scream and I didn't know what she was doing to you. Jakub had called into our house to borrow something and he raced up on his scooter to help you while I ran alongside him.'

Beth joins in the conversation to fill in the blanks. 'And it was a good job the front door was open,' she stresses. 'Or they wouldn't have gotten inside to help you.'

I nod at Beth and then look back at Jessie again. 'But it was you who cared enough to know something wasn't right,' I mutter. 'So, all I can say is, thank you, thank you, thank you.'

Jessie clears her throat and her big chest heaves. 'I rang the police before I left the house, but still wasn't sure what to do when we got to yours. Erin had already told me to stop interfering. But when I told Jakub, well, you know what he's like?' She pauses to take a deep breath. 'Then we heard the sirens and Jakub burst through the hall and into the lounge. I could hear the policeman running up the path behind us,' she says. Her eyes are awash with tears. 'Oh, God. It was horrible. There was blood all over the floor and settee and there she was with the knife.'

I realise they'd both put themselves in danger because Erin could have attacked them with the knife. I lean across with my good hand and squeeze her shoulder. 'I know, it's stuff that nightmares are made of. And I think I'm going to be having a few of them for a while,' I say. 'Thank you again, so much, Jessie.'

Beth nods and thanks her too.

A young nurse who doesn't look much older than Sally arrives to my bedside with a breakfast tray in her hands. 'Are you hungry,' she asks.

With the smell of toast in the room my stomach growls. I grin. 'You bet I am.'

She places the tray on the table then turns to Beth and Jessie. 'This is probably a good time to leave for a few hours so he can eat breakfast and maybe take a shower.'

Beth picks up her handbag from the floor getting ready to leave and Jessie pushes her chair back. 'Beth, you can always stay with us,' she offers. 'Although I will be at work all day and Mike is too.'

I frown. I will feel awful if Beth has to stay in a hotel. 'Beth, I'd love you to come with me. But the house will be in an awful state! I mean, the blood…' I shudder thinking about it.

Beth pulls her shoulders back and takes my key from inside the locker. 'Don't worry about the mess. I'll soon sort everything out,' she says and gets up from the chair.

Jessie stands up too. 'I'll drop you off at David's before I go into work.'

I watch them leave together. They seem to get along so well that they look like long lost friends.

Chapter Thirty

By six that evening Beth has arrived back onto the ward and I'm so pleased to see her. She has brought clean underwear, track suit bottoms and an old t-shirt. She cuts the sleeve to get it over the dressing on my arm and ties the sling around the back of my neck.

The nurse discharges me from the ward. I have an appointment for stitches to be removed, painkillers to take, and instructions to keep my arm elevated for another day. I hesitate near the bedside while Beth puts my few things into a carrier bag.

I've never liked hospitals. I've never liked the starched white coats and uniforms. I've never liked the clinical smell. And, I've never liked the enclosed feeling when you're confined to a bed.

This all reminds me of when I had my appendix out aged twelve. I'd had mam and Uncle Geoff with me. 'Come on, Davy, let's be having you,' Uncle had said. He'd put his huge arm around my back to steer me outside to the car.

I look around the room wishing he was here with me now. I feel safe here with the staff milling around. I know they have my best welfare at heart and won't allow anyone near enough to hurt me. I'm wishing I could stay. I feel quite spooked at the thought of going back to the house again. A porter arrives with a wheelchair to take me down to Mike in his taxi. Although I protest that I can walk down my legs start to tremble and I'm glad to sit in the wheelchair.

***

Mike's cheerful banter with Beth keeps me distracted during the short journey. But when we pull up outside the house, I can feel my heart begin to pound and my mouth dries. The last time I was here I'd thought I was going to die.

I'd been terrified.

When Beth jumps out of the taxi and turns to help me there's a large part of me wants to stay in the taxi and go back to safety in the hospital. I shake myself and follow her to the front door. Beth calls her thanks to Mike. And I give him a wave with my free hand.

It's just after six and the sun is still shinning. 'Look,' I say. 'Why don't we sit out in the garden for a while.'

Beth raises an eyebrow and I know I'll have to explain. I can't hide my true feelings from her. She'll see right through me. 'It's just, well, I don't want to see the blood on the carpet and settee. It'll bring all the foul memories flooding back.'

I know I sound pathetic. But the image of the knife and smell of blood fills my senses. I shudder.

Beth smiles and takes my hand squeezing it tightly. 'Don't worry about the blood,' she says. 'Mike has had a guy come to remove the settee and I've hired an industrial carpet cleaner who's done an amazing job.'

I nod warily behind her when we walk into the lounge. I pull my shoulders back and lift my chin. Man up, I think and brace myself.

There's no sign of blood anywhere. The carpet smells clean and fresh again. Apart from the space where the settee had been you would never know something awful had taken place.

'I've ordered another second-hand sofa for you until you sort yourself out,' she says. 'But it's not due to be delivered until six. So, maybe we should have a cup of tea in the garden until it gets here.'

Beth ushers me outside and settles me into a sun-lounger with my arm propped up on two cushions. She makes tea and brings biscuits that she has bought.

It is on the tip of my tongue to tell her that we never have biscuits in the house because neither myself nor Erin eat them. But I stop abruptly. I know my life with Erin is over now.

Beth is taking charge like I've never seen before. I think back to when we were married and how she didn't do very much organising. Was that because she didn't want to and was happy to leave it all to me. Or did I not give her the chance. I shrug my shoulders. Maybe that was just the way our marriage worked out. The way we'd moulded together.

'I'm more than used to doing things on my own now,' she says smiling. 'And I do like to sort people out.'

'I can see that,' I say smiling my thanks. I dunk one of the ginger-snap biscuits into the tea and sigh with pleasure at the sweetness. Obviously, she thinks I need sorting out. I nod in agreement because she's right, I do need help.

Thirty minutes later the green squashy sofa arrives, and the delivery men put it in the original place. Before Erin had re-arranged the furniture.

Beth offers. 'Shall I move this to where it was before?'

I shake my head. 'Nooo, leave it there,' I insist. 'This way the room will look different to yesterday.'

The sofa looks like it has been well used, but it does seem clean and is soft and cosy. I lie down with my arm propped on two cushions. Beth fusses around me insisting I take the painkillers the hospital prescribed. I relish in her kind and caring manner but try not to feel too sorry for myself. However, I've never been very good at the stiff upper lip especially when I'm poorly.

I lie with my eyes closed. I'm not asleep but try to enjoy the peace and quiet of the house.

Beth senses my need for a little me-time and heads off down to the village shop to buy food for dinner.

I allow myself time to go through the events from yesterday. When I think of what happened I feel like I'm having a horrible nightmare that I'll soon wake up from. It doesn't seem tangible now in some respects. As if it didn't really happen and it could be a figment of my imagination. But when I move my arm and feel the pain, I know it is real. And yes, my wife did try to kill me. And yes, I'd been absolutely petrified of her.

Erin had thrown so much information at me in such a short space of time that I hadn't been able to understand it all. Now I go through it piece by piece.

She had found her mother's diary the day before we moved down here but didn't tell me about it. Why? If we've always been such a close couple, why couldn't she talk to me about the diary. And yes, I'd have been devastated to learn what my father had done. But I would have coped because my sympathies would have lain with the victim: her mother.

Erin's mother had drowned herself and baby Neil. I shake my head. I'm amazed that I'd had a half-brother I knew nothing about.

They hadn't been killed in a car crash as I'd been led to believe and wonder if she'd been lying to me from the very start of our relationship. Was that the only lie she'd told me or was there more. Maybe, I'd just been so bloody gullible that I'd believed every word she said.

Erin had been pregnant and was carrying our child but had a termination in London. So why wait until afterwards to tell me: that was cruel and totally unfair. I sigh, knowing it was probably because I'd threatened to leave her.

She must have thought by telling me I was going to be a father it would stop me from going. I tut. She knew me well enough to know her plan would work.

I frown and rub at my eyebrow. Had I really known my wife at all. How could I live and love someone to that intensity without knowing her? Erin was a liar with an abnormal personality. And I hadn't seen it. I suppose, I could argue that she was normal when I first met her. It had only been the discovery of her mother's diary that had flipped her over the edge.

But, as Jessie had said, 'Erin must have been close to the edge in the first place because sane rational people wouldn't have reacted the way she did.'

I know Jessie is right.

I'd often wondered in our early days what my mam would have thought of Erin. Would they have got along together? Would mam have understood Erin's challenging personality. But, I sigh, no matter what mam thought about her as a person she would have appreciated the way Erin had loved me to distraction.

Alfie had said at the first Christmas party when he met her. 'It's obvious to everyone how much in love you both are. You're the perfect couple.'

I shake my head at our memories of true love as opposed to the way she'd glared with hatred at me yesterday.

But by far, and more than all of this, the biggest shock is what my father has done. I suppose Erin had a reason to become deranged. But what was my father's excuse. What reason could he possibly have to viciously rape and assault an innocent young woman. There are no reasons or excuses for this. Other than he was an evil man.

I think of his face on Beth's laptop. In a way I'm pleased he is dead. If he was still alive and I could find him in Scotland I'd be on the next train up there. Regardless of his old age I'd have him arrested for what he did.

I remember what Uncle Geoff told me about hitting the barmaid. That makes at least two other women we know he attacked. As well as mam, of course. Could there have been more. Had he fathered more children, and do I have more half brothers and sisters. My eyelids feel heavy and sticky and I yawn. I doze for a while then wake with a jolt.

The noise of pans clattering in the kitchen makes me hunch my shoulders. In my grogginess, I panic. Is it Erin? Has she come back? I feel my stomach lurch.

Then I hear Beth tunelessly singing along to a song on the radio. I smile and flop back against the cushions. It's so good to have her here with me and decide I've missed that awful singing. In fact, I realise how much I've missed having her in my life. I manage to manoeuvre myself up from the sofa and potter through to the kitchen.

Beth cooks a roast dinner and makes her delicious gravy. She cuts the meat up into pieces on the plate. 'Oh, my. I never thought I'd be doing this today,' she teases.

I can't help smiling back at her. She's lifted my mood so much today. I know if I'd had to return here alone, I'd have felt a hundred times worse.

I lay my hand over the top of hers and squeeze it. 'Thanks for being here, Beth.'

She nods then sits opposite me.

'Shall we have some wine?' I say.

She frowns and shakes her head. 'I don't think you should be drinking with that medication, Dave.'

I follow her lead and drink the cold water she's poured.

Whilst eating, although I try not to make comparisons, I know if Erin had wanted a glass of wine, she would have poured it out. Tablets or not. Whereas, Beth always has my best interests at heart.

I recap over other small incidents between me and Erin. Now I can now see how selfish she really was. Whatever the circumstances she would have thought only of herself.

I begin to talk and tell Beth everything that's happened since we moved down to Bexley and how Erin abused me. A couple of times I see Beth look down at her plate when I talk about the intimate assaults. I realise I need to choose my words more carefully and appreciate it can't be easy to listen to your ex-husband talk about another partner.

The last thing I want to do is make Beth feel uncomfortable. 'Look, Beth, I can't begin to tell you how grateful I am that you are here and listening to me.'

Beth places her knife and fork together on the plate. She smiles. 'It's okay, you don't need to say that. I know you'd do the same for me if I was in a fix.'

I smile in pleasure knowing she is right. Her familiarity soothes me, and I feel my shoulder and neck muscles loosen around the knot of the sling.

Jessie and Mike call for a drink and stay longer than they'd intended mainly because the two women get along so well together. When they leave, I check the lock three times before I move back down the hall.

Beth notices. 'Dave, you are safe,' she says. 'Erin is locked-up in a secure unit.'

I nod my head and frown. 'I know, I'm probably just overreacting.'

'Look,' she says reassuringly. 'We'll check all the window locks and the back door again before we go to bed.'

I follow along behind her into the lounge feeling like a wimp. Beth sits on the opposite end of the sofa with a fresh mug of tea.

Her mobile tinkles and she reads her text. 'Oh, it's from Sally. They're on the way home from Paris. I'd told her yesterday that you'd had an accident but that you were okay with a dressing on your arm,' she says. 'I also told her that Erin has left you and that I was with you in the hospital.'

I think of my conversations with Sally about Erin over the years and sigh. 'I don't think I'm up to the, I told you so, from my daughter just yet.'

Beth raises an eyebrow. 'That's not fair, Dave! I think you're being a little hard on her. She's grown up a lot in the last six months and I know she wouldn't say that,' she says. 'She sounds very concerned about you and she loves you to bits. She's bound to be worried.'

I bite my lip and feel my cheeks flush. It's Beth and Sally that really care about me. I shouldn't have made the remark and I apologise. 'Sorry, I'm upset and shouldn't be mouthing off without thinking first. After all,' I pause and notice the cat slinking along the windowsill looking for Erin, 'when I think back, Sally has been right about her all along.'

I can see Beth take a deep breath and wrinkle her forehead. She is obviously choosing her words carefully. 'Well, I think Sally would automatically have hated any woman that, in her eyes, took her daddy away,' she says with a slight shrug. 'I found it hard enough at times to break into your tight-knit pact.'

I turn to her. 'What do you mean?'

'Well, when she was little it was always you two together doing things.

First bike-ride, first ice-skating practise, and even when she was older, her first pop concert. It was you who took her everywhere.'

I sigh knowing Beth is right. Has she had this resentment simmering away in her mind all these years? And if so, why hadn't she said anything. I protest, 'But you could have come too. It's just that we thought you weren't interested.'

Beth shrugs her thin shoulders in the silky-green blouse she is wearing. 'Did you?' she says truculently then looks down at her hands. 'I gave up after a while because both our mams told me Sally was always going to be a Daddy's girl.'

I think about this and struggle to remember my feelings back then. It all seems such a long time ago. Obviously though, Beth had remembered and resented me for doing this. I'm thinking of words to apologise when she brightens.

A smile fills her face. 'But we are close now in other ways as mother and daughter should be. And thinking about her at the wedding, I reckon, between us we've done a damn fine job. Don't you?'

Although the smile is back on Beth's face, I can't help feeling that I should have given more thought to her in our marriage. Especially when Sally was growing up.

Beth starts to type a reply. 'I'll let Sally know that I will be home soon,' she says.

The thought of Beth leaving makes my palms sweat and I drag my free hand down my trouser leg. I have a sick note for two weeks and can't bear the thought of rattling around in this house alone. 'But you're not going, are you?'

She looks flustered. 'Well, I don't know, Dave,' she says and drains the tea from her mug. 'Do you want me to stay?'

'Yes, of course I do,' I say. 'I'm dreading being here on my own.'

I give her my best winning smile.

Beth frowns slightly. 'Well, I did leave a message for my manager at work to say I wouldn't be in today and tomorrow. I suppose I could ask to take the week off. I've got loads of holiday left and the practice is quiet…' she pauses then continues as if talking to herself. 'You won't be able to cook or shop for yourself and, you have to keep the dressing dry until the stitches come out.'

'There you are,' I say happily. 'You can't go yet.'

She smiles and tuts playfully. I know she will stay, and I thank her.

It's a big ask and if she refused, I couldn't blame her. She's my ex-wife who I left for another woman. I don't know if I could be this gracious if it was the other way around.

Beth yawns and looks pale with tiredness. I sigh. I could kick myself for not getting the guest room sorted and buying a single bed like I'd planned.

Beth offers to sleep on the sofa so I can be comfortable in my own bed. I refuse for two reasons. First, she has already slept in a chair last night at the hospital. Second, I can't face going upstairs to our bed.

The bed I slept in with Erin. I know it's going to take a while to put this behind me.

Beth reassures me that she has made the bed up with fresh linen. So, I know I won't be able to smell Erin, but I still don't want to sleep in it. Beth heads upstairs after bringing me a blanket and pyjamas.

When I try to close my eyes and go to sleep, I can still see Erin above me with the knife poised ready to plunge into me. The fear grips my throat making my chest jerk.

I can see her warped and twisted face. But more frightening is the revulsion I see in her eyes. The locking of our eyes or what I've always thought of as our look of love had been replaced with a look of utter hatred.

I toss and turn in broken sleep for most of the night.

Chapter Thirty-One

The shower the next morning is a challenge with one arm but I manage. I make breakfast for Beth with one hand. If I'd been able to carry the tray, I would have taken it upstairs. But within minutes she is downstairs and dressed in clean white shirt and trousers.

'Look at the mess you've made,' she scolds and banishes me back to the sofa with my arm raised on cushions again.

The police call in the morning and I go through my statement. The young police constable is patient with me. I flounder at some of his words. Paranoia, complex personality disorder, and psychosis are not words that I completely understand. There're not words I use in my day-to-day vocabulary. Beth tries to help with explanations.

He stares at me with his spotty young face and smiles encouragingly. 'So, did Erin experience any hallucinations?'

I hesitate. 'I'm not sure,' I say. 'She never mentioned having them but there again, I didn't know what she was experiencing in her mind. She wouldn't talk to me about anything.'

He nods reassuringly. Beth gives me a big smile which is a boost.

'So, you can always contact the staff at the hospital to see when you can visit her. And of course, she will need some of her belongings.'

Beth shows him to the door. I sit alone to think about what I've been told. I wipe the perspiration from my forehead. It feels like I've been interrogated about something I know nothing about. Last night's restless sleep catches up on me and I yawn.

In months to come I know there will be many decisions to make.

However, the only thing I do know for certain and will never change my mind, is that I don't ever want to see Erin again. Whether people think I'm cold and hard-hearted, I don't rightly care. I won't be visiting her in hospital and will refuse to have any further contact. My solicitor can do all the necessary.

I gulp down a dry sob of sadness. Erin was my wife and on our wedding day, I know I vowed that my love would be in sickness and in health. But I'm breaking that vow right now. I don't have the forgiveness to carry on any type of relationship with her. We are over.

When Beth joins me, I tell her my decision. 'I don't know how long the treatment will last and if she will want to come back here afterwards because there is another three months left on the tenancy,' I say looking around the lounge. 'But if she is still in the hospital when the tenancy date ends, I know I won't stay here. I can't re-live these dreadful memories a moment longer than I have to!'

'Are you sure?' Beth asks pulling her eyebrows together in concern. 'Maybe you should give yourself a while to think about it all. You've had a massive upset. In time you might feel sorry for her and want to give things another chance.'

I shake my head vehemently. 'No. I won't, Beth. I'll never have any sympathy for her. I'll never be able to think any different other than seeing her with that knife in her hand!'

Beth sits forwards and opens the palms of her hands. 'But she might get better with the treatment and bounce back to her normal self.'

'No!' I almost shout. 'Even if she appears to be back to normal, I know I will never be able to relax with her again. I'd never sleep on a night wondering if she's going to snap again.'

Beth nods sadly. 'Well, I suppose once the trust has gone, there's not much left,' she says.

She pauses and looks down at her hands. 'I know how that feels.'

I look at her and know she means her trust in me. It must have been very difficult for Beth to trust another man after the lies I told in our marriage. Is it too late to ask for forgiveness?

'Beth,' I say. 'I don't know if I've ever actually said this, but I am truly sorry for the way I behaved when I first met Erin. And for the lies I told you.'

Her eyes look watery and my heart sinks. I pray she isn't going to cry because I won't be able to cope with her tears on top of everything else.

I can see she is thinking about her reply.

'Okay, Dave. Let's park it up for now,' she says. Re-hashing our marriage today isn't going to do either of us any good. But thank you for the apology.'

I nod sadly and shuffle on the sofa feeling uncomfortable when Beth offers to do Erin's packing. I know I can't manage with one hand. And I don't want anyone else involved in this mess. We head upstairs.

Beth packs Erin's clothes and toiletries into two suitcases then places her handbag into the top of the case. I remove her set of house keys before she locks the case.

We head into Erin's paint room. I sit on the chair in the corner of the room while Beth stacks her canvases and materials into small crates from the garage. The smell of oil paints hits me. I know forever more this smell will always remind me of Erin from her hands and hair.

I look at the trunk in the other corner of the room with a shawl draped over it. The clasp is open.

'I've never known what was in here,' I say gingerly opening the lid of the trunk. I gasp when I see what looks like the diary lying on top of some clothes. There is also a red notebook underneath the diary. I lift them both out.

Beth stops with a canvas under her arm and warns me against reading it. 'You might find out more than you want to know.'

I can't stop myself and open the diary. My stomach twists and heaves when I read her mother's words about the rape. I slump back down onto the chair and shake my head. This poor woman had been tortured at the hands of my father. I simply cannot comprehend how any man could behave like this. I look at the wedding photograph of Erin's parents and can see her mother was a tiny slim woman, just like Erin.

My stomach knots with anger at my bully of a dad hurting a woman half his size. I sigh remembering how I behaved when Erin was abusing me. Jessie seemed to think I was a bloody hero for not retaliating. But I'm not. It's just that you don't behave like that to a woman. No matter what she does or however angry you feel, you don't hit women. It's not right. So, how come I know that golden rule but bully's like my dad, don't. I conclude that he was simply an evil bastard.

Although Erin's actions were the result of a warped and twisted mind I can at least see where her anger came from. I open the red notebook and recognise Erin's writing on the date that we moved here. I read some of the rambling sentences to Beth and show her the underlining's highlighted in red pen.

I shake my head and whistle through my teeth. 'God, she sounds completely deranged!'

Beth puts her head on one side. 'Did you not realise how unbalanced she had become, Dave?'

I shudder and rub the top of my shoulder which aches where the sling is tied. 'Well, there were the times when she was irrational and abused me, but in day to day conversations she seemed fairly normal,' I say looking around the room at her artwork. 'She could be very charming and engaging, especially when we first met. Afterwards, I'd simply decided her slightly haphazard behaviour was part of her character and arty-personality.'

Beth flops down onto another chair and shrugs. 'You're very easy to fool, Dave. You've always been too nice for your own good, as mam would say.'

I think of both our mothers then smile. I know that's what they thought of me and I suppose it's true. I usually try to see the good in people rather than their faults, but maybe being like this brings its own set of problems. Are they right? Am I a complete walk-over? And am I too simple to see danger coming until it has a knife at my chest?

I sigh and lay the diary and notebook back where I found them. 'Come on,' I say fastening the clasp on the trunk. 'Let's get this finished.'

Beth labels everything with Erin's name and address then we agree it is a job well-done.

We spend the afternoon pleasantly in the garden. Although the sun is not shinning and it is overcast, it is sultry. Beth enjoys weeding the borders of the lawn. We talk about the garden at home that we'd had laid with paving slabs in our early days.

However, I did notice at the wedding weekend that Beth has had half of the slabs lifted and has planted shrubs and flowers. 'I find it so relaxing pottering around in the garden,' she says. 'It's one of my favourite things to do now. I love a day to myself planting different flowers with the colours and smells.'

I grin imagining her pottering and singing along to the radio in the peace and quiet. I swallow a lump of longing to be back home in Kibblesworth.

She continues. 'I'm planning to uplift the rest of the slabs then try my hand at growing fruit and vegetables. It would be lovely to have new potatoes and green beans fresh from the soil, wouldn't it?'

I nod knowing there is a lot I don't know about this new Beth. She's not the same woman I left behind two years ago. The essence of her personality that I've always loved is still there, but she has a whole new life.

Shortly after five, Jessie turns up with a fold-up bed for the spare room. I am in the sun-lounger in the garden but can hear the women talking in the hall together.

Jessie joins me in the garden. 'I've got a surprise for you,' she says, and I raise an eyebrow. I'm not sure I'm up to anymore shocks.

'Ta-da,' she exclaims. I look past her to see Jakub bound through the door.

I've a lump in my throat which feels like the size of a tennis ball and feel quite tearful. Jakub grasps my good hand to shake.

'Jakub, I…I can't thank you enough,' I say thinking how feeble my thanks sound considering what he did. 'If it hadn't been for you, I…I might not be here!'

Jakub interrupts. 'Ah, it was nothing, boss,' he says. 'I told you I had your back, yes?'

But I know it was something. It was a great deal. Few men would tackle a crazed woman with a knife and risk their own life to help another. But he did. He saved my life and I'm not sure I would have had the same courage. I sigh and clear my dry throat just as Beth brings tea out for us all.

Sipping my hot tea, I look at Jakub's young eager face and smile. He gabbles his new idea for a chocolate smash cake and how amazing it will look. Jessie tells me the retailer has cancelled this week's presentation until next month. This is good news because it will give me time to get back to work and not let the team down.

***

Beth and I have had a good week together and I've really enjoyed her company. I'm not going to say we've slipped back into exactly the way we were in our marriage because we haven't. Beth is too much of a different person for this to happen. I guess I am too.

No one can go through what I have and not be affected by it in some way. But it's been an easy week of recuperation and Beth has taken much of the everyday worries from my shoulders.

She had been shopping with Jessie into London and enjoyed the hustle and bustle of the capital. 'Oh wow, Dave, there's some amazing shops in London. I've got some great ideas to decorate the lounge at home,' she'd raved.

I'd been surprised. The Beth I was married to would have been wary about hordes of people and the noise of a big city. But the confidence and enjoyment had shone in her eyes when she'd told me all about the trip.

We'd been out for dinner twice to different restaurants. Wearing new clothes from her shopping spree Beth had been assured and lively company with Jessie, Mike and Jakub.

I can see this new Beth has certainly come out of her shell. And it suits her. However, she has a train ticket to return home because she needs to go back to work. And I can't bear being here alone.

***

While we wait in the outpatient clinic area for the nurse to remove my stitches, I look at Beth. 'I'm dreading you going back home tomorrow.'

The hospital smell and memories of being here last week flood my mind. As we sit quietly, I watch the activity of nurses hurrying around the clinic and patients ambling from room to rooms. Beth nods in understanding. I can see her forehead frown slightly and know she is mulling something over.

She raises an eyebrow. 'So, why not come home with me for a while, you could stay in the spare room or in Sally's bigger bedroom.'

My heart leaps in hope then I remember the plan of care. 'But what about the physiotherapy treatment?'

'Leave that to me and I'll see what we can do,' she says then heads off to the nurse's desk at the end of the corridor.

I have the stitches removed and return to the clinic area where Beth is waiting for me. She is sitting with her legs crossed and looks lovely in a lemon cotton dress. She seems decidedly pleased with herself.

'Well, I've asked the medical staff if arrangements can be made for you to have your physiotherapy in Newcastle. The nurse can't see a problem if our hospital agrees,' she says and smiles broadly. 'But if they won't, you could always pay privately to have it done. I reckon you'll get better quicker at home than being miserable down here on you own, do you?'

I gratefully accept Beth's offer. My whole insides fill with delight and relief. I hug Beth as tightly as I can with one arm.

Chapter Thirty-Two

Once I'm settled at home Beth gives me daily jobs to do. 'Your stay isn't going to be rent free,' she jokes.

I've shopped online for the wallpaper and paint Beth has chosen to re-decorate the lounge. I've ordered curtains, carpet and a new three-piece leather suite which we've stored in the garage.

The decorators have been here for two days and will finish today after hanging the wallpaper. I've enjoyed having the guys in the house even though I've only been making cups of tea. I like the friendly banter.

Frustration has set in now because although my arm is healing quickly and the physiotherapy is helping me reach a good range of movement, I'm still limited. I haven't been able to move furniture around in the lounge and I'm not used to letting other people do the work.

Beth has chosen a striking mustard patterned wallpaper for the feature wall.

One of the decorators unrolls the paper and holds it against the wall. 'Oh, my, this is bright!'

'Yep, it certainly is,' I grin. 'But it's what the lady of the house wants.'

I wander outside into the garden and hold my face up to the early morning sunshine. I sip my coffee and take a sigh of relief and pleasure. I'm loving being at home in our village again. I try to read the newspaper but then lean my head back against the old deck chair to recap over the last couple of weeks.

The peace and familiarity feel like bliss and the villagers are overly enthusiastic to see me home again.

I've been stopped many times with their welcoming words as I've walked to the shop and pub.

I've seen my pals in The Plough regularly since coming home but haven't told anyone what happened with Erin. I know it's obvious that I'm no longer with her, but I haven't elaborated on the situation. All I've told them is that I've had an accident and have come home for my physiotherapy in Newcastle.

In time, I might tell them but not yet. My pals understand and haven't pushed me for answers. They know I'll talk about it when I'm ready. And for that I'm grateful.

I mull over my visit to Uncle Geoff which didn't help in any way. Unfortunately, he wasn't having one of his lucid days. I still have many questions to ask about my dad, and I'm hoping if I go to visit regularly, I might learn more about the farm. I sigh and rub my neck. I'm as much in the dark about my dad's history as I ever was.

Last night I'd lain in bed and done some serious soul-searching. I've faced death in the last few weeks and was very close to not being here at all. So, I felt the need to sort out my thoughts.

I'd thought of Bexley and admitted that although I really liked the job, the thought of going back and staying in the rented house filled me full of dread. I don't want to return.

I'd spent most of the time in Bexley trying to convince myself that I could settle in the south. Of course, being unhappy at home with Erin's assaults hadn't helped. But I truly believed that even if Erin hadn't changed, I still wouldn't want to live the rest of my life there. If I had stayed it would have been to please Erin and make her happy. Not myself. And surely, in time, this would have caused problems.

I'd started to drift towards sleep knowing the dreadful memories were not in my thoughts every minute of the day now and what Erin did, had started to fade a little. But I knew I'd never forget what had happened.

I drain my coffee and consider a refill, but the peaceful setting makes me want to stay still for a while with my thoughts. I want to appreciate everything I have right now. Right at this very moment.

While I'd waited for Erin to plunge the knife into my chest, I'd known I would feel pain. But I hadn't been frightened of dying and had been almost ready to accept my fate.

I remember the young doctor in the hospital, and know he was right. I am more than lucky to be alive. I owe it to myself to live every second of what life I have left to the full. I determine that going forward, my life will only be filled with the good stuff. Wherever possible I'm not going to do things because I must, but more because I want to.

I shake myself now as the decorator calls out and I hurry inside to the lounge.

'Are you happy, mate?' he asks then chuckles. 'You'll need your sunglasses to look at this paper.'

I grin. 'Yep, she'll love this. It certainly brightens the old place up again.'

Within the hour the carpet fitters arrive. I manage to sweep up the debris from the old floorboards while they carry the roll of new carpet from the back of their van.

Once more I head outside into the garden and leave the carpet fitters to do their job. I grin thinking of the zigzag wallpaper and bright mustard colour which is so striking. It's very different to what we've ever had in the house before and makes the room look much bigger.

There again, I muse, Beth is so different to what she was before. I love her new ideas. I mumble to myself, out with the old and in with the new.

The new cream and pale blue checked carpet is down. With my good arm I've managed to hang the new blue lampshade. I've hoovered and wiped clean all the skirting boards and windowsill then finish cleaning the window just before Beth arrives home from work.

From the bay window I watch her walking briskly towards the house swinging her handbag. I've already sent a text to tell her the decorators are done, and the carpet is down. I can almost see the adrenalin pumping in her stride as she hurries.

She dashes into the lounge and stands next to me then gasps. 'Oh, Dave, I love it!'

I slide my arm along her shoulders and grin at the delight gleaming in her eyes.

'Me, too,' I say. 'It's a great choice, Beth.'

I look out of the window to see Ian and Sally pull up in their car.

Amidst greetings, and Oooh's and Aaah's, we decide to get the room finished tonight. Ian drills the curtain pole into place and Beth hangs the cream silky curtains. Sally places a new blue table lamp onto the old bureau. Between the four of us we manoeuvre all the new furniture from the garage into place. Beth drapes a pale blue throw over the back of the cream settee and Sally squeals with delight.

'Mam, it's absolutely fabulous!'

My daughter's face is pink with exertion and glowing. I smile remembering her words when I came back up to the house with Beth. 'Having you home in Kibblesworth is the best wedding present I could ever have wished for, Dad.'

And I believe her.

Ian wipes his glasses on the bottom of his jumper and proclaims, 'It's a resounding success, Beth. Well done!'

I look around at my happy smiling family and feel a tug of emotion in the back of my throat. This is so much more than I'd thought possible. I realise how much I've missed them. How much I've missed the family solidarity. And their love.

I stand next to Beth and give her another hug. 'Beth, you really should venture into interior design because you've certainly got a flair for putting colour schemes together.'

I turn and look down at the happiness in her face. She gives me one of her shy smiles.

***

By chance the next day, when leaving physio in Newcastle, I see a woman who works in HR at the old bakery site. After we exchange pleasantries, I learn that Alfie is taking early retirement and how they'll soon be looking for a new manager. I head to the bus stop knowing this couldn't have come at a better time.

When I reach home, Beth is outside in the garden. She has a diagram in her hands and is studying the plot she's drawn out. The remaining slabs have been lifted and she is making a start with her vegetable patch.

I smile at her in green shorts and vest. Her hair is clipped back from her clean-scrubbed face and in the late sunshine she doesn't look much older than when I first met her at Uni. She grins at me explaining the outline of the vegetable plot.

Sally and Ian arrive with a good-hearted exchange. 'We'll help with the digging for a promise of an Indian take-a-way!'

We all muck in digging and planting under Beth's instructions.

I feel the sun on the back of my neck and the peace of the countryside around us filling me with tranquillity. I stop for a few minutes' breather and relish in the fact that I'm surrounded with people who love me. I know this is the good stuff in my life.

As if Sally can read my mind, she says, 'Ah, Dad, why don't you move back home?'

I grin at her, 'We'll see,' I say trying to sound non-committal as they leave to go and collect the Indian food.

Beth straightens up rubbing her back with one hand and holding a packet of seeds in the other. She wipes her forehead with the back of her gardening glove and smiles at me.

'I think Sally's right, Dave. This is where you belong,' she says. 'Here in our village.'

I wipe the soil mark from her forehead, and she tuts good naturedly.

We are different people now. Me, because of how I changed for Erin. And Beth, because she runs her own life.

I look into her eyes. I'm sure I see a glimpse of what looks like expectation. Or dare I think, hope.

Even though I'm still shell-shocked about Erin, I know somewhere deep down in my heart that I still have feelings for Beth.

Whether we can re-kindle our love and move forwards in any way, I don't know. But if she is willing to try then so am I.

If you have enjoyed this story - A review on amazon.co.uk would be greatly appreciated.

You can find more from Susan Willis here:

Ebook Cozy Crime Short Reads:

Christmas Intruder https://amzn.to/2pVmsBj

Megan's Mistake https://amzn.to/2pl88Sf

An Author is Missing https://amzn.to/2Mk20X8

Paperback Fun-Size Tales of Love & Family
https://amzn.to/qwgSpB

Website www.susanwillis.co.uk

Twitter @SusanWillis69

Facebook m.me/AUTHORSusanWillis

Instagram susansuspenseauthor

Printed in Great Britain
by Amazon

21939859R00169